MURDER AT EVERHAM HALL

BENEDICT BROWN

Storm
PUBLISHING

Ebook ISBN: 978-1-80508-137-1
Paperback ISBN: 978-1-80508-139-5

Cover design: Tash Webber and Marion Doin
Cover images: Shutterstock, Unsplash

Published by Storm Publishing.
For further information, visit:
www.stormpublishing.co

ALSO BY BENEDICT BROWN

Lord Edgington Investigates...

Murder at the Spring Ball

A Body at a Boarding School

Death on a Summer's Day

The Mystery of Mistletoe Hall

The Tangled Treasure Trail

The Curious Case of the Templeton-Swifts

The Crimes of Clearwell Castle

The Snows of Weston Moor

What the Vicar Saw

Blood on the Banisters

A Killer in the Wings

The Izzy Palmer Mysteries

A Corpse Called Bob

A Corpse in the Country

A Corpse on the Beach

A Corpse in London

A Corpse for Christmas

A Corpse in a Locked Room

A Corpse in a Quaint English Village

A Corpse at a Wedding

A Corpse at A School Reunion

To my wife Marion and our incredible children, Amelie and Osian.
You make the hard work worthwhile.

READER'S NOTE

Welcome to my new 1920s mystery series. I hope it's just your cup of tea.
At the back of the book you'll find a character list, a glossary of unusual terms, and a chapter on the incredible historical facts I discovered while writing *Murder at Everham Hall*.
Now get sleuthing!

ONE

LONDON, DECEMBER 1927

I would say that I was having one of those days, but I'd been having one of those days every day for the last year.

I had been summoned from my cave in St James's to the headquarters of Price-Lewis & Aster. As I stood there, imagining any number of punishments for my misdeeds, my publisher's office felt immense and imposing. Loitering in front of his desk like a young boy before the headmaster, I waited for a chance to explain myself.

Bertrand Price-Lewis took his time writing a note on the pad in front of him, but I'm sure he only did it to make me suffer. When he'd tormented me enough, he looked up with a half-smile on his face and nodded for me to begin.

I cleared my throat and did what I could to keep the wolf from my door. "Picture the scene; an owl hoots in the wind-whipped trees, but nothing else disturbs that lonely place. There are no car motors or laughing children. As a hooded figure runs into the shadows of the ancient manor, there is just the sound of the natural world."

"Excellent! So the book's set in a crumbling country pile?" he interrupted.

"That's correct." I shifted my weight from one foot to the other. "But would you mind not breaking my concentration?"

"Of course not. My apologies. Please continue."

I picked up the threads of the story once more. "The man stops to survey the scene before pressing on through the gardens. The air is crisp, and the moon is full in the sky. A silvery light bounces off the carpet of snow—"

"Oh, it's been snowing. I do enjoy a winter mystery." Bertie rubbed his hands together with glee. "This book will sell, though you should probably have mentioned the snow from—"

It was my turn to interrupt. "Do you mind? I'm trying to set the scene."

"You're absolutely right. Go ahead." He sat up straighter in his chair, as though to signal that, henceforth, the floor was mine.

"A thick carpet of snow lies on the ground. The moonlight catches the jagged edge of a lustful knife in the hand of the cloaked figure." As I said this, I could practically hear Bertie thinking, *Hmmm... there are a few too many adjectives for my liking!* "Just for a moment, we catch the outline of the man's face, but it's too brief to make out any detail. He pauses again, perhaps listening for the faintest sound that has been drowned out by the wind, before changing direction to cut across the courtyard of the old house."

I was gaining confidence as I unfurled the tale and, for a moment, I could picture myself there in the freezing environs of the tumbledown mansion. "He moves faster. The powdery snow kicks up beneath his feet and, as readers, we move with him, switching to the man's perspective as he continues his hunt. Reaching the covered porch, he pulls the door but finds it locked and has to skirt around the side of the building to another entrance. In luck this time, he tugs it open, and the groaning hinges almost deafen him. He is frightened of discovery, frightened for his life. And just then, we come to question who this man could be. Is he a killer? Is he some madman, hell-bent on revenge?"

My fuzzy-haired chief clapped his hands together appreciatively but said nothing.

"Inside the house, our mysterious invader navigates the labyrinthine halls, ever-aware of the sound of his own footsteps and fearful that the creaking floorboards will give him away. And so it dawns on the reader: this man must be a thief, looking for some valuable object in the dilapidated old place. He enters the drawing room and walks over to an ornate cabinet. Putting the knife down to free his hand, he unlocks the door with a small silver key from a chain about his neck just as a hammer comes crashing down on the back of his skull. The blood pools around him like lava, and the last thing he sees before his eyes close is the face of his killer smiling down at him."

I waited a few seconds to see how the chubby-cheeked fellow would react.

He didn't. He just stared at me expectantly.

"It's called *A Glimpse of a Blood Moon*," I revealed when he still wouldn't say anything.

"So?" he eventually replied.

It was not the response I'd been expecting. "What do you mean, 'So?'"

His wildly overgrown eyebrows knitted together in concern. "So what happens next? It's an exceptional beginning, but we're going to need more than that." He folded one hand over the other on his desk.

I laughed as though he'd said something terribly foolish. "Bertie, old thing! It's not just a beginning. In that one scene, you have the whole book. Can't you imagine it?"

His right eye twitched, and I knew he saw through me. "No, Marius. I'm afraid I can't." He pushed his chair back and rose to standing. Since he wasn't the tallest gent in London, this only gained him a foot or so in height. "How will you sustain the reader's attention over two hundred and fifty pages? Where's the intrigue? All this opening scene does is make me want to know more."

I swatted a dark curl from my forehead. "That's just what we want, isn't it? We need readers to open the book and not close it again until they finish the final page."

"That's perfectly true, but it would be better if the first chapter was not also the last." He walked around the desk to set his gaze upon me. Bertrand Price-Lewis was a small, stout man of sixty-five. I'm sure I could have given him a good walloping if we'd ever come to blows, but that didn't change the fact he terrified me to the quick. "Before we go any further, I'd like to know the main thrust of the rest of the story."

"All in good time, Bertie. All in—"

"Marius, do you have the vaguest idea of what happens after that first scene?"

There was a drinks cabinet in the corner of his well-appointed office. I wasn't thirsty. It was only eleven o'clock in the morning, and I don't normally drink alone, but I poured myself a measure of brandy nonetheless. "Of course I know what happens. I just told you the title—"

"Yes, I heard you. It's called *A Glimpse of a Blood Moon*. However, it doesn't appear that you've written much beyond the front cover."

I had started drinking, and so I continued until there was nothing left in my glass. My throat burned, but at least it delayed the inevitable for a few seconds longer.

"Marius!" His good cheer was forgotten. "Have you written a single page?"

"Your lack of faith in me is astounding. I've written a whole chapter." It's hard to fathom that I could state this so proudly, as it was the very thing I'd wished to conceal when I entered that room five minutes earlier.

"A chapter?" Bertie spoke in such a sorry, disappointed tone that I think I'd have preferred him to shout. "You've had a year, and you've only written a single chapter?"

Hiding the truth had done little good, so I did my best to devise a defence. "To be fair, it is quite a long chapter. And don't forget the snow. You liked the snow."

He couldn't look at me but collapsed into a red leather armchair. "But your advance... It was the biggest in this company's history."

"I was going to mention that. You see, I've spent it, and I could really do with a small sum to see me through the next few months."

"You've spent it?" He looked rather like an owl and peered up at me through his perfectly round eyes. "What about the royalties from the last book?"

"I spent them, too." Far from the dread I'd experienced on arrival, revealing my dilemma turned out to be oddly restorative. "I bought a flat in St James's, and now I'm quite penniless."

He shook his head before speaking. I was used to surprising the old boy, but he was clearly mesmerised by my stupidity. "Then sell it!"

"I can't do that."

"Why not?" The intensity of these two words made me shudder.

" I have my mother to consider. Not to mention my aunt and uncle. They'd be out on the streets."

"You live with your mother?"

"She was all on her own," I rushed to explain. "When she came to visit, she subtly mentioned how large the spare bedrooms were, and I'm not so cruel as to deny an old lady some company."

"Then how did your aunt and uncle end up there?" He really hadn't grasped what I was saying, and I didn't have much hope of making him see.

"It would have been rude not to invite them after Mother came to live with me. I was trying to be a good nephew."

He raised his hands to his head at this point, as though he no longer had the strength to support it. "Didn't you consider buying somewhere more economical? I hear there are affordable properties in Hackney these days."

"Well, my first book was such a success and, to be quite honest, I never imagined I could want for inspiration." I tried to move the conversation towards the topic I really wished to discuss. "Now, if I could get a loan to tide me over until the ideas start flowing, that would—"

"No more money!" These three words thundered out of him. He was no longer a five-foot-five publisher with a perfectly round belly. He was a Herculean warrior. "I've seen this problem before with writers. The only solution is to keep you hungry."

"I'm already hungry," I replied through gritted teeth. "I've even cut back on the essentials."

He seemed to materialise ten feet closer just then, like Zeus before a trembling peasant. "No more money, do you hear me? You must go home, take out that expensive typewriter I bought you, and write Chapter Two of *A Glimpse of a Blood Moon*, and then Chapter Three and Four and so on until you have something that might plausibly be described as a novel!"

As nothing else had worked, I decided to throw myself on his mercy. "Bertie, I need your help. The bank is already furious with me. I've got until the middle of January to pay my next mortgage instalment, or they'll take everything."

He was deadly still, having turned from a Greek god into a statue of one. "I'll give you a hundred pounds for every chapter you produce."

I sighed and looked down at the richly patterned carpet. "I stared at that typewriter for days, but it did no good. I think I've forgotten how to write."

He walked over to the door and opened it. "Those are my conditions. You know I'm terribly fond of you, boy. But I'd be doing you no favours if I handed over a few notes and sent you on your way. This is your hole, and you have to dig yourself out of it."

He jerked his head towards the reception, and I felt as though a surgeon had cut me open to rearrange my organs.

"But, Bertie," I tried one last time, "it's Christmas Eve."

"My compliments of the season, Marius. I hope that Father Christmas brings you a new chapter." He pointed to the door, and I was in no doubt as to what he wanted.

With my head bowed, I trudged from the room. Even his stone-faced secretary looked a little sympathetic to my plight and, when I got to the exit, Bertie shouted after me, "Wait, my boy. Wait just a moment."

I turned around to see the smile on his face, and my organs jumped back into their usual places. "My dear friend, Bertie!"

"As you said, it's Christmastime." He reached into his suit jacket, and I'd never loved the man so much in the three years I'd known him.

"You've changed your mind!"

"Pardon?" He looked a little puzzled as he extracted a card from his inside pocket. "Oh, no, no. It's just that Margery wants to make sure that you're still coming to our house for lunch on Boxing Day. My beloved wife worries about you if she can't make sure that you're alive from time to time. I can assure you it will be quite the feast."

He clapped the address into my hand and pushed me towards the exit.

TWO

"Ahhhh!" This was the noise I made as I exited the Bloomsbury offices of Price-Lewis & Aster Publishing.

"Gaaaa!" This was how it sounded as I aimed a kick at a rubbish bin, slipped on the icy pavement and missed.

"Oi! What's your game?" A policeman was inevitably on hand to chastise me. "That's the King's rubbish bin, matey. It's lucky you didn't do any damage, or I'd be bringing you before a magistrate."

I was lying on my back by now but felt obliged to respond to his ridiculous claim. "So the King doesn't just own all the swans in Great Britain. He can lay claim to the rubbish bins, too, is that right?"

"Yes, it is, young man." The blue-uniformed bobby was only a few years my senior, but his bushy moustache gave him the look (and apparently the attitude) of an old man. "That's public property, and who owns the public if not the King?"

I could see that his knowledge of monarchical power was less than extensive but decided not to argue with him. "Very well. Please send my apologies to King George. I meant no offence to him or his rubbish bin."

On hearing my softer tone, he relented somewhat. "To tell the truth, I'm not in an arresting mood this morning." He became quite jubilant and was clearly eager to tell me why. "You see, I've just become a father."

I held my hand out in the hope he might help me to my feet. Instead, he shook it enthusiastically and continued his prattling. "My little Kermit is a bonny lad. If you haven't got children yourself, I really must recommend it. There is no feeling in life like the moment you lay your eyes on the little cherub for the first time."

Marvelling at the miracle of human existence, he wandered away, whistling a lively melody and spinning his truncheon in his hand. Before I could stand back up, a line of businessmen stepped over me. I considered surrendering to my misfortune and going to sleep there on the pavement.

It was amazing how much had changed in a short period of time. I'd always considered myself a confident, capable sort of person. I'd got through the war with only a few shrapnel wounds, and when I'd bought my flat, I thought that all my troubles were behind me. All I needed was to write a second book, but there was something stopping me – something that would no longer tick along as it was supposed to. So there I was, lying really very close to the gutter, looking up at the stars.

"Are you quite all right?" a refined voice called from nearby. My publisher's office was next door to Hotel Russell and... well, it was a nice part of town, to say the least.

Whoever had spoken came closer. I was still too winded to look around but could hear the click clack click of her heels on the flagstones. A dainty hand entered my view, and I put my own out to take it.

"My goodness, Marius! It is you."

I was brushing dirt and ice from my officer's coat and didn't look at her. I should have known instantly. I should have recognised her from the first word, but it had been a little over a decade, and we had both grown up a great deal in the intervening years.

I finally looked at her, and there, standing before me, was my childhood sweetheart. In an instant, it was as though a cherry tree in full bloom had sprouted in the middle of London in the dead of winter. For a moment, I thought of running across the street and through the park to safety, but then I uttered her name, and I knew there was no escaping.

"Bella."

She was even more beautiful than I remembered. I know novelists are supposed to be good with words, but that doesn't mean I can capture the true, unfathomable magic of a person. She had doe-eyes, porcelain skin, silky black hair that shone to turn the dull morning bright and so on and so forth, etc., etc.

If I continue with that task, it could well turn into an epic poem. So for everyone's sake, I'll stop there. What I will say is that, the moment I saw her, I felt as though she was what had been missing from my life. In fact, I felt just as I had on our last encounter – as if my heart had stopped beating in my chest.

"My goodness, Marius," she repeated. "It's such a surprise to bump into you like this. I haven't seen you since—"

"It's been about ten years," I interrupted, to make sure she didn't speak of our final night together. I adopted my smoothest voice and hoped that she wouldn't think too hard about where she'd just found me. "Yes, it's a pleasure to see you."

She didn't speak then. She examined me like a student studying some curious sculpture in the British Museum. As her eyes searched my face for the inevitable adaptations that so many years will produce, I wanted to take her hand again to feel it in mine for just a moment longer.

We stood there for fifteen seconds – each one of them lasting hours – and, when she finally spoke, it was not what I wanted to hear. "Marius, you look dreadful. Is everything all right?"

I laughed then. I laughed a loud, ridiculous laugh that made everything worse. "I'm just having one of those lives," I said despite myself.

"Come with me."

Before I could object, she seized my hand and pulled me along the pavement past Price-Lewis & Aster. I wondered for a moment whether she would take me to a Salvation Army shelter, make sure I had a blanket and a mug of hot soup, then disappear from my life once more. Instead, she squeezed my hand a little tighter and led me across the road to the park at the centre of the square.

"Wait here for just a moment." Her eyes looked into mine, and I would have done any last thing she requested. She darted across the road, passing through the traffic as though mere cars and lorries could do her no harm.

In all the times I had imagined our reunion, I had not pictured myself lying on my back on a London pavement, nor foreseen the look of concern that had shaped her features as she took me to a safe place and made certain that I would not run away. I can only assume that she would have done the same for a stray dog.

I watched as she reached her Sunbeam 12/16, which she already had when we were younger. It made me happy to know that she'd never moved on to the Daimlers and Bentleys that the rest of her frighteningly wealthy family surely owned. A Sunbeam was the perfect car for her.

Less perfect, though, was her chauffeur, Caxton. The old misery had never liked me, and his gaze flew across the road like an arrow as I watched her speak to him. He was the sort who had an opinion on everything and, due to his position as a trusted employee of the Montague family, felt confident enough to express himself. Even from fifty paces, I knew just how he felt about me.

"It's good to see that some things haven't changed," I said once my old friend had returned.

She put her arm through mine, and my disastrous morning was all but forgotten. "Come along, you. It's been far too long." We followed the diagonal path deeper into the park, and she chatted away as though no time had passed.

I patted her hand softly. "Never a truer word was spoken."

"I'd ask you what you've been doing, but I already know the answer," she whispered in a conspiratorial tone.

I analysed every word she said for hidden meanings. If she knew what I'd been doing, did that mean she'd made an effort to follow my career? Or had she merely stumbled across my book in a shop somewhere?

Her guilty smile hollowed out two perfect dimples on her cheeks. "I must have bought twenty copies of *A Killer in the Wings*."

"That's half the total sales." I had hoped this would sound humble, but she tutted in response.

"You're too hard on yourself. We both know how successful you are."

"I'm doing quite well," I lied and then, against my better judgement, I attempted a boast. "I live in St James's Square now. Number fifteen." I felt a fool for trying to impress the daughter of a duke with such a petty claim.

"Lucky you," was her unexpectedly melancholy response. "I would love to spend more time in the city. Hurtwood House is a beautiful old place, but I never imagined I would be living there at twenty-eight."

If she was still living at home, this had to mean she'd never married. Unless, of course, her husband had moved into her family home, and they'd— Gloomy thoughts flooded my brain, and I wished that I could have been the suave, aloof chap I liked to imagine myself.

"Tell me, what have you been doing all this time?" I asked to hide what I was really thinking. The path we were on was lined with bronze statues of old lords and politicians, and she glanced at one of them before replying.

"Oh, I'm sure you can guess." She smiled again, and it was as though the sun had come out from behind a cloud. "I helped out during the war when the government turned our house into a recovery centre for injured soldiers from the Royal Engineers. I spent a few years working at the Home Office, but then Father fell ill, and I returned to help look after him."

"I'm sorry to hear that. I've always been very fond of Lord Hurtwood."

For a moment, a look of sadness troubled her pretty face, but it soon disappeared. "He speaks very highly of you, too."

We were both tongue-tied as we reached the fountain in the middle of the square.

It was Bella who managed to find her words first. "Why were you lying on the pavement?" A worried expression troubled her brow. "Is something the matter?"

"Something the matter? With me?" I directed a puff of air towards my fringe and attempted another fake smile. "I've never been better."

"Come along, Marius. I've known you since we were five years old. You can't dupe me like that."

"I promise. The only problem is that my publisher wanted to change the name of one of the characters in my new book, and I refused. And, yes, I slipped over on the pavement and lay there as several people stepped over me, but that was only because my mind was so full of ideas for new stories." I had little hope that she would believe this feeble explanation.

"Very well…" I thought it strange that she didn't challenge me, but she had another topic to broach. "Has there been any news about your father since he disappeared?"

I hadn't realised how many things there were that I had no desire to discuss. The war, financial hardship, the last night before I left Britain, my missing father... When daydreaming of such a chance meeting, I hadn't given nearly enough thought to the topics of conversation that should be avoided at all costs.

"There's no news, I'm afraid. He just vanished into thin air. Of course, if I was half the mystery novelist that my publishers like to claim I am, I would have solved the case myself."

She took a few steps away from me then and pulled the belt on her purple woollen coat so that it hugged her a little more tightly. "I have something else for which I must apologise."

I wanted to tell her that the very idea of such a thing was quite ridiculous. I wanted to say that people like her were beyond fault, but instead I stared blankly and waited for her to continue.

"I should have written to you on the front line. I should have—"

"You had a perfectly good reason not to," was all I could say in response, but it had none of the warmth I had meant to impart. I sounded bitter for some reason, and I wished that I could have taken back each syllable just as I erase words in my books.

I couldn't think what to say to reassure her but prayed she would not return us to the previous topic. My time in France had been a perfect, tragic distraction from that night before I left for war. I was only eighteen at the time, but the conversation we had shared had scarred me as much as anything I saw on the continent.

She glanced at the silver watch on her delicate wrist, and I knew what this would mean. "I'm afraid I must go. I still have to buy some presents and drive back to Hurtwood before dinner."

I clamped my mouth shut for a few seconds to make sure that I didn't mumble anything inappropriate. What I wanted to say was, *I've spent the last decade trying to forget you and can see now what a mistake that was. I should have come straight home to you after the war and tried again, but if there's anything*

I can do to make it right, I will. Instead, I reached out to touch her shoulder and said, "Merry Christmas, Bella. Send my love to your family."

"My dear old friend, I can't say how much I've missed you." She put her hand on mine, and it felt as though she'd just warmed it by an open fire. "There is no one quite like Marius Quin."

Have you ever had one of those moments when you realise that you've been living your life in entirely the wrong way? Well, this was mine.

She turned to leave without another word and, as I am a total buffoon, I stood there and let her go. Her jade skirt swayed about her ankles, and I willed her to look back, but it wasn't to be.

In place of soft white flakes to mark the season, icy rain spat down from the skies. I pulled my collar up to keep warm, though the weather was the least of my worries. I'd just said goodbye to that precious human being for the second time, and I finally understood what was wrong with me. Everything I'd done for the last few years was for Lady Isabella Montague. I'd never wanted to live in a fancy part of London, but I'd bought an expensive flat there in the hope she'd hear about it and think me worthy of her at last. I couldn't give a fig for high society or fancy cars, but I'd become fixated on the idea of bettering myself without really knowing why.

Instead of catching a bus or spending my last few coins on a taxi, I walked in the freezing cold through Bloomsbury and around the British Museum. I passed the bright glowing theatre signs on Shaftesbury Avenue and wished that my own play had remained at such lofty heights for a little longer than it had – and that I hadn't invested my remaining savings in it.

Piccadilly was packed with cheery shoppers piled high with parcels and bags as they made their way home for Christmas, and by the time I reached my ground-floor flat in St

James's Square, I was close to swearing off the holiday altogether.

I should never have bought that albatross of a property. I should never have thought that my address would be enough to charm a woman who had everything. By mid-January, I would be homeless, and I only had myself to blame. The whole situation was unbearable... until I saw a camel-brown, 1914 Sunbeam motorcar parked in front of the building with a fashionable young woman standing beside it.

"Marius!" Bella's voice was a beam of light guiding me home. "It wasn't until we were halfway across London that something occurred to me."

I ran to her, not thinking for one moment that she would confess her undying love. I was simply ecstatic to see her again.

"What is it?" I sounded more cheerful than at any other time that day.

As her furious chauffeur glared through his foggy windscreen, she held out a card. The very sight of it was alien to me. It was printed on gold paper that was as stiff as an iron sheet, and at the top were the words "Everham Hall".

"A friend of mine is hosting a party on the thirty-first. You will come for the weekend, won't you?"

I'd never had much fondness for New Year's Eve, but she kissed me on the cheek, and there was no way I was about to turn down the invitation.

"Of course I will, Bella. How could I possibly refuse?"

THREE

Oh what a fickle world this is! I had been staring into the blackest of winters and now I felt the rush of Christmastide invigorate me. I positively danced into my flat and, free from my dark cloud, I noticed that the place had been decorated for the season. In the lounge, a Christmas tree stood beside the hearth, and sprigs of foliage had been hung about the place. I did not question who was responsible for this small transformation and, as I sat down before the fire to meditate on everything that had occurred, the man in question came into the room singing.

"I'm learning a song for Christmas
To sing upon Christmas night.
Oh, oh, how does it go?
This is the only part I know."

Uncle Stan was in fine voice and, to my surprise, I decided to join in with him.

"Ha, ha, ha, he, he, he, I hope I shall get it all right."

Before the line was complete, my mother had rushed in with her accordion.

"Oh I shall look a mug with me little brown jug,
When I sing it on Christmas night."

We simply exploded with laughter, and my uncle went to wheel in Auntie Elle in her chair.

Mother wrapped her arm around me and was all smiles. "Who is this man and what has he done with my downhearted son?"

I lifted her off the ground – accordion and all – and gave her the hug she deserved. "That grumpy old crab-stick is gone, Mother. He is no more."

"That's excellent news!" My rosy-cheeked uncle took his wife for a spin around the armchairs. "And just in time for Christmas."

Auntie Elle tittered with glee. In fact, the only one of us who looked less than delighted was our basset hound, Percy Anderson II, but then my uncle had been convinced of the dog's depressed state ever since we'd bought him as a puppy. The dear creature lay in one corner with his chin on the floor, watching the scene without moving his sorrowful brown eyes.

"Dare we ask what inspired the change in you?" my aunt enquired from beside the fireplace.

"You may, and I may tell you." I had stolen my mother's instrument of choice and was making an awful, joyous racket. The three old dears stared at me to prompt an answer and I quickly relented. "Very well. I met with Bertie this morning. The meeting was a disaster, but as I was lying outside on the pavement—"

Mother immediately started fussing, as was her right. "My poor boy, are you quite yourself? Did you bang your head?"

"I have never been better, you dear, sweet woman. Now

listen to what happened next. As I was lying on my back on the frozen ground – my plight ignored by members of the Metropolitan Police and London's financial community alike – a beautiful young lady came to my aid."

"He's in love!" Uncle Stan declared with a clap of his hands and, this time, he took his wife on a tour of the Christmas tree. "The boy's in love. Come this time next year, we will hear the patter of tiny feet echoing about these fine old walls." As you may have noticed, the man was prone to enthusiastic rhetoric.

I believe that Auntie Elle was giddy by this point, as she raised one hand to urge her husband to slow down. "Tell us what happened, Marius. Did you discover her name?"

"I didn't need to ask." I believe I allowed myself a knowing smirk. "The woman who set me back on my feet again was none other than Lady Isabella Montague."

The triumphant cheer I'd been expecting never came and, all of a sudden, our glum dog was the brightest being there. He cocked his head to look at me, as the others reacted to my news.

"Disaster!" Stan bellowed, which triggered a lament from my mother.

"Well, Christmas was nice while it lasted. I think we should stay in our rooms until the New Year to avoid any more calamities." Her curly grey hair seemed to spring out a little further from her head as she absorbed the news.

"What on earth do you mean?" I froze where I stood as the pair of them carved a figure of eight around one another on the carpet.

My uncle stopped walking to speak in a murmur. "Whatever happened between you and Bella changed you immensely, Marius. We don't want to see you go through anything like that again."

"Come along, Stan. I thought I could at least rely on you to be happy."

My mother clasped her hands together. "Happy? He wants us to be happy!"

Of the three of them, the only one to whom I was not related by blood often spoke the most sense, and I was hopeful that Auntie Elle might take my side in the matter.

She wheeled herself a few paces closer before speaking in her usual considered tone. "Marius, you must look after yourself. It's not Bella's fault, but you invested all your dreams in that girl and look where it got you."

I wanted to tell them that things had changed, and I'd made a success of myself but, sadly, they knew the truth.

"It'll be different this time," I replied. "I'm not a child anymore. I won't foolishly rush in as I did back then. I will tread with the utmost fear, like the wise old angel I have since become."

As if to contradict me, Percy tipped his head all the way back so that his muzzle pointed at the ceiling. He unleashed an ear-troubling howl in his usual doleful fashion, but Uncle Stan brightened a touch. "We will talk no more of it." He stroked the stubbly white hair at the back of his head. "It's Christmas Eve and there's a dinner to prepare... just as soon as we finish decorating the dining room."

I would have objected, but my mother was already pushing me out the door as my uncle pulled me. Uncle Stan had been a baker and had arms like telegraph poles, so there was no resisting him. My mother had arms like knitting needles, but the force of her will was enough to push me on as Auntie Elle followed us through the flat.

Perhaps inevitably, Stan sang again as we went.

"The cock sat up in the yew tree,
The hen came chitterling by;
I wish you a merry Christmas and every day a pie."

I must say, it's terribly hard to be a brooding author when living with such people. In a perfect world, I would have popped next door to the writer's room of the London Library to think long and hard about my faltering attempt to write a second novel. Instead, I spent the afternoon threading boiled sweets onto a piece of cotton to hang across the room, then cutting carrots, parsnips and potatoes to the exact right shape and size that the bossy and boisterous self-appointed chef demanded. Sniffing around the kitchen as Stan created a culinary masterpiece was the only time Percy Anderson II ever looked cheerful.

We dined in style that night. Three courses of seafood were two too many for me, but I found enough room for a helping of roast pork with crackling and honey sauce. After Stan's patented rum baba, I felt more stuffed than a pillow but, once the table was cleared, we had to get to work on the following day's meals.

It was midnight by the time I retired to my room. My barely existent notes for *A Glimpse of a Blood Moon* were scattered across my desk, but instead of reading the first chapter for the thousandth time, I decided to tend to one last important detail. I had not lavished my three favourite pensioners with the presents they deserved that year, but I'd bought them what I could and, with the flat now quiet, I tiptoed back to the drawing room to place the prettily wrapped boxes beneath the tree.

In bed at last, with my candle burning down to nothing, I passed the next half hour studying every last detail that I could observe on the invitation Bella had given me. I would be spending New Year's Eve at the home of one Cecil Sinclair... whoever that might be.

FOUR

I must admit that I rose on Christmas morning feeling flushed with excitement. It was not just the thrill of that most joyous of days, or the idea of ripping open my presents. I had woken up with an idea for Chapter Two of my book, which meant I would soon no longer be penniless. One hundred pounds would not be enough to stave off the bailiffs, but it did mean I could pay a few of the most pressing bills and buy a new suit. The next time I saw Bella, I would no longer look like a down-at-heel vagabond, but a perfectly respectable gent.

It was she, of course, who had inspired me to write. I'd always known how I wanted the book to start – the cloaked figure running through the snow on the way to meet his fate in the dilapidated mansion – but I could never make sense of how to link that thrilling scene with the rest of the tale I had in mind. All it had taken was a gold-leaf invitation and a chance meeting with the most exquisite aristocrat in Great Britain, and I could finally see a path through the knotty forest that I had been exploring for months.

I dashed off an account of twelve invitations landing on doormats around the country, described the reactions of the invitees as they opened the embossed envelopes, and finished with the doubt of whether the twelfth guest would ever receive what was coming to him. Happy with my work, I called out of the window to the messenger girl who passed her day on the bench in front of the East India Club.

"Girl, what's your name?"

"Jamie, sir. How may I be of service?" She was a smart little thing of ten or so but spoke with all the gentility of a chimney sweep.

I held out an envelope through the window, and she scampered over the road and up the front steps.

"This must be delivered to 22 Cresswell Place, Chelsea. Tell Mr Price-Lewis that I expect him to have my money at lunch tomorrow, or I will not attend."

She wrinkled her nose. "You don't reckon he'll mind my bothering him on Christmas Day, sir?"

Up close, I could see that Jamie of St James's had bright, curious eyes and a rather wise air about her.

"It may well be the best present he receives this year." I raised my voice, as she was already racing away. "I'll have a shiny florin for you when you get back."

For the next few minutes, I held on to the hope that my meeting with Bella had permanently unblocked whichever part of my brain refused to do its job. I wrote the words "Chapter Three" on a piece of blank paper and was confident that the rest would come. The life of Marius Quin is never so easy, though, and I encountered the same mist in my head that had been there since I'd finished my last book. I had a vague idea of what I thought should happen next, but when it came to putting words together to form sentences and for those sentences to make up a story, the process ground to a halt.

And so, instead of accumulating words by the thousand, counting the money that would soon be deposited in my bank account and saving my family from penury, my head started nodding and I fell asleep.

It was not long before Uncle Stan woke up the neighbourhood with a rendition of "The Wassailing Song". He bumbled into the room with his band of followers. Mother had her accordion, Auntie Elle sang as she wheeled herself along, and even Percy was howling in time with the music. I would like to say that this was unusual behaviour for them, but it would not be true.

"Merry Christmas, dear boy," my mother said, as the musical accompaniment continued. "It is always a merry one when we are together."

I remembered my father saying much the same before he disappeared a decade earlier, and I wished, as I did most mornings, that he was there with us. Such moping was not permitted in the Quin family, though, and I was transported to the kitchen to enjoy a breakfast of oatcakes, eggs and sausages that Stan had cooked while the rest of us dozed.

Breakfast led to lunch, lunch to supper, supper to dinner and the night of Christmas Day soon turned into the feast of St Stephen. I shared a suitably grand and festive banquet with my dear publisher's family, and the message I'd sent him had the desired effect. Not only was there one hundred pounds waiting for me at Bertie's house, the food was exquisite. In fact, each day that week rolled into the next as though the delicious meals we were enjoying had the power to warp time.

In amongst all that roistering and jollification, there were trips to my tailor, further naps and the odd hour spent failing to write another chapter. I killed such time remembering the adventures I'd had with Bella when we were children and trying not to get overexcited by our imminent reunion.

On the afternoon of the thirty-first, I stood in front of the mirror to look at my new clothes. In my blacker-than-black three-piece, with mother-of-pearl buttons on the waistcoat and cufflinks to match, I couldn't help thinking I'd made a good purchase. My dark, curly hair needed a trim, but sat well on my head for once and, with the Christmas stubble I'd accumulated now removed, I thought I looked quite dashing.

When I got to the front door, my family were already queuing to say goodbye.

"Your dad would be proud of you." Uncle Stan was the only one amongst us who regularly spoke of his brother, and yet it still sent a shock through me whenever he did.

"Would he?" I asked, as such simple statements seemed beyond my comprehension when it came to my absent father.

"Of course he would. You're off to a lavish party. There'll be film stars and rich ladies in attendance." He apparently knew more than I did.

"Will there?"

"Haven't you heard of Cecil Sinclair?" Mother asked when my expression remained perplexed.

"No. Have you?"

"He's famous," she explained in the tone she reserved for explaining simple concepts to me. The biggest drawback to living with my mother was the fact she still treated me in the exact same way as when I'd lost my last milk tooth. "He was the actor in that one about the secret door, and that other one about pirates."

"Ah, yes," I gently mocked her. "My two favourite films: the one about the secret door and that other one about pirates."

Auntie Elle angled her wicker chair in order to glare at me. "Marius, even I've heard of Cecil Sinclair, and I'm ancient."

"We clearly have that in common." I didn't know what else to say to her, so I bent to place a kiss on the tight grey bun on top of her head.

Mother embraced me, Auntie Elle waved goodbye, and Stan handed me Percy's lead. "I know that you'll walk him from time to time. He doesn't need a lot of attention, but he does still like to explore."

"I hadn't planned to take the dog, Stan. It's a swanky party in a country pile, not a picnic in the park."

"But you know he's been blue recently." He slapped me around the back with his sizeable mitt. It hurt. "With a little holiday, he should perk right up."

I peered down at my beloved hound, who did look terribly sad that I was leaving. The great bags beneath his eyes were more distended than ever and appeared to have collected two pools of tears. I knew I couldn't resist his guilty look and was about to accept him as a companion on that weekend's adventure when Uncle Stan walked us both through the door.

"And you'll get your mother Cecil Sinclair's autograph, won't you?" He looked over his shoulder to check that he had not been overheard. "She wouldn't say anything, but she just loves his films."

After all the cooking the two of them did for me, this was the least I could do. "I will make it my highest priority to secure Mother her prize."

"There's a good lad." He pinched my cheek and gave me a hug goodbye. "Happy New Year, Marius," he said in that low, thundering voice of his. "We'll be thinking about you at midnight."

Singing as he went, he slipped back into the flat, and I found myself outside my own front door in the freezing cold.

I looked down at my canine companion who did not seem a great deal perkier than before. "Are you ready for a wild weekend, Percy? I hope you've brought your dinner jacket."

Percy said nothing because he is a dog.

FIVE

My glossy red Invicta 3 Litre is a sleek and beautiful beast that I bought at the same time as the flat. Much like my immodest abode, my car is gorgeous, impractical, and saddled me with a large amount of debt. The problem with becoming a successful author at such a tender age was that I was old enough to spend a lot of money, but not clever enough to realise that it would soon run out. I would have to content myself with the knowledge that, if we learn from our mistakes, I was surely on the path to great wisdom.

I opened the car door for Percy, and he glumly climbed into the passenger seat without even a thank you. Some snow had fallen over the last few days, but it was yet to stick in any great quantity. The trees in the centre of the square had a dusting of white, like icing sugar on a Christmas cake. My neighbourhood looked so pretty that I felt a little sorry to leave, but I started the engine, and we pulled off through the city. There were few other cars on the road. Most sensible people had stayed warm at home to welcome in 1928 with their families. Only dolts like me would drive to the middle of nowhere to meet a group of people I probably wouldn't like.

Everham Hall was forty miles west of London and, by the time I'd left the outskirts of the city at Hammersmith and threaded my way between those green and pleasant parks at Richmond and Kew, the skies opened, and several tankers' worth of white confetti fell to Earth. It is amazing how swiftly the world can transform. Those first few flakes led to thousands more, and the ground was soon covered with snow.

I'd started the chilly journey chatting to Percy, but he still wasn't saying anything, and so I fell quiet to admire the scenery. Well, that lasted for approximately two minutes before my head was full of the woman I was on my way to see. If I'd achieved anything since leaving my village of Hurtwood, it was the ability to not think about my last night there. Meeting Bella had changed that and, as the light died, I relived every excruciating moment of it.

I'm sure there are certain things you will already have realised. She was rich – the daughter of the local duke, no less – and my family was not. Dad was a solicitor, but he was the kind of man who would go out of his way to help those in need and rarely got around to charging his clients. This meant that, although we were occasionally in the orbit of the Montague family, based on the state of our clothes and the type of people with whom my father had dealings, we really shouldn't have been.

I fell in love with Bella when I was five years old and didn't realise it for the next thirteen. I'm aware that sounds like nonsense; five-year-olds don't fall in love. But that's only because most of them have never met Lady Isabella Montague. I've told you how beautiful she is – porcelain hair, glossy skin, etc., etc. – but it was her spirit which entrapped and enthralled poor infant Marius so intensely.

Her parents never objected to my presence at Hurtwood House, the sumptuous mansion that had been in their family for centuries. They didn't seem to mind that I followed around their firstborn, much as Percy follows Uncle Stan about the kitchen. I was her best friend throughout our childhood. After the war broke out – then dragged on for so long that I went from being a snivelling adolescent to a near-grown man – the friendship turned into something more. And just as we both acknowledged this unexpected change, I was sent off to the barracks at Aldershot for my initial training to fight in the war. As my companions faced their fears of death, injury and imprisonment at the hand of our Teutonic foe, it was the thought of never seeing Bella again that I found most frightening.

In the two days between the end of basic training and the boat setting sail for my enforced holiday abroad, I decided that what I really needed to do was ask the most precious and unique human being I'd ever met to be my wife.

Forget Cecil Sinclair. As I drove to Everham Hall, I was watching a film starring Marius Quin and his elegant leading lady, Bella Montague. But at the big finale, when the hero finally got the chance to ask his sweetheart whether she would marry him, should he be so lucky as to return from the war, the projector in my head malfunctioned. You see, that is the one moment in my life I simply can't bring myself to think about. It is too torturous, too painful to recollect.

When the war was over, I didn't go home as I should have. I stayed in the army for as long as I could, then lived in Paris and Berlin to put off the inevitable. I fell in love with women who weren't Bella and cities that I'd never dreamed of visiting. I surrounded myself with artists and bohemians in the hope that their talent would rub off on me, but when I sat down to write something bold and beautiful, I ended up with a mystery novel. My father had always enjoyed them, so it made perfect sense. But I returned to Britain at twenty-five with an unpublished manuscript, and any number of ghosts that I was determined to ignore.

As we've already established, Percy is no great conversationalist, but I'd have been better off talking to him than reminiscing on unhappy times. With the snow now thick under our wheels, we crawled through Hampshire in the direction of the Chiltern Hills before I saw the sign for Everham and turned off the road.

I didn't get far along the increasingly narrow lane before the way was blocked by an imposing wrought-iron gate with twisting metalwork and a stone phoenix on the pillars on either side. I couldn't make out anything of the house just yet, but there were what looked like bowls of fire running up the driveway and a high wall surrounding the property. I stopped the car, and a guard in a regimental black and gold livery tapped on the window.

"Your name please, sir?" He spoke in a manner which suggested that if he didn't like my answer, he would dispose of me as he saw fit.

I wound the window down a crack. "Marius Quin, I was invited by—"

"Do you have any identification to that effect?" His voice sharp and officious, he interrupted before I could finish speaking.

I searched under the seat for my wallet. My fingers were numb from the cold and I had to pull off one leather glove with my teeth before extracting my driver's licence. "I'm afraid the dog didn't bring his. But I can vouch for his identity."

The guard did not respond. He looked at the name on my card, then down at his list and then at my face again, as though trying to determine whether I looked like a Marius. He eventually passed my licence back through the gap in the window but kept staring at a certain basset hound.

"He's very well behaved," I reassured him. "Isn't that right, Percy?"

Percy said nothing.

"I suppose I'll have to let you pass." The guard did not look happy, but he opened the gate and waved us through all the same.

The branches of the elm trees that led up the driveway seemed to have been painted white by some careful hand. They entwined above our heads to make a tunnel through which little light could break. Between each pit of flame, we entered a short patch of darkness before emerging once more. Despite the neatly trimmed hedges that I could see up ahead, and the well-kept gravel path beneath the trees, for a moment it felt as if we would be stuck in that repeating loop of fire and darkness for ever.

Everham Hall came into view at last, and we broke free from the cover of the wooded path. Perhaps it was due to the snow-laden gardens that stretched across the estate, but it was as though we had entered some fairyland, and Everham was the castle at its centre. I had visited grander stately homes before, but this was definitely the strangest I'd seen. It was crooked, for one thing, with a huge tower on one side and a lower gallery on the other, which was dotted with tall chimneys.

There were irregularly shaped windows all over, and a mansard roof behind the tower, as though a Parisian housing block had been dropped in the middle of an English country pile. The one unifying feature was the zebra striping of brick and stone that covered the façade and, as the place had been re-sketched in winter colours, at first glance, it was hard to comprehend the building as a whole.

I drove around an oval courtyard to the front of the house, where the only sign of life was a small electric light burning over the front porch. I wasn't sure whether to get out of the car or double back and drive home as fast as I could.

I turned the engine off as the footman on duty rushed from the porch to guide us inside. He had no fear of the cold or the thick flakes that turned his dark hair white, but the same could not be said of Percy.

"Come on, boy," I urged the reluctant hound as the servant took my bag from the luggage compartment. "I can feel my ears freezing as I stand here. Could you please hurry?"

Percy only turned his chin up at the suggestion. In the end, I couldn't wait any longer and picked up the big lump in both arms to run inside. Even this short trip covered my trousers in snow and froze my toes, so I was relieved to find a blazing fire in the entrance hall and a butler waiting to greet me. What I wasn't prepared for was the starkly modern interior of that ancient house. In place of the wooden panels and the smell of beeswax I'd been expecting, it was all black and gold wallpaper, hard, angular furniture and strange metallic sculptures embedded in the walls like shrapnel.

"Mr Quin, I presume?" the middle-aged butler enquired. Like all butlers I had met, he had a well-rounded belly and a slightly superior attitude. "If you follow me, sir, I will show you to your room for the night."

"Thank you..." I cleared my throat to suggest that I wished to know his name, but he ignored me and led off towards the stairs. Percy has never been a fan of such things, so I had to pick him up again as the footman passed my bag to a similarly ranked counterpart, who followed at a discreet distance.

For all the modern touches in the entrance hall, it was impossible to disguise some of the traditional features of the house. The banisters on the twisting staircase were ornately carved with an old family crest on each post, and they had tall, skinny figures of knights and maidens in place of ordinary spindles. Above this, a rounded window that looked as though it had been cut straight out of a nearby church and stuck to the side of the building gave a view of the dimly lit gardens. Much like the façade, nothing was quite uniform in this strange house. The medieval rubbed up against the modern, just as Victorian paintings were displayed in Baroque frames.

I could only assume that it was as much for atmosphere as

anything else, but all the corridors I saw were lit with candles and gas lamps. We reached a long, straight hallway that carved through the house and, at intervals of a few yards, large candelabras spilt light (and wax) across our path. Perhaps there was a man in Cecil Sinclair's employ whose sole job it was to tend to the maintenance and illumination of these fixings. There were so many that, by the time he lit the last one, I could only imagine that he had to start again with the first.

"Here we are, Mr Quin," the grey-waistcoated butler said with a bow of the head. "Your room."

He held out a gloved hand to point to the door then turned away without another word.

"I'm sorry," I called after him when the silence of that corridor deafened me. "But where is everyone?"

He stopped and, in the same slow methodical manner in which he'd led us there, turned back to me.

"In the games room, of course, sir." He said this as though it was the most obvious thing in the world.

"Of course," I echoed without thinking. "Thank you for your help."

"You are most welcome." He recommenced his journey, and I got the distinct feeling that he believed I should be incredibly grateful for his time.

Puzzled by more or less everything that had happened so far, I watched the butler retreat as the footman opened the door for Percy to have a sniff about inside. My designated home for the weekend contained the largest four-poster bed I'd ever seen. It was big enough for a family of eight, and I was worried that I might get lost inside it when I went to sleep. The décor of the room was as old-fashioned as the hallway, and each wall held a series of small sketches that looked as though they dated back to the dark ages.

"What do you think?" I asked Percy but, quite understandably, the footman assumed I was talking to him.

"It's one of the nicest rooms on this floor, sir." Something in his voice suggested that, although this was true, there were grander parts of the house in which to stay. He put my bag down on a low table between the two windows, bowed and scuttled from the room before I could ask him any more stupid questions.

In the meantime, Percy had taken his place on an ottoman at the foot of the bed. It didn't look strong enough to hold his weight. His head, paws and tail spilled over the side, but he evidently found it to his liking.

"I don't think I've ever set foot in such a curious house," I told him, and in response, he closed his eyes and went to sleep.

I sat down on that giant-sized bed and sighed. "I can only hope the other guests are chattier than you are, old friend."

SIX

I was already wearing my best outfit and, after a quick wash, decided to search the house for livelier company than Percy. As I navigated that corridor once more, I had to wonder what ancient spirits walked the curious old place. Between the narrow, round-topped windows on several of the walls, there was that same crest I'd noticed on the banisters. It had two interlinking phoenixes and the word "Cornwallis" inscribed at the bottom. I took this to be the name of the original family who had built Everham Hall, and I mused on how the grand old place had ended up in the hands of some gaudy film star.

The more I looked, the more I noticed that crest. It was there on the stained-glass windows, carved into the doors of various bedrooms and, perhaps most visibly, on ornamental shields that were dotted amongst old portraits in the corridor. I found it curious that they hadn't been thrown out when the place was redecorated.

Thankfully, there was more of interest in Everham Hall than its interior decoration. By the time I got down to the entrance hall, two other guests were arriving.

"Hullo there, new friend." A neatly coiffed man in a camel-hair coat and silk scarf stood at the bottom of the stairs . "I'm Anton Cavendish, and this is my wife, Alma." He rushed forward to seize my hand and shake it profusely. "And you would be?"

"Marius Quin. I'm an old pal of Bella's."

"Ah, so you're the author." He was still shaking my hand, and it was beginning to hurt. "I've heard that your book is rather good. Really, top-notch stuff. We should discuss the possibility of turning it into a film."

The petite, yet rather forceful woman next to him shook her head and released a critical tut. "Really, Anton? We've only just stepped through the door and you're already talking business. Can we at least find the others before the evening gets too dull?"

He dropped their bags to the floor, tossed his coat towards the disgruntled butler and fell to one knee. "My sweet, kind, generous wife, will you ever forgive me?"

She couldn't stay angry for long and tittered as she pulled him to his feet. "Get up, you sillikin." She turned to address me. "It's nice to meet you, Marius. I'm sure that Anton here will have you slaving away on a script in no time."

It was hard not to like them, and I had to bite my tongue to stop myself revealing just how useful any scriptwriting fee would be. Perhaps sensing my struggle, Anton set about putting me at ease. He placed his arm around my shoulder and directed me through the house as he chattered away about his work as a director and his biggest star, Miss Alma Cavendish herself.

"She was working in the millinery department of Selfridges, and I knew I had found someone special. Unlike her, I instantly fell in love."

"Ignore every word this man utters, Marius," the actress instructed. "Unless you want to be a director, in which case you should do all you can to learn the gift of the gab from him."

"You needn't fear that," I told her. "I tried my hand at

theatrical directing and it wasn't for me. As a matter of fact, I've been so busy since I published my first book, I haven't had the chance to go to the cinema in years."

"Nose to the grindstone, no doubt." Her husband giggled at this. "Still, I don't blame you. Film is the medium for artists who wish to tell stories to simpletons. You authors are the real thing."

Not wishing to dissuade him from offering me a job, I didn't know how to respond to such a comment. Luckily, we'd reached our destination, and Alma opened the door to an opulent salon where a few of the other guests were already engaged in a game of darts.

"You came," Bella called from beside the billiard table.

I can't describe the sensation as she sped across the room. I don't think I'd ever felt important enough to have inspired such a reaction. Sadly, it didn't last long.

"Alma, it's been forever," my old friend said as she embraced the woman beside me.

Anton was afforded a kiss on each cheek, whereas Bella just smiled in my direction. She evidently considered it unnecessary to offer any superficial display of affection to the man she'd known longest. Well, that's what I told myself, and to lend this idea a sliver of credibility, she became quite animated as she described me to the others.

"Everyone, this is Marius. We're friends from back in Hurtwood. Of course, Marius left our backwater behind for the bright lights of London when he returned from the war." She paused before revealing one final titbit. "He's a mystery writer."

"Quin!" a young man holding three darts in one hand declared. "You're Marius Quin!"

"That's right." I should probably have blushed or pretended to be embarrassed that he'd recognised me, but I wasn't used to this kind of attention and looked back blankly as the sallow-faced character in the cheaply assembled suit rushed over.

"I loved *A Killer in the Wings*. It's simply the best mystery

I've read in years." He gave me a jovial slap, thankfully with his empty hand. Even I thought he'd gone too far with his praise, but he had more to say. "The final scene where the killer turns out to be—"

"This is Carl Wilson," Bella interrupted with just a hint of apology. How could I not adore her after she stopped him from finishing that sentence in a room full of potential readers? "He's a colleague of Gilbert's."

Before I could enquire who Gilbert was, Wilson forced me into an armchair and proceeded to interrogate me for the next half an hour about my writing process. He was in his early twenties and was one of those people who never question that you might not want to discuss whatever it is they want to discuss. There was a strange intensity to him, and his deep brown eyes were forever moving. He was also rather boring, and dear Bella glanced across the room at me to sympathise with my plight.

As Wilson prattled, I had a chance to take in the other members of our party. I had somehow assumed that, as Bella had so freely added me to the list of invitees, it would be a grand event, but I could see now that it was an intimate affair. In addition to the exuberant pair I'd already met, there was a woman in a sparkling red beaded dress with matching lipstick who didn't seem capable of standing still. When she wasn't dancing, or playing darts, she draped herself over Anton and Alma, then moved on to Bella and back again. I didn't learn much about her – as Wilson was both chatty and terribly loud. All I heard was that her name was Poppy, and I got the definite impression that no one liked her.

I spotted one last figure on the telephone in the far corner of the room. He was approximately my age (twenty-eight on my last birthday for those who put much stake in such things). Despite his businessman's attire, there was something sporty about him. He was broad and muscular, much like the boys I'd known as a child whose only topics of conversation extended to rugby, cricket and football. I couldn't hear what he was saying over the noise of Wilson's chattering, though the man's grave expression told me he was not enjoying the conversation. At first, I took him to be our host, but then the door flew open, apparently of its own volition, and I realised my mistake.

"Ladies and gentlemen..." The doorway was unoccupied. There was merely a dark space where the speaker should have been. "Here comes the man you've all been dying to see. It's Cecil Sinclair!"

In walked one of those Spanish-looking fellows who've appeared in just about every film since Rudolph Valentino first graced the screen. He had a cocktail in either hand, and bright red liquid splashed onto the carpet as he waved them through the air.

"Cecil, you show-off," Alma chastised him, and I knew exactly what role she occupied in the group of friends.

"Merry Christmas, old boy," Anton declared with a hoot.

"It's too late for that." Cecil sipped from first one drink, then the other, though the contents looked identical. "I am only interested in the coming year. And what a year it will be!"

Poppy stalked over to him, and the pair commenced a truly horrific display of physical affection. They were all legs and lips and made such a noise that it sounded like someone was trying to force a cat down a plughole. I didn't like to watch but felt it was necessary to get a picture of the man who had convened this soiree. It wasn't just his dramatic entrance that I found eccentric. He was dressed in a red velvet suit with a floral neckerchief and, quite unlike any man I'd met before, had a diamond stud in either ear. He was evidently no enemy of extravagance, and he even had matching gemstones on his leather Oxfords.

"Why are you staring at me like that?" he screeched when he finally pulled away from his paramour.

I was glad that I wasn't the focus of his ire, but poor, dull

Carl Wilson didn't know where to look. "I'm sorry... I'm just a huge fan, Mr Sinclair. Really, I am."

"Cecil, it's only early and you're already drunk." Bella stepped forward to tell him off. "Try to be civil, or I'll take my friends and leave."

The film star had lost his swagger and wore a cheerless grimace as he addressed his young admirer. "As you're a fan, I can forgive you for gawking, but don't let it happen again." He had a rather piercing voice, so it was a good thing that he didn't need it for his career on the silent screen.

"Of course, Mr Sinclair." Wilson was a born groveller and bowed his head.

Cecil searched the room for something that might interest him. He had a hunter's gaze, which soon came to rest on the man on the telephone. "Gilbert! You've already crossed me once this Christmas. Would you hurry up and join the party?"

"You tell him, darling," Poppy cheered him on and, when Gilbert continued with his call, Cecil really lost his temper.

"For the love of all things pagan! Would you hang up and come over here?" Everything the man did had a stagey quality to it. If I was being generous, I would say that he was in his late thirties, but now that I could see him more closely, it was clear that he wore a layer of make-up to hide the lines around his eyes.

"No one ever takes my parties seriously enough." He deliberated over each word to ensure that whatever he said had the greatest possible impact. It was evident that he wanted us to pay attention to him and him alone. What I couldn't fathom was why my dear, smart Bella would want anything to do with such a character.

"I'll be one minute," Gilbert covered the mouthpiece to respond, but this concession was not enough for the fabulous Cecil Sinclair.

"You'll finish this moment." Throwing down one of the now

empty glasses, which bounced across the carpet hard enough for the stem to break in two, the actor was across the room in a flash, and his hand darted out to cut the connection.

"You swine," Gilbert responded. "That was an important call. You have no right to..."

Sinclair had already spun on his heel to return to his beloved. "This is my party, my house, and you are my guests. I can do whatever I like." He sounded like a spoilt child. In his brightly coloured palace, he was definitely spoilt, and it was only his youth that was lacking.

From Bella's restrained reaction, I could see that this behaviour was nothing new. I would have expected the fiercely brave young woman I had known to put an end to such poor conduct. Time had clearly affected us both, but she'd changed more than I had previously realised.

In the end, it fell to the director, Anton Cavendish, to prevent Gilbert from punching the actor in the mouth.

"What a scene!" He clapped his hands in appreciation. "You know, Cecil, I'll have to find you a part as a villain in one of my films. You are simply so convincing." His silver-tongued compliments were bound to have a bigger impact than any attempt to censure the drunken star. "Truly, you've put on quite the act for us."

Sinclair's eyes disappeared up into his skull. "I do my best." He collapsed onto the black leather sofa and pulled Poppy on top of him with a joyful whoop.

I looked at the chap in the pinstripe suit who was still staring at the telephone as though he could will the operator to reconnect the call. Apparently unable to react to what she'd witnessed, Bella loitered not far away. There was something terribly hesitant in her manner, and I had to wonder how the years we'd spent apart had treated her.

With Sinclair and Poppy canoodling on the sofa, some calm had returned to the room, but no one looked particularly relieved about it. Alma was clinging to the billiard table as though she were afraid it might blow away. Even that quivering jellyfish Carl Wilson, who did not appear to have met the uncouth actor before, looked quite terrified by his encounter.

Bella came to stand behind my chair and spoke in such a low voice that I could barely hear her over the sound of fervid kissing. "Cecil's not always like this. He can be quite sweet when he's sober."

I turned back to her, but she wouldn't look at me directly and kept her eyes on the window to watch the falling snow.

"What did you expect he would be doing on New Year's Eve if not drinking?" I softly demanded, so that she alone could hear me.

She didn't have an answer, and I once more had to question how any of these people had ended up at Everham Hall.

"You must be Marius." Gilbert had given up on his telephone call and crossed the room with great strides to talk to me. "The brave and gallant Marius Quin who went missing on the continent and has finally turned up again." He let out a knowing laugh that cut through me like a cold shower on a winter's morning. "Don't worry, pal. Bella didn't tell me too many of your secrets. I'll try not to be jealous if you do the same."

I was taken aback that he knew this much about me and found myself completely unprepared for what happened next. Passing my chair, he went to put his arm around a woman who was evidently so superior to him in every way that I considered cutting his arm off with one of the hunting knives that were attached to the wall between the windows.

"This is my..." Bella began by way of an explanation. "This is Gilbert Baines. Perhaps I mentioned him last week?"

She jolly well hadn't mentioned a muscle-bound boyfriend, or I would never have accepted her invitation to the party. It was lucky that I was as rigid as a long-dead rabbit, or I might have told her just that.

"It's a pleasure to meet you," Baines continued. He had a nasal voice and a face that looked as though it had been ironed flat. I didn't like one single thing about him, and I'd known him for less than a minute.

I had to question how I'd fallen into such a nasty trap. I had entered a haunted house on New Year's Eve with a group of people who clearly didn't like one another and the doppelganger of a woman I had once loved. It was hard to know what else could go wrong, but the nervy silence was even worse now that Gilbert had introduced himself.

In the end, it was Cecil Sinclair who broke the hush. "Why do you all look so miserable? This is supposed to be a celebration."

There was a button on the wall behind the sofa and, a short while after our host had pressed it five times, the snooty butler pushed a trolley into the room.

The dashing, though despicable, thespian rose to seize a bottle of cognac. "We should be drinking, dancing and having fun."

"You promised you'd be good, old boy." Anton's judgemental tone had no effect, but he wouldn't give up. "Are you sure that's a good idea?"

Cecil pulled the stopper out with his teeth and spat it across the room. "No, it's not a good idea. It's an excellent one."

He tipped the bottle down his throat and, when he could drink no more, wiped his mouth with the back of his velvet sleeve and collapsed face first onto the carpet.

SEVEN

To most people's disappointment, Cecil Sinclair had not been poisoned.

Poppy checked that he was still breathing, then let out a high-pitched laugh that rattled the snooker balls. "He told me tonight was going to be fun, and I'm certainly having a riot." She clapped her hands together and went to help herself to a glass of wine. I found it odd that the butler hadn't stayed to pour the drinks, but perhaps our incapacitated host valued his privacy.

As if there weren't enough prickly guests by this stage in the evening, two more members of the group had arrived just in time to witness Cecil's disappearing trick.

"I see my son is as upstanding as ever." A tall, barrel-chested man in his sixties walked over to prod the actor with the end of one hobnailed boot. "You used to be such a charmer, boy. Now look at you!"

A much younger woman in a simple cream dress lingered in the doorway as though afraid to step inside the room. The man who, it did not take a great detective to determine, was Cecil's father, hauled his son to his feet in one smooth movement. Cecil had neither the strength nor the desire to stand and was soon deposited on the sofa once more.

"I'm Edith Havelock." The girl was a dainty, nervous sort of creature who looked quite out of place as she finally crossed the threshold. She went round the group introducing herself and repeated her name to each of us in case we hadn't heard.

"I'm Carl Wilson," the next youngest member of the group responded with wide eyes as he took in the enchanting sylph. "I work at the bank with—"

"I'm Poppy," Cecil's brash and bright paramour interrupted without the hint of a smile. "Just Poppy. It's my stage name."

"Are you in films, too?" the ethereal young woman replied.

"I will be soon. Cecil says I could be the finest actress of my generation."

"Well, I was a secretary." Edith spoke with such hesitation that she only just managed to get the words out. "Until I met Ross."

Wilson seemed most excited by the delicate young woman's presence, and I could only assume that he'd failed to realise what her role there was. I didn't entirely blame him. There must have been forty years between Cecil's father and his pretty companion. If I hadn't been such an eager observer of my fellow men, I might have mistaken her for his daughter. The good thing about being so far removed from this group of eccentrics was that I could follow everything without the others paying me much attention. Even before I became a writer, I'd always enjoyed studying those around me, and one thing that struck me for certain was that Cecil's father and Miss Edith Havelock were sweethearts.

I'd known such pairings before, but theirs was most unusual. He was not one of those lithe, outgoing sorts who sometimes attract young admirers. He had a gruff manner, a fisherman's beard and a bulbous nose that was the colour of a good Burgundy wine.

In the end, it fell to Bella to introduce him. "This is Cecil's father, Ross Sinclair."

Sinclair senior briefly glanced across at her, then returned to his task of looming over his inebriated son. A rough-voiced, scurvy fellow with no manners was just what this party was lacking. A few minutes earlier, I'd been planning to fetch my dog and drive off into the snow, but I was warming to the thought of the fireworks that would surely be unleashed.

Alma evidently had a wiser head on her shoulders than most there and, when she approached the old man to speak, I finally understood something of this mismatched congregation. "We only came tonight because Cecil told us that he'd stopped using that stuff."

"He promised he'd put it behind him," Anton added and came to wrap his arm around his wife's waist so that a row of spectators now formed to inspect the actor's sorry state. I noticed that she flinched a mite as he touched her.

"What was it this time?" Ross Sinclair's eyes were still fixed on his son.

"Chloral hydrate, I'd assume." Anton rubbed his wife's side absent-mindedly. "It almost ruined the last production we worked on together. I had to use doubles and film them from behind when he couldn't come to the set."

This sad recollection was interrupted by Poppy's grating laughter. "Oh, you are such bores. Cecil was just having a little fun. There's nothing wrong with that on this of all nights."

Ross shot the girl a nasty look and signalled to Anton that he would need help to move Cecil somewhere more private. They were about to pick up the sleeping actor when a series of loud bangs came from outside. Edith Havelock jumped at each one, but Bella ran to the window to take in the view.

Bright explosions in various colours lit up the sky. The nearby town must have been making the most of a break in the bad weather to enjoy the night's firework display. The snow had provided a white screen on which to project and, across the courtyard of Everham Hall, reds, yellows, greens and blues mixed together to colour the ashen landscape. It was quite spectacular and, in a few seconds, every last guest had come to the window to marvel.

"It's beautiful," Wilson said in that strangely cautious voice of his.

Gilbert was standing alongside me and made a point of pulling Bella tightly against him, thus disproving his claim that he had no desire to make me jealous. This brief moment of unity added to the sense of separation among us. When the sky fell dark again, that same uneasy tension returned.

"Will you help me take him up now?" Ross Sinclair asked the director.

Anton considered the request in pensive silence before nodding, and the men took an arm each. Cecil's head rolled about and there was a faint smile on his face, but he did not stir.

"Don't leave without me," Edith cried to her inamorata, as though he was the only one who could keep her safe.

She scampered after the three men, and together they disappeared from the room. The remaining guests glanced at one another before the decision was made to disperse.

"I'm going to change before dinner," Alma declared, and her announcement triggered further departures.

"I'll go to the office to make my call," Gilbert told Bella, whereas Poppy floated from the room without an explanation.

Only Bella, Carl Wilson and I remained. I hoped that he would follow the others, and I could finally quiz my friend on what she was doing with these people, but Wilson wasn't the sort to take a hint.

"Perhaps we could go for a walk, Bella?" I suggested with my eyes on our unwanted companion.

"I'm fine here, thank you." Wilson released his high-pitched laugh. "I've got a book to finish and plenty of time before dinner." He sat back down in his armchair, and I marvelled that any man could fail to gauge the mood around him to such an extent.

"Of course," Bella replied in that nervous tone that apparently characterised her these days. She took a long-sleeved silk kimono from the back of one of the chairs and led me from the room.

"We don't need to go far." As I spoke, she opened the door to the next room, and we found ourselves in a large, airy salon with an unusual combination of Queen Anne furniture and ever so modern artworks. I noticed a brightly coloured Cézanne and what I took to be a Metzinger. This raised an important question that had only skirted around the periphery of my brain until now.

"How could Cecil Sinclair afford a place like this?" I asked Bella as she pulled the door shut and stood with her hands pressed against it. "Actually, no. First tell me why you ever imagined it would be pleasant for me to come here this evening. I thought you were doing me a favour by introducing me to a group of people who could further my career, or that you simply wanted to make sure that I was getting out of the house enough. That's not it though, is it?"

In one quick movement, she turned to look at me. "I'll admit that I'm glad you're here, Marius." She went to stand at the immense windows that opened onto that garden of white. "Gilbert has been Cecil's advisor for some time. He provides him with financial guidance, but there have been some problems recently."

"Oh, so your boyfriend is here to guard his investment." I couldn't just stand there, so I marched across the room to a drinks cabinet with a crystal decanter filled with... something more or less drinkable. "Thank you so much for involving me."

"I'm sorry, I should have told you the whole story before you came. But I couldn't bear to face this evening without you."

"That's not an explanation, Bella. You seem to have plenty of other friends as it is."

She bit her lip, and I believe she would have drawn blood if she'd pressed much harder. "I've said I'm sorry, Marius. I'm sorry that I didn't share my fears over this party. And I'm sorry that I told the man I love who you are." She paused for a moment, perhaps to give me the chance to die a little at her words. "And, yes, I'm sorry that Gilbert acted the way he did in there. I will take him up on the matter as soon as I can, but it's hardly surprising after everything we were to one another."

I snatched my drink and took a gulp, but in my head, I was screaming, *What were we to one another?*

When I said nothing, she continued. "No matter what he might say, Gilbert is jealous. He's worried that he can't compete with the past. But he's a good man and, if you take the time to get to know him, I'm sure you'll see that."

I looked straight at her, and in that moment, I wanted to tell her everything. I wanted to apologise for what I had done and get down on my knees before her to explain that I'd spent much of the last decade trying to become the man she deserved. Instead, I maintained my stern expression and said, "You've made it perfectly clear that he's got no need to worry. And after tonight, he won't have to put up with my presence in your life anymore."

She gasped then, and I had to hope that it was not just the cruelty of my words that had alarmed her but the thought of never seeing me again.

"I've only just found you," she whispered and then peered about the room in search of something to keep me there. "You asked me about Cecil," she said rather desperately and hurried over to the Cézanne. Her golden dress shimmered as she went, and one bare arm shot out to draw attention to the opulence all around. "He didn't buy this place on the back of his acting. He married a rich widow who swiftly died and left him a fortune.

He bought Everham Hall from some old family who were clinging to the estate as a last sign of their faded wealth. I didn't just invite you here because I needed an old friend for support. I thought this house could help loosen the cogs in your head. I thought it might inspire your next book."

Before I could lie that I didn't need anyone's help to write a mystery, we heard three short bangs. The surprise must have shown on my face as she walked closer to check that I was all right.

"It's just more fireworks," she assured me.

"Listen." I held one hand to my ear a little theatrically, but it made my point. "Nothing more – just silence. Those weren't fireworks. The fireworks have finished and, if children in the village were still playing with them, they wouldn't have sounded as though they were coming from inside this house."

Bella followed behind as I ran from the salon back to the corridor. We peeked inside the games room, but Wilson was engrossed in his book and didn't appear to have heard anything.

"Where are you going?" Bella asked. I didn't know the answer, but I followed my ears.

"The shots sounded like they came from the front of the house. That would mean the tower, I assume?"

"Shots?" Bella had always been smart. "How can you be so sure that's what they were?"

"I would say it was obvious considering the japes I got up to back in 1918."

We'd arrived in the entrance hall, and I was about to take the stairs when she seized my arm to stop me.

"Not up there. The tower is this way." She led me to a door on the other side of the parlour.

"This isn't the first time you've been here, then?" I was still trying to make sense of why she would choose to spend her time with such people.

"No, of course not. Since I became friends with Cecil, I've

enjoyed coming here as a respite from my time looking after Father. Though it may not appear that way after the events of this evening, Cecil can be a gracious host when he tries."

Behind the unremarkable door was a narrow set of stairs that led up to the first level of the tower. We came to a large dressing room that was far less organised than the rest of the house. There were piles of clothes all over the Chesterfield sofa and Cecil's extensive shoe collection appeared to have been emptied across the floor.

Bella cut across the dimly lit room to a spiral staircase on the other side of it and began the climb. Her scream came back to me before I could reach the upper level. It was a hollow, trembling sound that pulled me onwards up the stairs.

When I emerged in Cecil Sinclair's garishly decorated bedroom, Bella turned back to me. The distressed expression on her face told me all that I needed to know, but I darted past her to see for myself.

The bright shining star of *The Door With no Key* and *The Wicked Sailor's Lament* looked at peace for the first time since I'd met him. I suppose that three bullets through the frontal lobe will do that to a person.

EIGHT

Perhaps it was the morbid curiosity that all mystery writers possess, but I couldn't resist walking closer to inspect the body. I underestimated my nerve, of course, and all of a sudden, I was eighteen years old again, looking down at my lifeless captain, who had taken a bullet from a German sniper. I was back in the trenches, with the smell of mud and rats and death in my nostrils. I could feel the same tangible fear and that burning in my throat as terror and sorrow ripped through me.

Bella released a cry, and I was transported to Everham once more. I put my arms around her as she sobbed, but I couldn't pull my gaze away from Cecil. He was lying on his back. His eyes were closed and there were black marks around the bullet holes that suggested he'd been shot from close range. I imagine that one bullet would have done the trick, and my first inference from this was that whoever killed the flamboyant actor really must have hated him. Of course, the fact they'd shot him in the first place told me much the same thing.

I didn't have to look far for the murder weapon. It was positioned neatly beside him, atop an old photograph on the satin sheets that covered his bed. It was a small pistol with a mother-of-pearl grip and a silver barrel. Such a weapon was a perfect example of style over substance; it would have looked more at home in a jewellery box than on a gun rack.

"It doesn't make any sense," Bella finally said when the silence had become unbearable. "Who did this to him?"

"I was wondering that myself." I didn't know whether this was the moment for questions, but she seemed to have found a burst of resilience. If the truth be told, comforting her had made me feel a little stronger, too. "Do you recognise the photograph?"

She leaned forward to inspect the picture of a glamorous elderly lady in fox furs. Partially obscured by the pistol, it was lying in its frame an inch from Cecil's outstretched fingers.

"It's his wife, Hortensia." I could feel her body tremble as she spoke. "She died several years ago."

I scanned the old woman's bold features and upturned mouth in the hope it could tell me what had brought the killer to that bedroom.

Bella's voice was as fragile as she herself looked at that moment. "It's just awful. For what possible reason would someone murder him?"

"Do you really have to ask? I've only just met the man, but I can already think of a number of motives." I was no longer certain that she wanted me to hold her so closely, so I took a step away. "Anton's film was nearly ruined because of Cecil's habits. His father apparently doesn't think too highly of him, either. And during his brief appearance downstairs, he succeeded in insulting almost every person there."

She found the courage to look back at the body. "He really did have a nice side to him, no matter what you might have seen."

I sighed and wished I hadn't let go of her. "You always did see the best in people."

I felt terribly sorry for her then. She'd been caught in the middle of everything, and it was no wonder that she'd looked so nervy. Bella had suffered Cecil's outburst as much as she had gauche Gilbert's behaviour, and now her friend was dead.

"There's a telephone in the dressing room. I'll call the police." She floated limply back down the staircase, and I watched her go. The further she walked, the more that familiar pain inside me stung.

What an odd chap I was to be worrying about matters of the heart whilst a man lay murdered mere feet away from me. In my literary career to date, I had murdered three poor souls, and yet here I was with a real mystery to solve, still moping because of an ill-fated adolescent romance that came to a conclusion a decade earlier. My writer's instincts kicked in and I tried to look at the scene more analytically.

"Pull yourself together, Marius," I said aloud, which only made me feel more irrational. "Clues. There must be clues here. Now, how does one go about finding them?"

I considered what my detective, Inspector Rupert L'Estrange, would have done in the situation, but as there were no traces of suspicious powders on the floor, or footprints marked out in a particularly rare shade of paint, this didn't help me a great deal.

To let you into a secret, we mystery writers are all cheats. Oh yes, everyone thinks we're clever to craft such devious plots, but we do it all backwards. As I had recently discovered – thanks to the brief tutelage of former Superintendent Edgington of Scotland Yard – starting with the killer and working towards the murder is far easier than the other way around. Writers can set their own rules. Police officers have no such luck, and there was nothing to say that I would make a competent sleuth.

I fell to my knees and hunted for ticket stubs. I looked through the books on the nightstand in the hope that they would provide some great insight. I even inspected the posters from Cecil's films on the walls around the room in case a speck of blood or bullet hole could reveal the identity of the killer. It was no good. None of the evidence that typically appears in mystery novels was there at the scene of the crime.

All I had before me was a man in a fancy outfit, lying dead in his own private palace, with an old photograph and an expensive pistol at his side. I was about to give up when I noticed another of those ancient family crests. This one was not on a painting or chiselled into the brickwork. It was etched on the butt of the gun, and I could only conclude that I'd finally discovered something worth discovering.

This surely meant that the murder weapon had been taken from somewhere in the house. To me, this suggested that the culprit was an opportunist. Perhaps he had witnessed the intoxicated actor's passive state and hatched a plan that very night.

I kept searching the room, but the only other thing of interest was a photograph of Cecil Sinclair right beside Cecil Sinclair's bed. It was even signed "Cecil Sinclair"; the man was clearly his own biggest fan. I was tempted to rip it from its frame and put it in my pocket, but I doubt the police would have approved of my removing potential evidence from the scene of a crime before they'd identified the killer.

Throughout my very nearly fruitless search, I could hear Bella on the telephone below. She spoke in a calm, controlled manner, but I was sure that she was still struggling with the emotion of it all. I couldn't make out exactly what was said but got the impression that the local authorities were being less than helpful.

"Very well," she said as I returned to the dressing room. "I understand... Yes, of course, officer. Thank you..."

"That didn't sound promising."

She hung up the earpiece on the candlestick receiver and peered glumly back at me. "At least the sergeant at Everham police station can't be accused of being impolite. He wished me a Happy New Year."

"And what about the body?"

She sank into the one free armchair in the room. "He says they can't get anyone out to us in the snow. The road is blocked from here to Reading."

"That's insanity." In detective novels, the local bobbies tend to be a foolish bunch, but I was struggling to believe they could treat a murder investigation so lightly. "You did tell them that Cecil has been murdered? I mean, it's not as if there's room for doubt over what happened. He didn't just fall down the stairs. And the fact he was shot three times must rule out suicide."

"Of course I told him, Marius." She adopted a harder tone. "But the sergeant said that, even if it wasn't snowing, most of his colleagues are off duty for the holiday."

I couldn't believe it and so I cleverly said, "I can't believe it. What if there was a real emergency like a—"

"Like a murder?"

"Well, exactly." I walked across the room to gaze out at the snow. It really was thick on the ground, and I could hardly blame the police for not donning galoshes and going on an arctic expedition.

"We should tell the others," Bella suggested when I failed to think of anything more useful to say.

My eyes shifted focus, and I could see her reflection in the window. "You're right, only..." There was something I couldn't put my finger on – something that didn't quite fit together. "The killer didn't have long to escape."

"What does that prove?"

"Once the job was done, the killer would have had to run down two flights of stairs and out into the entrance hall without anyone noticing. This was hardly the perfect place to stage a murder."

There was a flash of excitement in Bella's eyes. I knew that look. It showed a hint of the magic that she'd been missing. "You're right, but then perhaps it was never meant to happen like this. Perhaps Cecil's inebriation scuppered the killer's plan." She walked closer to the spiral staircase and peered up into the space above. "It's possible that…"

I understood what she meant and walked over to listen. "Are you suggesting that the killer could still be up there?"

Her brain was suddenly in a higher gear. She tucked a long lock of silky black hair behind her ear and, in that one movement, she became a different person. "How long was it between the shots being fired and the pair of us leaving the drawing room?"

"Perhaps ten seconds. Fifteen at most."

"Exactly. And we didn't hear anything from that point onwards. More importantly, we didn't see anything, either."

I nodded in appreciation. "You're right. If the killer had left the tower, we'd have seen him from the corridor. The time he had was too short. He must have known that someone would come looking."

We hesitated to ascend the stairs once more, afraid that the killer had been listening to everything we said and did.

"No, that's not quite right," I intervened before we had to explore the instantly more menacing space within Cecil's bedroom. "There's no way anyone could be hiding up there; I even searched under the bed. The blighter would have had enough time to leave the bedroom, then probably heard us coming. To avoid being detected, it would have made more sense to hide in here."

"You clever thing." It was perhaps a touch rude of her to be so surprised by my intelligence, though I tried not to be offended. "There's nowhere to hide upstairs, but he could have gone into the wardrobe, or simply hidden behind the curtains."

I think we were both glad that we wouldn't have to climb the stairs again. The thought of peeking into the double doors of the wardrobe was frightening enough. The only good thing was that we knew the murder weapon was lying safely on Cecil's bed.

"You're right. And in actual fact, I believe the wardrobe was half open when we first passed through here." We walked over and took a handle each.

"On three?" she said and began the count.

I stopped her at two. "There is another option which is less likely to get us murdered."

She let out a relieved sigh. "Thank goodness for that."

NINE

When we turned the key in the door which led to Cecil's suite, I believe we both felt some deal better.

"Now all we have to do is call everyone together," I suggested. "Unless the killer has already escaped, whoever doesn't appear must be to blame."

Bella was already moving away. "Another great idea, Mr Quin. I'm impressed."

"You keep saying these things as though you're shocked to discover I have a brain. Wasn't I clever when we were children?"

She didn't answer until we'd left the entrance hall. "I knew you were tenacious when we were children, but I was happy to overlook just how smart you were."

I could have taken offence again but decided not to say anything. She looked back the way we'd come. Her mind was clearly still focused on the loss of her friend.

"We should go to the dining room," she said, to help us concentrate on our task. "It's this way."

As we walked towards the state rooms of Everham Hall, I listened once more to the sounds of the house. It was disconcerting to know that there was a killer in the building. Although I'd spent countless hours over the last few years plotting crimes and thinking about corpses, I couldn't say I was keen to spend the evening with a murderer.

The dining room contained the first signs of Christmas that I'd encountered since I arrived there. On the ceiling, garlands of green foliage and red berries dangled from one corner of the rectangular room to the other. The walls were hung with long curtains of silver strings that glinted in the light of the electric chandeliers above the dinner table. They swished up into the air as we entered the room then swayed, like debutantes waiting to be picked for a waltz.

"Now what do we do?" I asked my companion, who had evidently taken my plan and improved upon it.

"We'll call everyone to dinner." Bella was energised by this new focus. She positively rocketed through the room to the far wall, where an antique gong sat on a chest of drawers. "Open the door. We need to make sure everyone hears."

I did as she requested, and she seized the immense beater in order to strike the hanging bronze disc. It was a huge instrument, just as you would find in a Buddhist temple, and the reverberating sound it produced brought the place to life.

The first people to appear were not guests, but the two footmen who had (for want of a better word) welcomed me to the house. The older of the two poked his head into the room as though eager to discover who he would have to rebuke.

"Ah, Lady Isabella, I didn't know it was you." He even bowed when he saw that the beater was in the hand of the elegant aristocrat. I sometimes wished that I was a baron or a duke for the deference people would show me. Oh, and the money! Most of the landed set seem to have a fair bit of that, too. "Madam, if you require refreshments, you can always ring the kitchen."

"That's not the problem, Matthew," she explained in her

most authoritative voice. "We need to call everyone in the house together before dinner. I'm afraid we have some terrible news."

The younger chap who had carried my bag to the room looked particularly disturbed by her words. "Is there anything we can do to assist in the matter, madam?"

"Thank you, Philip. I may require your help if the guests don't all appear." As she spoke, the first suspect stepped into the room.

Wilson strolled over to us, now bookless, and looked at the table expectantly. "I admit that I'm feeling peckish, but I was sure that Gilbert told me dinner wasn't until nine."

"We didn't call you here for dinner," I began, but Bella's blasted boyfriend arrived at that moment to cut my explanation short.

"What's all this? I've been telling everyone that dinner's not until nine."

"We're not eating just yet, darling." This was Bella, obviously, not me.

"I thought dinner was at nine?" Anton arrived with his bow-tie still loose around his neck, and Alma trailing behind him. Her hair wet, she was pulling a black bolero over her nude silk gown as she appeared in the doorway.

"Dinner is still going to be..." I tried one last time before the dead man's father appeared to make the same observation, and I gave up entirely.

If they made this much fuss about the evening meal, I dreaded to think how they would react to the news of our host's murder.

Ross Sinclair had entered the room with his arm around young Edith's shoulders. On finally realising that the pair had come together, Carl Wilson's face crumpled in on itself in disappointment. I'd rarely seen such a disillusioned creature. Unlike the other guests, the uneven couple had not made much effort to dress for dinner, and the pretty, though less than glamorous, young woman was still in her cotton dress. I had to wonder whether she was so poor that she couldn't afford a second outfit for the weekend, or perhaps she wasn't familiar with high society's incessant demand for regular costume changes.

"There's still one person missing," Bella told me as subtly as she could while the dinner conversation continued to rumble.

The butler turned up at this moment, but presumably that wasn't who she had in mind. "Just Poppy" was the only one of the guests not to have appeared. I would have nabbed a couple of the larger men (i.e. rough Ross Sinclair and that human rugby ball Gilbert Baines) and run to the tower to see whether we could flush her out, but the demand for answers grew too loud.

"The table hasn't even been laid yet," Alma noticed. "Why did you call us if the meal isn't ready?"

Her authoritative tone was enough to cut through the hubbub, and Bella was free to answer the question in something approaching calm.

"I called you here because..." Evidently, she had the same doubt that I had. Did it make sense to tell them about the murder, or would it be best to test them first? "...we needed to see where everyone was." She'd answered their question without answering their question. It was rather neatly done.

I was struck just then by a brilliant (or, at the very least, adequate) idea. I walked to the spot where they had convened and looked them over, much as our lieutenant had examined my platoon during the war. His very voice had the power to inspire fear and obedience, and I was hoping this approach would have a similar effect. "We're going to ask you a series of questions."

"I love games," Edith Havelock replied, and there was a smile on her face which I hadn't seen before.

"I can tolerate games if I have to," Gilbert echoed. "But please get on with it. If we're not sitting down to eat by nine on the dot, I'll go to the kitchen and scoff whatever I can find."

"This isn't a game," I told them, in that same military voice. I'd spent several years in the army and never taken to it like some men, but I could still do a first-rate impression of my commanding officer. "Something has happened and there are important facts that must be established."

Bella raised one eyebrow. She clearly thought I was mad but refrained from interrupting.

"My first question is for Anton. Did you let Alma out of your sight at any moment between leaving the games room and coming downstairs?"

He looked as though he would answer but changed his mind. "Wait a second. What's going on here?"

Everyone in the room – including the three members of staff who had stayed to find out what we'd discovered – glared at me as though I was trying to trick them.

"Tell us right this moment what's happening." Alma stepped forward just as timid Edith retreated into the arms of her towering lover.

The others in the group began to complain, but before I could provide answers, there were footsteps in the hallway, and we waited to see who would appear. After a few seconds of creaking floorboards, Percy Anderson II waddled into view. I must admit that I was relieved to see the adorable hound. I'd half expected a cloaked figure with a glinting blade in his hand.

"Hello, boy." He padded up to me as I spoke. "Who let you out of your room?"

Percy said nothing, but he was not alone.

"I did." Poppy followed straight after him into the room. "He was howling like a wild thing, so I took him outside for a walk." She peered around at the other guests as Bella and I glanced at one another. I was disappointed to discover that we had not locked our suspect in the tower after all.

The calm was instantly forgotten, and an angry racket kicked up.

"We want answers, damn it!" Gilbert Baines was railing even as he placed an arm around his visibly shaken girlfriend to comfort her. "Marius, tell us what's going on here or I'll... I'll..."

It was lucky that Anton answered him. I wouldn't have been so polite. "Perhaps we should all simmer down and hear what they have to say."

After the sadness and shock of finding Cecil's body, Bella and I had been invigorated by the idea that we had trapped the killer in the dead man's suite. Disabused of this belief, and with our plan only serving to vex everyone else there, I felt quite thwarted. This was nothing compared to Bella, though. She looked as if she was back in the tower, standing over the body of her departed friend. There was only one way to put things right again. It was time to admit what had really happened.

"It's Cecil," I told them, and my words plunged the room into silence. "He's been murdered."

TEN

Seeing the pained reactions of Cecil's friends and loved ones brought the tragedy home to me. Pretty young Edith attempted to hide even deeper in the folds of her boyfriend's jacket. Anton raised one hand to his mouth in apparent shock. Alma gasped, Poppy flinched, and Percy said nothing.

The atmosphere in the room had changed in an instant. I know that's the kind of thing that authors always mention in books. In real life, it isn't something you normally notice, but I swear that I felt a physical shift just then.

And yet, it was the sight of the dead man's father that really affected me.

"My boy?" Ross asked. "You're saying that my boy's dead?"

Bella moved closer to reply in a soothing tone. "Yes, but it would have been so quick that I'm sure he didn't suffer."

"How did it happen?" Anton asked, and I noticed that, far from going to comfort his wife, he'd moved away from her.

"Not here." I stepped around Bella to accept their stern looks. "There must be a comfortable salon somewhere that we can use for such a discussion."

Alma nodded and, clearly familiar with the house, was the

first to leave the dining room. We trailed after her in single file to walk twenty paces along to a door on the opposite side of the corridor.

Judging by the opulent décor, I assumed this was the main sitting room of Everham Hall. The wood-beamed ceiling was divided into squares, and there were intricate murals on each panel. Elegant paintings of knights and damsels hung on the walls – their armour and jewels picked out in gold leaf. And, wherever I looked, red velvet furnishings completed the picture. There were velvet curtains, sofas, armchairs, ottomans and stools. It was a touch excessive to say the least.

One thing I hadn't noticed in any other room was a Christmas tree. In keeping with the luxurious feel of much of the house, the decorations were all in gold. I spotted golden bells and rocking horses, angels, stars and kings. It was a perfectly festive scene and, at the foot of the tree, there was a slew of presents neatly wrapped. The paper, in a stunning twist, was silver.

"I think you should all take a seat and help yourself to a drink," Bella told her friends, so I went to the drinks cabinet in that sea of velvet and began to pour them all tumblers of whisky. I decided I'd drunk enough for one evening, though, and did without.

"This isn't nice," waiflike Edith Havelock mumbled, and she wasn't talking about the drink. "I feel awful."

I might have pointed out that she'd largely seemed terrified ever since she'd set foot in the games room an hour earlier. Her big, hairy protector helped her onto one of the sofas and held her tight. Ross Sinclair clearly cared for the girl, but his strangely paternal display was at odds with the rough fashion in which he'd hauled his inebriated son off the floor.

"We've no wish to frighten anyone," Bella said once I'd passed out the glasses.

I moved to a spot in front of the fireplace and did what I

could to help her. "Perhaps some of you heard a few bangs after we dispersed."

"There were some explosions," Ross replied, his nostrils flaring. "I assumed they were fireworks."

"Well, they weren't." I gave them a moment to make sense of this before telling the full story. "Cecil was shot three times in the head."

Bella added an extra detail as I watched the suspects' shocked reactions. "Marius recognised the sound as being more like gunfire than fireworks. We went to the tower to investigate as soon as we heard it."

"But you didn't catch the blighter?" Gilbert was already suspicious and looked at me as though I were to blame.

"There was no sign of anyone in the hall." I suppose that Bella was worried about making her beau jealous, as she went to stand at his side. "The killer must have hidden in Cecil's wardrobe and escaped when we went up to the bedroom."

I wouldn't be bossed about by a self-important banker and addressed the rest of the suspects. "We need to know what happened when you took Cecil back to his room."

"We?" Gilbert objected. "What's all this 'we'?"

The man was an idiot, so I ignored him. "Anton, can you tell me all you remember?"

As I'd decided from our first meeting, Anton Cavendish was a reasonable man and nodded thoughtfully before describing the last moments of Cecil's life. "Ross and I carried him up to the tower."

"Just the two of you?" Bella asked, and he considered the question before replying.

"No, no. Edith was with us, and Alma was waiting in the entrance hall when we came down."

"It was a struggle to get him up there," the older gentleman explained. "He's a big man, like his father. And I admit that I banged his head pulling him up those infernal spiral stairs."

The odd bruise was the least of Cecil's worries, but I didn't think his father needed to hear that, so Anton continued the account. "We managed to carry him to his bed. He stirred a little as we put him there, and I thought he might wake up, but he hugged his pillow and fell fast asleep again."

"That'll be the chloral!" Poppy replied with a loud sniff that set off Percy's sympathetic howling. "Chloral hydrate is fun to begin with, but it soon knocks you out." Sitting in an unusually large velvet armchair that made her look like an elfin creature, the dead man's girlfriend was quite distraught. If she was the killer, she was just as good an actress as she claimed to be.

My canine travelling companion had somehow obtained a plate of scrag ends and was eating them by the fire. Whenever he managed to catch my eye, he would send a guilt-inducing glance in my direction. I considered telling him that he was the one who'd chosen to stay up in the bedroom, but he would only have looked surly in reply.

"Very well," I intervened, to return us to the main topic. "And after that, I imagine you left him to sleep?"

"Correct." Anton's gaze darted over to look at his wife. I couldn't fathom what this meant, but I knew there was more to the story than he was willing to reveal.

"We all left," Ross added. "I took Edith to her room, and the Cavendishes followed along behind."

"That's right, Alma and I went to get changed." Anton's oddly insistent tone returned.

Poppy was in tears by now, but not for the reason I'd expected. "It could have been me!" She was shaking so much that she had to go over to the hearth to cuddle Percy for support. He really didn't mind and closed his eyes as she lay down next to him. "If I'd gone up to the tower, it could have been me!"

Ross Sinclair showed the thornier side to his personality of which we'd only seen hints in the games room. "Which raises the question of where you were, you little trollop."

"Oh, and you clearly treated him so well! Is that what you're saying?" This point would have come across a little more forcefully if she hadn't said it into a basset hound.

I loved seeing the speed at which Bella's mind worked. Like a gymnast at the Olympic Games, she hopped away from her sweetheart to quell the nascent argument. "There are questions around each of your whereabouts."

"Please don't," little Edith wailed. "I can't take this. My nerves aren't strong enough."

"There, there, my sweet darling. There's no need to worry." Ross gathered her up like a baby kitten in his arms. Once his girlfriend had been pacified, he turned back to me. "The fact is, my Edith was in the room next to mine the whole time. So you've no reason to suspect her."

Carl Wilson still looked offended by this May-to-the-December-after-next romance. I could understand why he was so upset. He and Edith would have made a far more suitable couple. They were closer in age and were both wispish and handsome in their own way. What hope did novices have if the old fellows were snaffling up all the women? Carl must have felt it acutely.

In a low, dispirited voice, he provided his alibi. "I imagine you're aware that I had nothing to do with any of this. I didn't even know where they'd taken Mr Sinclair, and I doubt I would have had the time to go there, shoot him three times and get back to the games room without anyone seeing me."

This was all true, but Alma found a hole in his argument. "That's only if he really was killed when the shots rang out. You're a fan of Marius's book, aren't you?"

The nervy fellow nodded. "Yes. You must have heard me say that very thing when you arrived."

"In which case, you'll know all about killings that play with time. Murders in detective novels often appear to have happened at one specific point at which the killer has an alibi, when, in reality, the victim was already dead some time earlier."

"It sounds as though you know something about the matter yourself, my dear." Gilbert Baines really was a smug so-and-so, and I will not tire of pointing that out.

"You're missing the point," Alma explained. "If Wilson was the killer, he could have done the deed, set the fuse for a few minor explosions to go off somewhere and run back to pretend he was in the games room the whole time."

"No, he couldn't," I told her, as Wilson didn't look capable of defending himself. "He would never have had time to do all that between our leaving him and the moment the three shots were fired. Bella and I went to talk in the salon next door, then looked into the games room on our way to Cecil's tower."

"Well, I didn't do it." Alma must have taken my correction as an attack. She folded her arms and looked at the smouldering fire. "As Anton has already explained, he and I returned to our room to get changed."

I looked at her husband to see his reaction, and that same curious expression still gripped his face.

"I'd never even met Cecil before tonight," Edith proclaimed to strengthen the defence that Ross had presented on her behalf.

I was surprised that it was the previously meek Carl Wilson who tore into her argument. "That doesn't mean anything. He was the son of your unsuitable suitor. It's more than possible that you decided to kill Cecil before he could come between you."

"That's impossible." Ross Sinclair was not a man who suffered easily panicked fools sitting down. He got to his feet, and it was as though a new mountain had formed. "I don't believe for one second that my sweet girl was involved in Cecil's death."

Wilson had more fight in him than I could have predicted,

and he held his ground. "You would say that, wouldn't you? But if you didn't have your eyes on her, she has no alibi."

It came as no surprise that Bella should be the one to intervene. "Perhaps we should all calm down."

"Not likely," Gilbert replied in a stoic tone. "The best solution is to get our differences out in the open. It's the only way we'll find the truth."

"Stop!" Edith shrieked as Wilson rose to meet Ross Sinclair's gaze. "This is horrible. Just stop."

Anton looked as though he wanted to step between them but was afraid of the older man's impressive range. Alma retreated to safety behind the sofa, and the rest of us could do nothing but watch – like spectators at just about the most uneven contest since Christians fought the lions in ancient Rome.

"Ladies and gentlemen." A voice from the doorway interrupted the chaos, and there stood the butler with a disapproving expression on his face. "Dinner is served."

ELEVEN

It was the worst possible moment to break bread with one another. As we walked back to the dining room, we couldn't bring ourselves to look our fellow diners in the eye.

The only person who seemed comfortable with the new hell we were about to endure was Gilbert, who looked quite pleased with himself. I had to doubt that he was particularly fond of Cecil Sinclair if he behaved in such a manner so soon after the man's death.

"Has anyone called the police yet?" sensible Alma asked, which was hardly the ideal start to a dinner party.

"I did." Bella had retreated into her shell. Her voice was weak and her skin pale. It was hard to know whether the changes I'd observed in her were due to the years she'd spent caring for her invalid father, or this was simply what happened to the women Gilbert Baines courted.

"And?"

"And they're not coming." I thought it only fair that I should share Bella's burden. "If the snow continues, we'll be lucky if they get here before spring."

"That's insanity." Anton no longer looked quite so cool and

composed as when we'd first met. "You did tell them that a man has been murdered?"

Bella nodded. "The sergeant explained that his officers are on holiday. I tried to reason with the man, but he insisted there was no way through the snow."

A painful hush took over the room. It was as though our heavenly overseer had put His finger to His lips and forbidden anyone from making a sound. Glances rebounded from person to person like India rubber balls. I could see the more reasonable members of the group searching for something to say, but no one had the courage to speak.

When the first course was served, the silence was punctuated by the cracking of lobsters' claws. The only conversation was an occasional request to the haughty butler, Perkins, to distribute bread, butter or more wine around the table. It was a shame that the cook hadn't opted for prawns to start the meal; they wouldn't have been so noisy.

The one advantage to the choice of dish was that it gave me the opportunity to see who belonged in these refined surroundings. Lady Isabella Montague, the beloved daughter of the Duke of Hurtwood, had no trouble whatsoever and wielded her knife and lobster cracker like a professional chef. At the other end of the scale, Alma sent several pieces of shell flying off the table for Percy to inspect, and Ross Sinclair was similarly handicapped. I was fairly impressed by a few of the diners. Edith, Poppy and Wilson managed to eat without covering themselves in crustacean, and Anton was incredibly well mannered throughout.

We were spaced out around the long rectangular table. Cecil had obviously been planning some piece of theatre, as there were props and disguises beside each place setting. I had a pirate's hook and patch. Sitting opposite me, Bella had a mask from a Venetian ball and, glancing around the table, I spied various other accessories. I believe it would have been a real scream, but any such frivolity was now denied to us.

I could see that Gilbert was saddened by the loss of this diversion perhaps even more than the death of his friend. He mournfully pawed the green Robin Hood hat beside him with one large hand, which triggered a reproachful look from Bella.

"Oh, come along, Belly." Faugh! What a horrible pet name. "I wasn't going to put the hat on, but we mustn't forget that it's New Year's Eve and Cecil more than anyone would have wanted us to have a good time. In fact, it seems to me that he's left us a game to play."

Anton was the first to object to Gilbert's clumsy comment. "That's enough." He brought one furious fist down on the table. The impact rattled cutlery and made the wine glasses around him sing. "This isn't a game, man. Cecil's dead."

Gilbert was shocked to be censured so and struggled for his words. "You misunderstood me, I was only suggesting that—"

"You don't care that he was our friend, do you? He may have been a drunk and a druggard. He may even have been the most unreliable actor I've worked with in my twenty-year career, but he was a good man and that should be enough for us not to be joking around the dinner table tonight."

All eyes were on the indignant banker. We stared along the table at him, and I realised that what made the sight particularly striking was that Gilbert was sitting where Cecil would have been. There was no place laid at the opposite end, and I couldn't imagine our proud, peacocking host being anywhere but the head of the table.

"If you'll all listen—" he tried once more, but he was soon interrupted.

"If anyone should be upset, it's me." Poppy decided that she deserved more of our sympathy. "I loved Cecil. Simply loved him. I don't know what the future holds for me now."

"Oh, please!" Alma was so incensed she nearly spat out her

wine. "You'd only been together a few weeks. It wasn't so long ago that you were hanging off Alec Pemberton's arm."

They'd finally mentioned someone I knew! Pemberton was another famous face on the silver screen. He was very much in the Cecil Sinclair mould, but I'd read somewhere that he no longer enjoyed the popularity in British cinemas that he once had.

Poppy was appalled. "The way I felt about Cecil was different. No one can replace him. He was my star, my guiding light, and I am quite lost without him." This poetic statement would have been more convincing if she'd managed to cry over her loss for more than a few minutes of cuddles with Percy.

As far as my ability to interpret human behaviour informed me, Ross Sinclair was truly distressed. As arguments flared up and quickly died around him, he rested his forehead on his fist and stared glumly at his plate.

"This is not a competition," he growled without looking at us. "We all loved and hated Cecil in different ways. He was just that kind of person."

"That's it in a nutshell." Alma tapped her fingers on the red tablecloth for a few seconds before continuing. "And instead of bickering, a more constructive use of our time would be to see if we can identify the killer."

"That's what I've been trying to say," Gilbert put in. "The game that Cecil left us has got nothing to do with these disguises. The game is a mystery, and it's down to us to crack it."

Bella shook her head and sighed. "Then perhaps you could have expressed yourself more diplomatically from the beginning."

"My apologies, my love." Gilbert bowed his head and put his hand out towards her across the table. "I should have chosen my words more carefully, but that doesn't change the fact that the police aren't coming, and the killer is most likely still amongst us."

His proposition drew a host of blank faces and a few soft tuts, so he appealed to his underling for support. "I thought this would be right up your alley, Wilson. You're forever reading those blasted mystery novels. And you were desperate to see out the year in style, well now's your chance."

Wilson emitted a self-hating laugh to appease his superior, but he maintained a serious mien. "There's a big difference between stories and real life. I don't think I have the stomach to investigate an actual murder."

He looked queasy just mentioning it, but there were more interesting reactions to witness around the table, and I turned to spy on Ross Sinclair to see what impact Gilbert's suggestion would have on him. My father used to say that you could never trust a man with a full beard, as they hide too much. I assumed that the dead man's father would react as he had to Wilson's rude remarks in the sitting room, but he observed the scene with cold detachment.

As no one else spoke, Gilbert continued to lay out his case. "It appears to me that unless the servants got tired of Cecil's histrionics and decided to kill him, one of us must be to blame."

"It's unlikely that an Everham employee would be guilty." All heads swivelled in my direction. I'd been silently observing the scene until now and some of the guests looked surprised that I would have an opinion on the matter. "For one thing, if they truly found Cecil unbearable, they could have simply looked for work elsewhere."

I could see that, even through her sadness, Bella was excited by the task before us. "Unless he caught one of them up to no good." She gave us time to consider the possibility before expanding on the idea. "Perhaps a scullery maid stole from him, Cecil discovered what she'd done, and so she killed him to stay out of trouble."

She'd always had a head for riddles and puzzles, and I replied with a challenge of my own. "It's not impossible, but why would she have done it at that moment? Why not wait until we were asleep instead of committing the crime in a three-minute window, right after Cecil was taken to his room?"

"You're smarter than you look, Marius!" Anton declared with a clap of his hands.

"I'll try to take that as a compliment."

"As you should." He wagged one finger as he considered the implications. "It seems to me that if anyone's going to investigate, it should be you."

"Now wait just a moment," Gilbert began, clearly frustrated by the possibility of his "game" being stolen from him.

Alma spoke over him. "Anton's right. Out of all of us, Marius is the perfect detective."

I stifled a laugh then as, in my mind at least, I was the perfect person to seek out the library and while away the rest of the weekend with a pile of books.

"What's so funny?" Cecil's father demanded, and I regretted my reaction. "That's the kind of thing you do, isn't it? You solve mysteries."

"No, I write mysteries." I cleared my throat and, in the most polite tone I could muster, did my best to explain. "I'm not a detective, I'm a fantasist. I make up silly stories in my head and, when my brain allows it, I scribble them down on paper. I dare say I could create a mystery that no reader could solve, but that doesn't mean I can solve a real-life murder that has everyone flummoxed."

"Marius is being too modest, as ever." Bella looked a little proud of me just then. I think she might even have blushed on my behalf. "My father always said that he was so clever he should become a politician."

"Well, politicians are certainly fantasists," Wilson quipped and received several wry smiles for his effort.

"Come along then." Gilbert stroked his hairless cheek as

though daring me to react. "If you're so clever, who do you think is responsible for Cecil's murder?"

"I just made the point that I don't think I'm particularly intelligent, so you're baiting the wrong bear there, chum."

I would like to have told him that he was the obvious suspect, but beyond my finding him a distasteful dullard, there was nothing yet to incriminate him.

"There's no getting out of it, Quin." Ross Sinclair sounded less than relaxed himself, and Edith put one hand on his immense arm to soothe him. "I want to hear what you think."

The atmosphere had changed once more. There was excitement in the air. Those who cared about Cecil wanted to see his killer brought to justice, and those who didn't mind either way were curious to see what stroke of genius this novelist chappy might produce.

"I can't just tell you who the killer is, you know. Even the great detectives aren't expected to do that. I met Lord Edgington back in the autumn, and he needed more than an evening to solve the murders he was investigating."

"That may well be, Marius," Anton took up the baton again, "but it seems to me that you have the brain for tricks and stratagems. In the absence of the police, you're our brightest hope."

"You're also one of the few people here without a connection to the victim." Bella was already talking in the cold, impersonal terms of a murder investigation. Her friend was no longer Cecil. He was "the victim".

"He's not the only one." Gilbert was quick to point out. "Edith and Wilson hadn't met him before tonight, either."

Carl Wilson looked surprised to be included. "Oh, umm... I do like word games and that sort of thing, but I don't have the brain to solve a cryptic crossword, let alone a murder." The frightened tone entered his voice again. "And just so we're clear, would I actually have to look at the body?"

"I've heard enough." Big salty Ross scraped his chair back,

but it caught on the carpet and tipped over to add more drama to the already theatrical moment. "Quin will investigate Cecil's death." With no further ceremony, he turned to leave the room. "Come along, man, you can interview me first."

The truth was that I rather fancied trying my hand at solving a murder, if for no other reason than to get on Gilbert's wick. I pushed my chair back, rose to standing and, in the firmest, most official tone I could muster, issued an order to the remaining suspects.

"I'm sure it goes without saying that you must all remain here until I return."

Gilbert almost burst a blood vessel when I strolled past him on the way to the door. As he realised that he would not be the heroic detective who would save us all from the crazed killer, the look on his face was priceless.

TWELVE

There are always plenty of spare salons, parlours and lounges in old houses like Everham Hall. Clearly knowing the lay of the place, Ross Sinclair led us to yet another one. I never learnt its name, but I will refer to it as the mirror room. I imagine you can guess why.

There must have been twelve of the big, shiny, mercury-backed panels covering the four walls of the room. They made me feel like I was being watched by an army of Mariuses. The salon was less comfortable than others we had visited, and it was hard to know what such a space was meant to be used for. The furniture was all hard, modern and uncomfortable, and there were no curtains over the narrow windows. It was a curious place indeed.

Ross took a high-backed seat in the middle of the room and urged me to get on with the interview. "Well, what do you want to know?"

I took a few steps across the polished floor to look at him, but was uncertain where to begin. "Well..." I froze quite still, as that often helps me think. "I suppose what I should ask..."

"You should ask me about Cecil. Surely something from his past could explain what happened tonight."

"Surely, it could." I was happy to be led by him. "Right, yes. Tell me about his childhood and that sort of thing." I felt like an alienist, probing the dead man's mind.

"Well, Cecil was nothing like his three brothers. They were all quite different, but he was by far the most flamboyant." I could tell that he did not think this a positive quality to possess, and I instantly had a picture of Cecil's upbringing. "He was forever acting and putting on shows. I don't just mean in his school or as a diversion. Cecil never stopped performing. He was born to show off and flounce about the place."

I made no response but he evidently felt the need to defend this view. "I suppose I didn't like it at the time. One of Cecil's brothers went into the army, another joined the navy, and the third was a pilot in the war. What did Cecil do?" I didn't say that he did a very good job defending himself. "He joined the blasted theatre."

"I see," I replied, still not moving, but concentrating on each word he said. Due to his briny delivery and that impressive beard, I once again wondered whether he had spent his life at sea. "I imagine he was young when he first appeared on the stage?"

"That's right." He paused to remember his son, and I believe the reality of Cecil's death returned to him at that moment. It must have been difficult for him to accept that he'd not only lost the man that Cecil had become, but the boy he'd once been. "He was sixteen when he went to London and took up with a theatre company."

"How did you feel about that?" I was hoping for a reaction and certainly got one.

"I felt it wasn't normal, and a year later his mother died. The poor woman was only forty-three. I told Cecil that he'd killed her, and he didn't speak to me for the next decade."

It was difficult to be a detached, neutral detective if my witnesses insisted on making such statements. "How could a boy's decision to become an actor have killed a woman?"

He poked the end of his tongue through a gap in his large, crooked teeth. "I was angry, and I shouldn't have said it."

"How did she die?"

"Typhoid."

"Then you really shouldn't have said it. If she'd had a heart attack, you could have made a case for such an innocuous act having brought about her death, but typhoid!"

I looked at him in disbelief. He stared back as though he wanted to knock me out, so I hurried to move on to my next question.

"So, Cecil joined the theatre, his mother died of typhoid, and he stopped talking to you for some years. Did you at least follow his career?"

"He was my son," was the cryptic answer that came back to me. "I might not have spoken to him, but I heard what he was doing. I never told Cecil but, in my own way, I was proud. You see, he travelled to America and found work on a film set. He had his mother's good looks and my build, so he quickly moved from small parts in Westerns to romantic films where he was the star. Once he'd made his name in the States, he came back to Britain."

There was something in his voice that told me this was not the right decision. "I'm assuming that was when things went wrong for him?"

"You could say that." He released a tired breath. "He should have stayed in Los Angeles. I don't know whether it was the climate here or the people around him but, though his star continued to rise, his behaviour deteriorated."

I doubted my abilities as a master interrogator, but I was beginning to see connections between the picture he was painting and Cecil's sordid swan song. "Was that when the two of you reunited?"

He sniffed and rubbed one rough thumb across either nostril before answering. "He said he wanted to make it up to me. Said he wanted to put things right." He put his head back and looked up at the ceiling. "I should never have treated him so coldly just because he wasn't like me. I expected my boys to follow my example, but Cecil never wanted to be like anyone else. When he was a tot, me and his ma loved that about him. We treated him differently to the others, and so it was no surprise he turned out the way he did."

"You mean a drug addict?"

"No. An actor!" He said this with no small amount of anger, though I believe it was directed at me for failing to understand him rather than his son's choice of career. "Listen, when Cecil came back into my life, I'd drunk myself halfway to death. My boy paid for me to get out of the house where I'd been mourning his mother for so long. He went and bought me a flat of my own in Chiswick. He even gave me a salary, so I didn't have to work no more. If it wasn't for him, I would have served out my time on this Earth as a bitter, lonely man." In a quieter voice, he added, "And I would never have survived to meet my Edith."

I was deeply curious over how such an affair had begun, but decided to keep my focus on Cecil for the moment. "He helped you even as things got worse for him."

"That's right. As I got better, he went off the rails. He was already drinking a lot when he came back to Britain, but then he developed these other interests. Each time he took things too far, I was there to pick up the pieces – not just because he was my son, but because that's what he did for me."

It was strange to see that giant of a man suddenly lose his composure. He produced no tears, but the light from the chandelier rebounded off those elegant mirrors, and I could see that his eyes were glossier than before.

"You didn't seem interested in helping him tonight, though," I had to point out.

"That may be true." He sniffed more loudly this time. "It wasn't very nice what I said to him. I took him up to bed with Anton, and I assumed he'd be able to sleep it off. I never expected..." He didn't need to finish that sentence and his words faded out for a moment. "I regret it now, of course, but I didn't want anything to do with him when he was in that state. Even as an old rummy myself, I can criticise another for the way he behaves."

I saw another pattern emerging. "Even after all this time, you still didn't approve of the way Cecil conducted himself."

He shook his head but accepted the point I'd made. "He wasn't all bad, but except for his films, he had nothing of value in his life. He'd married for money rather than love, sunk his fortune into this pit of a house, and then really lost control all alone out here."

If I'd been writing this interview in one of my books, my detective would have put cruel, hard allegations to this suspect until he cracked under the pressure. I'm happy to say that I was not such a heartless operator. The man had just lost his son, and I had no wish to make him feel even worse about it.

Instead, I shifted to a different topic. "I believe that Cecil married an elderly widow and inherited everything from her?"

He pulled his neck in, as though surprised at the question. "Cecil was a lot of things, but he wasn't a murderer, if that's what you're implying. Hortensia Alcott knew exactly what she was doing when she married my son. She was already sick and had a year or two of fun with a dashing young husband in exchange for her inheritance. Cecil always felt bad about it, but the whole thing was a transaction; they both got what they wanted."

I remembered the photograph of Cecil's wife on his bed and wondered whether he had kept it nearby out of guilt.

"So that's how Cecil got the money to buy this place?"

"Exactly. The Cornwallis family who previously owned it were drowning in debt. He got the whole estate for a song."

I remembered the silver pistol on the other side of Cecil's corpse and wondered what impact his bargaining over the house had on the former owners.

"Do you know what happened to them?"

"I know that they didn't all agree with his plans for the place. Some of them even tried to take him to court. They said he'd ripped the family estate from their grasp, but it didn't do them any good. The fact is that Cecil had made a deal with the old couple who lived here, and they were able to move somewhere more comfortable."

"You mean that they were stowed away in a cottage to live out their days in relative poverty." I knew just what happened to grand old families who fell on hard times. As he didn't deny my claim, I put another to him. "It seems that Cecil upset people wherever he went."

"I'm not here to defend him." Ross caught his reflection in the mirror behind me. He didn't seem to like what he saw and stared at himself disdainfully. "As I've already told you, my son wasn't perfect. He could charm the watch from your pocket and the money from your wallet, but you'd have a great time while he did it."

"If he was such good company, why were you so firm with him? How was tonight different from all the other times you've supported him?" I kept going back to this point, as it seemed to undermine so much of what he said.

"I was furious with him."

"Because of Edith," I concluded and, even as his gaze fell to the floor, he nodded.

"That's right. Because of Edith." He needed a moment's silence to gather his thoughts. "When Edith came into my life, I was content for the first time in years. I wanted to shout her name in the street and write odes to her beauty. I told Cecil about her, and he said she was only after my money. He said no girl like that would be interested in a bloke like me."

"I bet you wanted to strangle him."

"You're right, I did. He wouldn't even meet her. I arranged a dinner in London to announce our engagement, and he didn't come."

"You're getting married?"

"That's right. I asked Edith to be my wife, and she agreed."

This had knocked me from my train of thought, but I quickly climbed aboard once more. "So Cecil refused to meet his future stepmother—"

"And that's not all." The man kept offering me evidence that would count against him. It was not at all what I had expected. "He said he would change his will if I married her."

I would like to have responded to this but just sat there in stunned silence.

"He promised that he'd leave me nothing. I told him I'd probably die before him anyway, but he said that I shouldn't count on it." His face fell and his eyes examined the bare floorboards at our feet. "Turns out he was right."

I was struggling to keep up with the pace of information that was pouring from him but managed to select one key point. "Cecil refused to meet his future stepmother, and yet you're both here together this weekend?"

Ross became circumspect once more. "He didn't know Edith was coming. And if the truth be told, she didn't want to come, but I convinced her. I thought that, if the pair of them could meet, he'd calm down and see how wonderful my girl is."

He kept leaping over important points, and so I tried to fill in the gaps. "Had you argued? It sounds as though it wasn't just that he objected to your marrying a young wife. You fell out because of it."

He turned to one side of the room and then the other but,

wherever he looked, he couldn't escape me. If I ever redecorate my flat, I'm fairly confident that I won't include a mirror room.

"Yes, we argued. The last time I saw him he was drunk and belligerent, and we both said things we didn't mean."

"Are you sure you didn't mean them?"

He fell quiet then and stared at his hands. I wondered what deeds they had done to make him react in such a fashion. I thought I would have to soften my tone to convince him to answer but, in the end, he spoke without prompting.

"It broke my heart to have my son back in my life and then almost lose him again. I made a mistake when he was young. He was a good boy and, for all I know, every last problem he had was down to the way I treated him."

It was at this point that the weight of his guilt and misery overwhelmed him. He hunched his shoulders, and his whole body seemed to pulsate as the emotion passed through him. I could never have imagined him in such a state.

"I wish I'd been a better father. I wish he wasn't dead!"

I'm not the kind to communicate what I'm really feeling to anyone. I'm more of a stiff-upper-lip sort of chap, and it was quite bizarre to see big, burly Ross Sinclair show such vulnerability.

My detective Rupert L'Estrange would have ignored the tears and put it to the man that he was the one who'd shot his son. He would have suggested that Cecil was going to stop giving him any money if he married Edith and that was why the actor had to die. Luckily for Ross, I couldn't bring myself to be so cruel.

Instead, I walked over to put one hand on his shoulder and told him, "I'm so sorry for what you must be experiencing. It's simply too horrible." I may not have extracted every last secret from him, but it felt like the right thing to do.

THIRTEEN

If I'd had a notebook with me – which, let's be honest, all writers should keep about their person seven days a week – I might have noted down some areas in which I could improve my interview technique. Number one on the list would have been to focus more on the suspect and not just the victim. While I was happy to find out plenty about Ross's dead son, I still didn't know much about the man himself.

Unable to trouble him with more indelicate questions, I left Ross to have a bit of a cry on his own and slipped back out to the corridor.

I must say that I was rather enjoying this detective lark and I could see why so many amateurs went in for such a pastime. It would have been insensitive to say this so soon after a man had been murdered – and I certainly didn't want to come across as a total Gilbert – but there was fun to be had on this sort of adventure, and so I set off to explore.

Before I joined the others in the dining room, there was something I needed to confirm. It seemed to me that, if the killer had spontaneously decided to kill Cecil having seen how intoxicated he was, the gun would originally have been found behind one of the doors between the games room and the tower. I tried the first that I came to and discovered where we would be having breakfast the next day. The next door along was a day room with a small selection of comfortable furniture and plenty of newspapers. It was of little interest, so I continued my search.

In all, I found a study, a nook, a cupboard full of ancient crockery that must have belonged to the previous owners, and a room that was all black and white except for one red chair in the middle and the mounts of several stuffed cats on the wall – which, to be honest, was far too creepy and I did not step inside. There was a room with a giant phoenix painted on one wall, a sewing room, and a scullery, but in none of them did I come across a gun.

I'd worked my way along the corridor and back and was about to give up when I decided to inspect a few more doors in the other direction, just to be on the safe side. And would you believe it? The first room I tried, directly opposite the mirror room, was an armoury. It had been given the inimitable Cecil Sinclair look, of course. One wall had a selection of brightly coloured paints daubed all over it, but on racks all around were knives, swords, pikes, spears and, yes, guns. A few of them bore the Cornwallis crest and, best of all, there was a small space in one of the displays which was just the right size to hold a pistol.

The murder weapon had surely been there. However, I now faced a different problem. I pulled down a few of the remaining guns to check, but none of them were loaded.

"Where did the blighter find the ammunition?" I mused aloud.

There was no sign of any bullets in the room and so my grand discovery didn't seem so helpful after all. I was hoping I could rule out the possibility that the murder had been planned in advance, but unless the killer had stumbled across the one weapon that happened to have bullets, this didn't seem to be the case.

One mystery had led to another and, though I might have found a needle in a haystack, what good is a needle when looking for a killer? I returned to the party, feeling a mixture of excitement and exasperation.

Despite the open fire which Matthew the footman was doing his best to make roar, the atmosphere in the dining room remained chilly. This was particularly noticeable as dessert had been served, which really should have improved the mood.

"Meringue," Gilbert proclaimed for no one's benefit, "I don't like meringue."

"I missed the main course, so I'll have yours," I said as I sat down to enjoy that singularly sweet and fruity pudding. There was thickly whipped cream, various winter berries and a dark chocolate sauce which, while in no way traditional, added a new level of complexity to an already beautifully balanced dish. I don't normally have a sweet tooth, but I was so hungry that I didn't notice what a spectacle I was making.

"Delicious!" I declared when not a speck of white sugary base, nor a morsel of fruit, cream or chocolate remained in my bowl. Upon finishing the delectable treat, I looked up to see that nearly every eye was trained upon me. "What is it?" I felt my face in case I had a crumb of food there. Nothing.

"Well...?" Wilson tried and, when that failed to shed light on the situation, Bella explained.

"We were wondering whether you've come to any conclusions."

"Conclusions? About the case you mean?" I strangled a laugh. "I've only conducted one interview – and eaten one helping of dessert. What do you expect from me?"

Everyone's gaze shifted to look at Ross, who was back in his place at the table. He had fallen into some kind of trance and was staring into his bowl as though it were a magic mirror. It was evident that he would not be revealing anything significant for some time, even after his fiancée put her hand to his cheek to comfort him.

"There's nothing to tell," I finally revealed as I leaned across the table to help myself to Gilbert's bowl. "I had a discussion with Cecil's father, and I now know his son a little better." There was some quiet mumbling at this, as they apparently needed more reassurance. "The investigation is only just beginning. I have no doubt there will be more to discover once the meal is complete. It's one thing to appoint me as your inspector, but it's quite another to force me to go hungry." I was beginning to sound like a cake-loving boy I'd recently met, and so I decided to stop talking about food.

"Marius?" Bella said, just as I was about to raise my spoon to my lips and float away on the tastebud-enchanting delicacy.

"Oh, what now?"

"A word, please." She marched from the room before I could complain.

My stomach rumbled, but I threw my napkin down to follow her to the corridor. She opened the first door she came to and was about to walk inside when she discovered it was a small cupboard for storing glasses, bottles and decanters.

"This won't do at all!" she complained and continued on to the next room.

"Are you going to tell me why you dragged me from my dinner?"

Instead of answering the question, she found a way to criticise me. "You should make do with one helping of any sweet at your age. It's not healthy."

"What do you mean, 'at your age'? I'm twenty-eight."

"Yes, and twenty-eight is nearly thirty. And thirty is nearly forty. And my father wasn't much more than fifty when he fell ill." The cause of the Duke of Hurtwood's illness was another fact I'd yet to unearth.

"My dear Bella, will you please tell me why you are making such a fuss?"

She shook her head, and I remembered how often she had treated me like a dim child back when I was actually a very bright child. "Really, Marius, I would think that was obvious. I'm not the one shovelling meringue down my throat."

"But I didn't get to eat my—" I decided to give up before I'd started. "It's a good thing that we didn't get married if this is how you would have treated me."

Every word I uttered was like a nail through my skin. It was the first time I'd even indirectly referred to my last night in Britain before the war. The night when I'd gone to the woods on her family estate with armfuls of flowers to decorate our tree house and waited in that happy spot to see her.

She could hardly look at me as she changed the subject. "I brought you here to talk."

I hadn't taken the time until now to examine where "here" actually was. The perfectly square room was more functional than the others I had entered. There were desks at either end, and a low bookshelf on one wall held paper files and folders as though it belonged to a resident accountant.

I hadn't said anything and so Bella continued. "I'd like to know what you plan to do next."

"I would have thought that was obvious. I plan to finish dinner." I can't deny that I enjoyed teasing her.

She scoffed and I was transported back to any number of such playful exchanges between us when we were children. "I was referring to the investigation, Marius, as I'm sure you know."

"Ah, the investigation." I smiled at her. I'm sure it was in terribly bad taste considering the dead man in the tower and all that, but I was simply having a lovely time. "I rather hoped the killer would crumble under the pressure and pop by to confess."

I was playing the fool and so she fell into the familiar role of my conscientious friend. "Really, Marius, you must take this more seriously. You do realise that our lives could be in danger?"

I became rather distracted at this point and my eyes drifted to the elaborately carved alabaster fireplace. It bore various figures who all resembled Guy Fawkes and, at the top, high above the unlit fire, was a statue of some long-deceased matriarch. She was dressed in flowing robes that made her look like a cross between Queen Elizabeth and the Virgin Mary.

Hanging on the wall of the chimney breast was a portrait of what I could only assume was the Cornwallis clan themselves. Three generations of the family stood in a large group, with grandparents in the middle and their many descendants all around. It wasn't a particularly old painting, and it was hard to imagine what change in fortunes had forced such an eminent dynasty to sell their home. Some families had been wiped out by the war. Whole male lines had been extinguished, but that wouldn't have explained where their money had gone. Whatever had brought about their downfall, they were a pasty lot, and I could see the family resemblance to the carved figures on the fireplace.

"Marius, are you listening to me?" Bella asked, and I foolishly told the truth.

"No, sorry, I was staring at the fireplace. It's rather curious, don't you think?"

She held my chin to twist my head around. "I'm terribly sorry to distract you, but I was trying to explain how important it is that you keep up your efforts. Who knows what could happen if you don't."

Her sea-green eyes were still on mine, and I knew that, if I didn't look away, I would give in to whatever she wanted.

I spoke more seriously all the same. "I can't say that my interview with Ross was the grand success I might have imagined." I bit my tongue as I considered why this was the case.

"It's not so easy as I had hoped to extract the truth from people. I'm not like you and your fancy friends. I don't believe in lying to people just to charm them. I'm simply Marius, and it's hard for me to be anything else."

"Which is why you'll be so good at the job." She made it sound as though I'd be getting a salary at the end of it. "You won't be swayed by the suspect's clever manipulations, but you must be quick about it. Perhaps whoever murdered Cecil has a list and he'll tick us off one by one. That's the sort of thing that happens in your book, isn't it?"

"Wait, I thought you'd read my book? You told me you'd bought twenty copies."

"That's right. I bought it for all my nearest and dearest." Her voice faltered for just a moment, but she was soon her confident self again. "I fully intended to read it too, but I never found the time."

This was hard news to take, and so I sought a silver lining. "Did you give Gilbert a copy?"

"I did as it happens." Even she smiled at this, and then everything felt better.

I could just imagine that dryasdust unwrapping his present on Christmas Day to discover that he'd been given my novel! Fellows like him were as likely to read a half decent mystery as I was to take up fox hunting.

"Now stop changing the subject." She was serious again and, though an inch shorter than me when last measured (aged seventeen), she managed to tower over me. "What's the next step in the investigation?"

In that moment, I knew exactly what needed to be done. "You're going to help me."

She took a step away to perch on a filing cabinet. "I beg your pardon?"

"Come along, Bella. You know exactly what I mean." I studied her reaction for a moment, and she looked as nervous as she had for most of the evening. "I'm saying that our best hope of catching the blighter who killed your friend is if we do it together."

I could see just how much this idea frightened her, but I couldn't say why. She stared back at me, as if trying to make sense of what I'd suggested, and then began to drift across the room towards the exit once more.

"Bella, wait." Even the possibility that I could lift her spirits sent a jolt of energy through me. "I might not be the best at talking to people, but you are. Perhaps I can sniff out the contradictions in our suspects' accounts while you make them talk."

Instead of smiling, a flash of anger showed on her face. "Are you suggesting that I couldn't sniff out a lie myself?"

I bowed my head in apology. "You're right. You're right, you can do the whole thing solo. You don't need me after all."

Despite my own clever manipulations, she was still cautious. "I wouldn't know what to say any more than you do." She lingered in the doorway as though she were caught on a hook.

"Of course you would. You've always been a great talker. When we were little, you charmed the adults while I just mumbled. People adore you. It's as simple as that." I could see this hadn't convinced her, and so I quickly searched for something that could. "It will be just like our time together in Hurtwood."

Her response was so quiet that it only just reached me. "How do you mean?"

"We became friends because we both loved adventures. Do you remember all those summery, and not so summery, days we spent running through the woods around your house? Do you remember the time we stole your mother's sausage dog and replaced him with the stuffed boar from your father's study?"

She stared into space for a moment as she recalled our youthful high jinks. "I'd forgotten all about that." Her face finally brightened. "Mother was furious because we'd hidden Jonesy in the stable, and Father was up in arms at the idea of anyone touching his favourite hunting trophy."

"Yes, but they forgave us in the end. They always did because you persuaded them." I paused to see whether my words had swayed her. "It seems to me we have a stalemate. You want me to poke about in your friends' business until we can identify the killer, and I can't do it unless you help me. It's the perfect solution. This is our chance to be adventurers again. You do the talking, and I'll spend too long thinking about everything, just like I always used to do."

"I'm not sure it's a good idea," she began, but something in her tone told me she was about to change her mind. "Oh, why not? We'll do what we can and probably fail, but at least we can tell the police we gave it our best shot."

She held her hand out, and a strange sensation ran through me. I really don't know the word for it. It was somewhere between love, fear and excitement and was probably a combination of the three.

"Where do we start?" She leaned back against the door with much of her youthful vim now restored.

"With you, Bella. We'll start with you."

FOURTEEN

Until now, I'd been collecting doubts rather than clues, and I felt confident that Bella would be the one to set me on the right course. She sat down in a chair in front of the grand old fireplace, and I considered where to begin. I fell still once more, but it did little to help me.

"Marius, are you quite all right?" She must have been wondering whether the war – or spending too much of my life staring at a blank page – had turned my brains to mush.

"Yes, yes, never better," I insisted. "There's just so much I don't know." This made her laugh, and so I hurried to clarify. "Not in general, I mean. But about the friendships and rivalries of your associates in the dining room."

"So you'd like me to tell you who everyone is and what they do? That sort of thing?"

"No, I've garnered a lot of such basic information. What I need to know is how long you've all known one another, what Cecil Sinclair was up to that got him shot, and how far you trust each suspect."

Immediately excited by the challenge I'd presented, Bella

pushed her shoulders back. "Fire away, Mr Quin. I am ready for my interview."

"Exceptional." All I needed now was to decide upon the first question. I held on to the mantelpiece and allowed all those threads that I had been picking at since Cecil was killed to untangle.

"Are you sure you're feeling yourself?" she asked in the meantime. "Would you like me to call Philip for some bicarbonate?"

"No, of course, I wouldn't." I might have snapped just a little. "I didn't even get to eat my second helping of meringue." It was at this point that I decided to say the first thing that came into my head, if only to stop her thinking that I was suffering from indigestion. "How did you and Cecil become friends?"

"I met him at a party a couple of years ago and we got on well, so we started spending time together. He was the one who introduced me to Gilbert."

"Then what exactly does Gilbert do for him?"

The mildest panic crossed her face, and I finally realised that it was her boyfriend's involvement in the case that had been worrying her. "Gilbert is in charge of investments for Hargreaves Bank in the City. Cecil was tired of making tiny films with little return, so he approached them for a loan. The first one they made together was called *The Casebook of Dr Featherstonehaugh* and it was a wild success. After that, Cecil met his rich widow, Hortensia Alcott. They got married, and he had enough money to fund any film he wanted to make."

I was fairly certain that the picture Bella had just painted was different from the one that Ross Sinclair had of his son's career.

"Did the marriage upset anyone in this Alcott woman's family?" I remembered the photograph on Cecil's bed and thought this a rich seam to tap. "She evidently left him the majority of her fortune. Could some vengeful heir have resented it?"

She considered the possibility for a moment, before shrugging. "Well, it's possible, I suppose. But Cecil insisted that the only family Hortensia had was an estranged daughter she hadn't seen for several years. He felt quite guilty over the affair, but it wasn't his fault that the pair had stopped talking."

"In which case," I began, "if he had so much money, why did Cecil and Gilbert continue working together? I can only assume that this is your boyfriend's office in which we're talking?"

She nodded in one quick movement. "Cecil was so wealthy he didn't know what to do with all that he had, and so the two men were still useful to one another. In fact, even before I knew them, Gilbert had become Cecil's full-time advisor."

Everything she said made sense, of course, and my only disappointment was that none of this greatly implicated that blue-bore Gilbert in the murder.

"I'm surprised Cecil had the forethought to control his money so carefully. He didn't seem like the organised type."

She pushed her long, black fringe to one side. "He really wasn't by the time you met him. But when the pair first met, Cecil was far more astute. The effect that his hedonistic lifestyle had on him was quite pronounced." She looked about the room then, as though expecting to spot Cecil's ghost raising a glass to her. "When I first came to Everham Hall, he usually managed to go a week or two without drugging himself into a stupor. Over the last year, it had become a nightly occurrence."

I attempted to sort through everything she'd told me and pluck out the most relevant points. "You've clearly spent a lot of time here. Why was that?"

She became nervous again and seized a handful of the glossy gold material that covered her lap. "Cecil and I were simply good friends. We had fun together while Gilbert was working. I spend five days a week looking after my father, and Everham Hall served as my escape from real life on my days off."

There was a question I wanted to put to her, but I didn't know whether I should. Being rude old me, I asked it anyway. "But why were you the one to look after the Duke? Surely you could have paid a nurse to care for him?"

A sad smile turned up the corners of her mouth. "I discussed the possibility with my family. We even interviewed a few candidates for the job, but I knew from the beginning that I wouldn't be happy unless I did it myself. You see, Father had a stroke not long after you left Hurtwood. Mother doesn't have it in her to help a great deal, and my brothers have lives of their own. I'm glad that I can be at home when he needs me, and Gilbert has been terribly understanding about how little we see of one another."

I'd finally heard something positive about Gilbert Baines.

"I'm sure that Lord Hurtwood appreciates the care you offer."

For a moment, silence fell between us. I reflected on the thought of losing my joyful collection of old people to the ravages of age. The thing that I couldn't bring myself to think about just then was my own dear father and whatever had happened to him. As sad as the Duke's illness evidently was, I would have given anything to visit my old man, even if it was only in a hospital bed.

"I doubt that Father's condition had much bearing on Cecil's death," Bella said to pull us back to more pressing matters. "Now, what else would you like to know?"

"What about Poppy? I heard that she and Cecil hadn't been together long. Had you met her before tonight?"

"Yes, I certainly had." She did not make it sound as though this was a good thing. "Poppy has been hanging around film sets for months. I occasionally visited Cecil when he was at work, and she was there when he made *The Devil Dances in Darkness* with Alec Pemberton. For a while, the two men were great rivals, always going for the same parts, competing with one another to see whose films would make more money. It was all rather juvenile really, and Alec lost. His career has been on the brink of extinction for some time, and it was only out of the goodness of his heart that Cecil offered him a part on that film."

I realised something important then. "You were very fond of Cecil, weren't you? It was hard for me to understand why you would spend so much time with such a person, but I can see it now. You were always a believer in lost causes."

The smile she gave me was not so sad this time. "You were never a lost cause, Marius."

"I wasn't thinking of myself but thank you all the same." I had to laugh. After the dramatic evening we'd lived through, it helped me relax a little. "I lost count of the times you charged off to defend the downtrodden and in need when we were children. I imagine you did the same thing for Cecil."

She looked across at the painting above the fireplace as though projecting Cecil's features onto the oddly blank family portrait. "That wasn't the only reason I liked him. Cecil always did his best to make me happy." She must have known how this sounded after the way he'd behaved that night, as she added a caveat. "When he was sober, he could be a real darling. He was loyal and considerate."

"That's not the impression I got from Anton and Alma."

"Yes, but they had to work with him. That's different. They'd been trying to keep him away from drink and drugs so that he could make films and maintain their business. Cecil promised that he would be more moderate if they came tonight, but you saw how things ended."

There was an implication to this that she was too polite to voice. "Do you think that Poppy was to blame for his intoxication?"

"She certainly didn't help the situation. Even when they met, she was known as a girl who liked a drink or two. She cast Alec Pemberton aside and fell in with Cecil quicker than I could read off the text on one of their posters." Her voice fell quiet for a few seconds and, when she spoke again, she was more confident. "You think that she's the likely suspect, don't you?"

"It would make a lot of sense. It sounds to me as though she set her sights on Cecil from the beginning. Who's to say Alec Pemberton isn't behind all this?"

This suggestion instantly set the cogs in her brain to whir. "You mean that Alec sent his girlfriend to murder his rival in order to clear his path back to stardom?"

I couldn't say how likely this was, but it sounded like the plot for a book I'd happily read. "Yes, why not? Cecil was getting all the best roles, so perhaps Alec decided to put the kibosh on him. The fact that Poppy went from one man to the other so quickly is certainly suspicious. She's been acting as though she's lost the love of her life."

Bella put her hands together in excitement. "I knew you'd be good at this!"

I was only too happy to impress her. "We know she trailed after Cecil when he was carried from the games room. We also know that Ross and Anton didn't see her again after that. So perhaps she waited for them to leave then sneaked in there with a gun she'd found in—"

"How do you know the gun was from the house?" she asked before I could finish my big revelation. One of the reasons I so admired my old friend was because she didn't need to have everything broken apart and explained. It was probably a good thing she'd never read my book. She was far too good at filling in gaps and would have spotted the killer from the first few chapters.

"It had the Cornwallis crest stamped on it, and so I went

looking for the armoury and found the space where the gun must have been."

Her smile grew a fraction. "That doesn't surprise me. It's harder to find a pencil than a pistol in an old house like this one."

"When the deed was done, Poppy could have hidden in the dressing room as we went to look at Cecil's body, then slipped out of sight to freedom."

"Of course, she'd have to find bullets too, and they're hardly kept on display the way that guns, knives and swords are." As she spoke, she pointed behind me where a pair of crossed swords were fixed to the wall.

"Yes, I've considered that, and it may be an important point. I wonder if she brought bullets with her and looked for a matching gun. Or perhaps the one she found was already loaded."

"No, no. That doesn't sound plausible." Bella had such a keen look in her eye then that I knew it wouldn't take much to get her running around after clues, just as we had imagined ourselves doing as children. She got up from her chair to discuss the matter further and it was clear that this was no longer an interview. She was already my partner on the case. "We'll leave Poppy aside for one moment and see who else might have wanted Cecil dead."

"Is it certain that Cecil had never met Edith or Carl Wilson before tonight?"

"It certainly seems that way." Standing in front of one window, she tapped her pointed black shoe three times on the carpet before continuing. "I must admit, I rather like Carl. He started working at Gilbert's firm and the three of us have become pals. He's sociable in his own way, but he wouldn't say boo to a mouse, let alone a goose."

"Does he have any connection to the other guests?"

"Not that he's mentioned. His parents died not so long ago,

and I don't think he's got too many friends. His family aren't
from London, and he seemed ever so alone when Gilbert took
him under his wing." She spoke in an almost maternal tone just
then. "I really can't imagine he's got anything to do with what
happened."

"Which means he's probably the culprit." I smiled at this,
though I wasn't about to rule the idea out altogether. "And what
about Edith?"

"We've heard about her for some time, but Cecil wanted
nothing to do with a potential stepmother who was little more
than half his age."

"Yes," I mused. "That's exactly what Ross told me. He's an
odd chap, don't you think?"

"How do you mean?"

I leaned on the mantelpiece as I tried to translate my
thoughts into words. "The idea that a man like that could have
fathered a son like Cecil. They were both broad chaps, but they
barely looked alike. Chalk and cheese surely have more in
common."

"Their differences had pushed them apart for years, but I
always got the sense that Cecil loved his father." The line of her
lip became a fraction softer as she thought back on previous
visits to Everham. "Whenever they were here together, they got
on famously. They could be quite nostalgic when looking back
through old photographs or reminiscing on Cecil's youth."

I gave her a moment to enjoy these thoughts, before dark-
ening the mood once more. "He also mentioned Cecil's will. Do
you have any idea who would benefit from his death?"

"Well, Ross presumably."

"It does seem that way." A feeling that I'd been unable to
express before found its way to the tip of my tongue. "There's
an edge to Ross that I don't quite trust. Of everyone here, I
could imagine Cecil's father possessing the fury required to
murder another man."

She came to stand next to me, and I could tell that she would disagree. "Shooting someone with a pretty silver revolver is hardly the obvious method for a man like Ross Sinclair. I'm sure that, if he were to murder someone, he'd use his bare hands."

"Unless he knew everyone would assume such a thing and wanted to get away with it. Killers are rarely as clever or as stupid as we wish to believe."

A burst of laughter broke from deep within her. "Is that the conclusion that you've formed during your long career as a detective?"

I had no shame and smiled back at her. "Yes. Yes, it is. Or rather, it's what I've learnt scouring famous cases in the archives of the London Library. You wouldn't believe the stories that I've discovered. One of them inspired my first novel."

She was only a foot away from me now and, in the exotic films of Cecil Sinclair, a man like me would have kissed a woman like her. In Britain on the eve of 1928, however, I was bound by propriety, modern manners and personal history to stand there, in quiet awe of her beauty.

"Which is yet more evidence of your suitability to lead this investigation."

Did she know what she was doing as she stared so deeply into my eyes? Did she know the effect it had upon me? I very much doubt it as, when the comfortable silence broke, she said, "Oh, Marius. I'm so glad I found you on the pavement last week. When you didn't come back to Hurtwood after the war, I thought you would never talk to me again."

In another world, these words would have given me hope that she wished things were different between us. Despite the presence of her boyfriend a few rooms away and everything my instincts told me, I've no doubt I could have used this brief comment as evidence that we were destined to be together.

Though I may be a romantic, I'm not a complete idiot and

managed to fashion a reply that was free of any such hope. "Of course I still want to talk to you. Who else will look out for my waistline if you don't? My family are as intent on fattening me up as the witch in *Hansel and Gretel*. You should have seen what we ate on Christmas Day."

Before my resolve wavered, I cut short that dreamy moment and moved towards the door. "Now, if I'm not mistaken, Lady Isabella, it is your turn to lead the investigation. So, where should we go next?"

FIFTEEN

The diners had finished their dinner in the dining room is a tongue twister that I will not be saying three times fast. Our return silenced the quiet mumbling between the suspects, and I was once more aware that my presence in any room would, from now on, be the cause of discomfort.

My partner came to a stop at the free end of the table and stood confidently before them. People like Bella are born public speakers. For my part, when I'd won an award for my first and, as yet, only book, my acceptance speech had stretched to three sentences and one of them was "Thank you".

"Marius has asked for my help with the investigation, as I know you all better than he does."

"Wait a moment," Poppy screeched. "How can we be certain that you aren't the killer?"

Bella was not intimidated by the question and provided a quick answer. "Because I was with him when we heard the three shots."

"And how do we know that the two of you aren't working together? Perhaps you hatched a plan to provide one another with alibis. There's nothing to say that one of you didn't kill the man I loved." The longer the evening went on, the stronger her feelings for Cecil became.

Bella was not intimidated, but she was a mite vexed by the accusation. "Because I've only seen Marius once in the past decade. Do you really think we plotted to kill a close friend of mine after we bumped into one another in Russell Square?"

Poppy was at least partially placated by this and asked no further questions. When Bella was certain that she would not be interrupted, she spoke again. "I will be helping him interview you one at a time. I was planning to start with Anton, but as you have so much to say for yourself, Poppy, you can be first."

She looked surprised to be summoned but, after a moment's hesitation, the aspiring actress rose from her seat. "I suppose I can spare the time."

Poppy had an unusual walk. It's not the sort of thing I'd normally notice, but there was a lazy, lolloping nature to it, as though she wished to communicate that she would get to where she was going in her own time. Perhaps more remarkably, my dog Percy appeared from under the long red tablecloth and trotted after her out of the room. His muzzle was covered in crumbs, and I could only imagine that Poppy had been throwing him scraps throughout the meal. I cast him a judgemental look, but he ignored me entirely.

"There's a room down here which Gilbert uses as an office," Bella informed our suspect as we reached the corridor. "We won't be disturbed if we—"

"Not a chance." Poppy was not one to tread lightly. "I need a cigarette or five, so we're going to the smoking room."

She marched off in the opposite direction to Gilbert's office, leaving Bella and me where we stood. With no other solution available, I shrugged and walked after Poppy (and Percy – who had clearly taken a liking to her).

The smoking room was, like most such spaces, woody, musty

and rather worn-looking. It did not have the grandeur of the state rooms I'd visited and looked to be one of the few places in that wing where Cecil hadn't left his mark. I very much doubted it had been decorated in fifty years. In fact, the most modern thing in there, after Poppy herself, was a painting of soldiers on horseback coming under heavy fire in the Crimean War. It brought back memories that I had no wish to revisit, and so I immediately looked away.

My dog curled up in one corner to have a nap, and the would-be star went over to an octagonal wooden table in the centre of the room. It was surely the most interesting feature in there and opened in various ways, with hinges and extensions popping left and right like a devilish puzzle box. It took her a few tries to find the right section, but she eventually extracted a handful of cigarettes. She did not offer us one but, to be honest, I didn't mind. The air, carpets and furniture were so infused with the scent of tobacco that it felt as though we were taking a drag with every breath.

"I'd much rather be in here with you two and away from those awful people. First things first, one of them killed my darling Cecil, but even worse than that, they're terribly dull." One thing you could say about Poppy was that she knew how to start a conversation. "The thing is, Cecil promised me a fun evening. He said we'd celebrate the New Year in style, but this isn't at all what I had in mind."

It was amusing to see Bella's attempt to recover from the barrage of words that had been fired in our direction. Poppy looked perfectly innocent and blinked repeatedly as she awaited a response.

"I can't imagine that it has been pleasant for you," my friend began in as diplomatic a tone as she could muster. "Even just after we found the body, people were casting aspersions on you."

"People?" Poppy snapped before Bella could even utter a

question. "I wouldn't call Alma Cavendish 'people'. She's just one of those animals that lives on the side of things."

Bella glanced at me then in the hope that I might know what she meant.

"Are you referring to koalas?" I could only guess.

"No, not those sweet little bears. I mean in the sea. You know... Barnacles or limpets or what have you."

"And that's a bad thing?"

"Yes!" Poppy took a few seconds to feel the smoke billowing around her lungs before jetting it back out again. "She's a clinger-on. She is without talent or humility."

"Just like a barnacle," my friend replied, somehow with a straight face.

"Precisely. And her whole sweet-little-mother act is just that: an act. I don't believe for a second that Anton discovered her in the hosiery department at Debenhams or wherever it was. She has the look of a calculating little madam all over her face."

"Are you saying that you think she killed Cecil?" There was shock in Bella's eyes then, and her mouth fell open as she awaited the answer.

Poppy certainly took her time providing one. She picked a strand of tobacco from the tip of her tongue and then took another drag on her cigarette to really make us wait. "She might well have. After all, they were in films together, weren't they?"

Bella didn't realise this needed a response at first, but when the brash woman in front of us said no more, she murmured, "Yes, obviously they were."

"Well, there you go then." Poppy slowly drew her hand through the air, as though the implications of this were plain to see. "Cecil always said that the Cavendish woman was a terrible co-star. She was forever telling him what to do."

"I'm sorry, but I don't see how that proves Alma is the

killer." Bella was more than shocked; she was bulldozed by the strange woman in our midst.

"Because she was evidently jealous. Cecil Sinclair was one of the best loved actors in the country. But tell me this: who would want a cigarette card with Alma Cavendish's dour face on it?"

Bella turned back to me, and I felt a little sorry for her. Facing Ross Sinclair in my first interview had been a picnic compared to a clash with a woman like Poppy.

"That's an interesting theory. It really is." She took a deep breath and found some confidence. "But have you come across any evidence that proves Alma was involved in the murder?"

"No." Poppy stubbed out her first cigarette and leaned back in her chair to cross her slender legs at the ankle.

"What about the history they shared? Can you tell us anything about Cecil's thoughts on Alma or the rivalry that existed between them?"

"No." Before Bella could ask another question, Poppy changed her mind. "Or rather, I could tell you, but it would be disloyal to Cecil. And I do not wish to speak ill of the dead."

"Of course not. We never would," Bella insisted. "Would we, Marius?"

I was just as bamboozled as my partner, and it took me a moment to realise I'd been addressed. "No, no. We never would."

"That is a relief." Poppy seemed to have already forgotten her previous qualms. "In which case, I don't mind telling you that Cecil called Alma a despicable little snake."

Bella leapt on the comment. "Do you know why?"

Instead of answering, Poppy lit another cigarette and looked a little pensive. "No, I don't think that I do. All I know is that when they were filming *The Devil Dances in Darkness*, Anton stormed off set one day and wouldn't talk to Cecil for a week.

Or at least, that's what Alec Pemberton told me, and he always spoke highly of Cecil. I can't imagine he was lying."

It was hard to know whether this would turn out to be an essential point in the case or an entirely irrelevant digression. The same could be said for almost every word that had fallen from Poppy's painted lips. She was a real puzzle; the kind of person you could know for a lifetime and still never fathom.

"So you've stayed friends with Alec Pemberton since the end of your relationship?" I had to ask before she could change the topic again.

"Oh, yes. Alec and I are bosom pals. It's not his fault that Cecil was just a morsel more ravishing." If her previous beau was the evil manipulator who was pulling her strings, she appeared entirely comfortable talking about him.

"And what about Cecil's director?" Bella spoke quickly to keep the conversation moving.

"Ooh, what about him?" Poppy reacted as though we were about to let her in on a secret.

"Do you think he would have hurt Cecil?"

Our suspect tipped her head back and gave off a laugh like a fire alarm. It was not just that it was loud; it was equally shrill and repetitive. It seemed to poke into my head from one side, drill right through my brain and shoot out the other.

"Anton? Kill his golden goose? Not likely." She laughed again, and my headache worsened. "What is a director without a star? In fact, they all fed off poor Cecil. Gilbert, Alma, Ross, even you, Bella. You were all reliant upon him in different ways. Surely you can see that?"

I thought that this might be difficult for my friend to hear, and I was about to point out that Poppy was hardly a disinterested party herself when Bella spoke again.

"That may be true. But that was because of Cecil, not us. He told me on a number of occasions that he liked to feel important." She paused for half a moment to consider this point. "I know that may be common among actors – and Cecil certainly didn't shy from the limelight – but, more than anyone, he loved giving people what they needed."

"That's just it. He was generous and selfless." The woman in red rocked from side to side. I thought that she was dancing to music that only she could hear, or that whatever substances she had consumed that night were still flowing through her, but I was wrong. It was him; Cecil was with her for a moment as she recalled the man she'd (briefly) loved. "He wanted to be all things to all people, but he was no sap, either. He stood up for himself when it was required."

Bella's next question was delivered with such precision and such force that it knocked our suspect back in her seat. "What about you, Poppy? Did you kill Cecil?"

She looked uncomfortable for the first time since we'd sat down. "Whyever would I have killed him? If he was worth anything to me, it was for the contacts he had. How can he influence people and make me a star now that he's dead?"

"That's a good point." Bella was growing into the interview and the tidal wave that had crashed over us had all but subsided. "But you keep assuming that whoever killed Cecil had her wits about her. I believe that the majority of murders are committed out of passion or anger. Surely it is more common for a woman to see red and rid herself of an abusive lover than to plan and scheme and kill with calm determination?"

Poppy just smiled. "I might not think that Alma's very innocent, but you are, aren't you, my dear?" Poppy couldn't have been more than a few years older than Bella, but she spoke to her as though she was far more worldly. "It would be nice to believe that murders are only committed in a fugue-like state, but you clearly underestimate just how wicked humans can be. It is highly likely that one of the people in the dining room right at this very moment came here with the intention of killing my beloved Cecil."

There was a pause then as Poppy directed a glare straight at Bella. I thought we'd finally found a chink in her defences, and so I asked a question of my own.

"Even if you didn't kill your boyfriend, you're hardly an open book. We still haven't learnt anything about you."

There was a long pause, a long draw, and a long puff. "What would you like to know?"

Bella leaned closer. "You could start by telling us your full name."

Our suspect was sitting in a grey cloud by this point. The smoke from her cigarette had no desire to dissipate and hung in the air as though Poppy was a witch who could control the atmosphere around her. "Why would you care about such a minor detail? I'm just Poppy."

Bella threw a telling glance in my direction. "I think it's normal for two people investigating a murder to want to know as much about a suspect as possible."

"And it's only natural for me to wish to maintain a certain secretive allure. All I can say is that I was born without love or care. My family took no interest in me, even when I was a child, but when I discovered acting, I felt as though I'd been born again. Cecil offered me a second chance. So, no thank you. I have no wish to revisit my past. Like I said, my name is Poppy, and that's all you need to know."

"Perhaps we'll find out your full name when Cecil's will is read." Bella looked rather proud of herself, and I didn't blame her. "If you were hoping that, by killing him, you would inherit the estate, I can promise that I will do everything in my power to prevent that from happening."

Poppy no longer looked so indignant. In fact, she looked scared, and I had some information that could only add to her worries. "Ross Sinclair told me that Cecil intended to change his will if his father and Edith married. Is that what happened? Did you become the beneficiary when they got engaged?"

"Oh, please. I know nothing about Cecil's finances, and I have no reason to believe I would benefit from his will." The fear remained in her eyes, even as she changed the subject. "Now, who else haven't we considered?"

As she watched our main suspect's shifting glances and even faster puffing, Bella took some seconds over her response. "Of the suspects?"

"Yes, the suspects in the dining room. There's that skinny young boy, Carl, isn't that his name? What a masculine name for such a little runt." A sourness had entered her voice since we'd raised the possibility of her guilt, and she was no longer trying to pretend she was on our side. "He seems like the type who would kill out of jealousy. Perhaps the odd little fellow was envious of Cecil's house and money, and beautiful girlfriend."

She clapped her hands together and looked ever so pleased with herself. "That must be it! Did you see his face when he discovered that the pretty waif belonged to Cecil's father?" Some of her phrasing was clearly designed to shock. In this day and age, we don't normally talk about women as though they are chattel. "I bet baby-faced Carl was so upset that he wouldn't be kissing Edith at midnight that he took his rage out on poor Cecil – who, I must admit, had been rather rude to him. How marvellous! How simply marvellous!" She clapped once more and hooted her appreciation for this improbable scenario.

Perhaps it was this overt cruelty which helped Bella steel herself. "You do realise that speaking in such a sadistic manner is never going to convince us that you're innocent of your boyfriend's murder?"

"And you do realise I'm no killer and that, by bringing me in here, you've wasted everyone's time?"

"Then tell us where you were when Cecil was killed?"

Her third and final cigarette had burnt down to nothing,

and she reached forward in her chair to stub it out in one of the compartments in the strange cabinet. "I've already told you."

"No, you haven't," I was quick to reply. "When Ross Sinclair asked you, you made a fuss about nothing and managed to avoid answering the question."

Bella showed that she approved of my interruption and we both awaited our slithering suspect's response.

"How can I answer such a thing?" Poppy replied inscrutably. "How can I tell you where I was when it will only incriminate me?"

Bella had a sly glint in her eye that I could only admire. "Were you busy polishing your pistol? Or did you have a tête-à-tête with Cecil's father?"

"Don't be disgusting." For someone who, just a short while earlier, had been parading about the place like a bacchanalian reveller and proselytising on the thrill of illegal drugs, our suspect had an oddly repulsed reaction to these mild insinuations. "I can't tell you where I was when Cecil was killed because I don't really know. I was wandering the halls upstairs and lost track of time. I'm hardly going to tell everyone that I can't explain where I was when poor Cecil was killed."

"You haven't an alibi, because you were the one who killed him." Undeterred, Bella detailed the grand theory we'd formulated. "I put it to you that you killed Cecil Sinclair on the behest of your real love – his rival Alec Pemberton. I say that you only ever started seeing Cecil in order to carry out this wicked plan."

Poppy rose from her seat to look down at us with something approaching sympathy. "Oh, you dear, dear creature. What a pretty little theory you've hatched. Good luck proving it." With her piece said, she closed the cigarette cabinet so that it became a small, compact coffee table once more and strolled over to the door. "Come along, Percy."

Despite the pleading face I made for him to stay, my dog waddled out of the room after his new friend. When we were alone and their footsteps were no longer audible, the two now slightly more experienced detectives turned to one another with a look of pure befuddlement on our faces.

"The woman's mad," Bella declared, and I needed a moment to think before delivering my own verdict.

"Mad or extremely clever. I wonder if we'll ever work out which it is."

SIXTEEN

"Would you like to know what I've realised?" I asked my esteemed assistant when we stepped out into the hall once more. It was a rhetorical question, and she took it as such. "I see now that it will do no good to ask our suspects to incriminate themselves."

"How wise you are, Marius Quin. It's no wonder you write such complex and compelling novels."

"Thank you, I do like to think of myself as something of a genius," I lied... or at least exaggerated.

"Of course you are." The sparkle hadn't left her eye and there was a boldness to her that made my heart beat just a tiny bit faster. This was my Bella. The girl I had loved as an adolescent was always full of life. "Go ahead then. What did you learn from our interview?"

I stopped between a pair of wall sconces that held two burnt-down candles. "It may sound obvious but, when we asked Poppy where she was when Cecil was murdered, she could have told us anything."

"Except to say that she was with another suspect." Bella leant against the wall opposite, and the flickering light lent her dress an orangey hue. "She couldn't just make up an alibi, as no one would have confirmed it."

"Evidently, but it's also true that, by taking us off on so many tangents, she did a good job of distracting from the fact that she could still be our culprit. From now on, we'll have to be smarter with our questions."

Bella's hands linked loosely together in front of her. "Does that make her a likely choice, though?"

We peered down the corridor, even though Poppy was no longer in view. "My dog doesn't seem to think so. Maybe she's not such a monster after all."

"I can't say that I think too highly of her. A few weeks ago, Cecil was doing all he could to keep his life together. He might have slipped from time to time, but he was trying his damnedest. Not long after that woman got her hands on him, it all went to pot. It seems to me that the killer's job would have been more difficult if Cecil hadn't been inebriated at the time he was murdered."

"And you blame Poppy for that, at the very least?"

She nodded and then shook her head. "I don't know. I really don't. Cecil was a grown man. He might well have been the one pushing them down that slippery slope of excess. Poppy is a lot soberer than he was."

"Perhaps what we have to do..." I began without knowing whether this was a good idea or a genuinely terrible one. "What we have to do is stop thinking of these people as a group of your friends and start looking at them as characters in a detective novel. Maybe by identifying the different roles that each of them plays, we can work out who is the most likely killer."

Bella immediately stood up straighter. "That does sound rather clever. But wouldn't it simply reinforce the idea that Poppy is our woman? She is the money-grubbing interloper, after all."

"Is she a money-grubber?" I had to ask, as we'd seen no

evidence to prove such a theory. "I think what you mean is that she's a young woman who spent time with male film stars. In mystery novels, such scarlet women are condemned for their moral degeneracy. In fact, they are far more likely to be victims than killers. I'm not saying that Poppy can't be the culprit, but there's a strong possibility that we think so badly of her simply because she doesn't fit our expectations of how a young lady should behave."

Bella was amused by my moralising. "Very well then, which other stereotypes do our suspects fulfil?"

I moved off along the corridor as we talked. "Well, in the absence of any parents tonight, Alma is definitely the mother figure. She was protective of me from the moment we met and has shown concern for many of us over the course of the evening."

"Does that make Anton the father of the group?"

"Possibly, but he's also an impresario and an artist. He's a more difficult character to pin down and—"

"Marius," she interrupted, "I believe that we have moved from detective work into the realm of literary criticism." We had reached the dining room, and she placed her hand upon the door.

"Ah, you may have a point." I tried to remember why I'd started on such a path in the first place. "The main thing I wanted to say is that we shouldn't judge Poppy based solely on the vibrant shade of her lipstick or the hemline of her dress."

"Duly noted," she replied with a wink and opened the door to discover that the room was empty except for the younger of the two footmen who was clearing the table.

"You will find the other guests in the sitting room, madam," he told us politely before continuing with his task.

"Thank you, Philip, and while you're here, I should probably put some questions to you."

"To me, madam?" He froze then and looked a little confused. "I'll do what I can, but I doubt I'll be much help."

"Don't worry, you're not in any trouble." Bella had been trained from birth in how to talk to people and it was impressive how swiftly she set the man's mind at ease. "I was merely wondering whether you could contact the guard on duty at the gatehouse and confirm whether anyone could have entered the estate after the last guests arrived?"

Philip was clearly happy to be of service. "I rang Oscar as soon as we heard the news about poor Mr Sinclair. No one came through the gate except the people on the guest list. Oh, and Ross Sinclair's fiancée, Miss Havelock, didn't have a formal invitation, but Oscar made an exception and let her pass."

"What about the front door?" I asked. "Were any of you stationed there at the time of the murder?"

"I'm afraid not, Mr Quin. Once everyone was here, we returned to our duties in other parts of the house to prepare for the party. But if you're wondering whether anyone could have got in without us seeing, there's a high wall around the estate that wouldn't be easy to breach in any weather, let alone ice and snow."

"That's wonderful, Philip." Those pretty craters on Bella's cheeks hollowed out in a smile. "You've told us just what we needed to know."

"It's my pleasure, madam." He bowed to us both, and we turned to leave the room.

We walked on along the corridor and a thought occurred to me that we hadn't had time to explore. "I know that we dismissed the possibility of the staff being involved in the killing, but it's a little odd that they've continued with their jobs as though nothing has happened. Are you aware of any ill will they have held towards Cecil?"

"Far from it," she replied with great finality. "I've always had the impression that he treats them rather well. He's given half of them the night off to be with their families, for a start. The old butler disappeared at ten o'clock on the dot, too, and I haven't seen a maid since I got here. Aside from the footmen, I imagine there are a couple of women in the kitchen and the rest were sent home."

"I did assume that to be the case, but I can't help finding it close-minded when authors simply overlook servants as possible killers. I'm not suggesting that the butler should be to blame each time, but at least give the man his due as a human being."

I was rambling, which was not a problem, as Bella wasn't listening. She had made it to the sitting room and was staring through the open door with horror etched on her face as the sound of a commotion travelled out to us.

"Come back here this instant so I can wrap my hands around your throat and choke the life out of you!"

SEVENTEEN

I ran into the room ahead of her to see whether anyone needed saving. It turned out that this furious threat had come from Ross Sinclair, who was chasing Gilbert around the furniture. That was fine by me, so I left him to it.

"I didn't mean to upset you, old boy." Gilbert's face had turned a shade of puce. "You know full well that I thought Cecil was a top-notch fellow, but you can't deny that he stepped on a few toes from time to time."

"Please don't fight," poor little Edith fussed, and I was worried for a moment that she would faint from the stress. If I had to pick an archetype with which to label her, she reminded me of a damsel in distress or some birdlike heroine in a Victorian novel.

"I never meant to put my foot in it," Gilbert attempted to reason with the man as they came to a halt with a sofa between them as a barricade. "But you know me, I can't open my mouth without saying the wrong thing."

This was not enough to stop the big sailor, who somehow vaulted over the sofa. He would have grabbed his hapless rival, but Gilbert spotted an escape route and ran to hide heroically behind his girlfriend.

"Everyone, stop!" Bella definitely held some sway in the house. I'm sure that, had I attempted such an intervention, they would have ignored me. "That's right, now calm down."

Ross was still huffing out steam from his nostrils. He reminded me of a bull in the middle of a Spanish corrida. What remained uncertain, however, was whether the immense creature would gore the matador, or the caped antagonist would find a way to stick in the knife.

"He said that Cecil deserved to die." Despite Bella's instructions, Ross had definitely not calmed down. "That's a despicable lie, and I won't have my boy's name besmirched. If it wasn't enough that he's been murdered, now I have to listen to insults and slurs."

"I didn't mean it like that." Gilbert was not a clever man and did not know when to surrender. "Cecil was a lot of fun, but it's no secret that he wasn't everyone's cup of tea."

Ross lunged forward again, but Anton was there to keep him away from his target.

"Now, now," the director purred, looking straight into the big man's eyes. "There's no need to resort to violence. We're all friends here."

The raging bull looked dubious. "Except that's not true, is it?" His voice ripped through the room like the horn on a boat. "We're not friends. We hardly know one another. And on top of that, one of you is a killer."

It wasn't as if any of us had forgotten this, but his blunt reminder underlined the reality we were facing. Our problem did not end with the dead man in the tower. There was a homicidal devil hiding amongst us, and any attempt to ignore him would only lead to woe.

"That's just what you would say if you wanted to deflect suspicion." It really was impressive how dim Gilbert could be.

Couldn't he see that he'd only escaped being pummelled because his sweetheart had appeared in the room at the right moment?

"I'll deflect my fists into your face if you're not careful."

Anton put both hands on the old man's broad chest to hold him back, but I doubted it would work for much longer if Gilbert kept talking.

"Mr Quin," Alma began, "have you identified the killer? We could certainly use some good news."

I rather liked Alma. She was kind-hearted and down to earth. And yet, at that moment, I wished for nothing more than to roar, *Have none of you ever read a mystery novel? Detective work takes time!*

"I'm afraid we're still in the early stages of the investigation," I replied more diplomatically.

Before Gilbert could say anything else that was both stupid and incendiary, Bella pulled him from the room.

"It's not long until midnight," I continued. "I think it would be best if you all stay here for the moment and..." I didn't have anything to add to this, so I repeated myself in a graver tone. "Just stay in this room."

I left them to discuss the skirmish. I had no doubt that everyone would sympathise with the bereaved father over that inflated windbag Gilbert Baines.

Even as I left the room, he was still chattering away. "I must get some fresh air. I'm quite shocked that one of my fellow men could act in such a fashion. Really, I have never been so offended in my life." If he'd given me a few moments to think, I felt certain that I could have produced a better insult than anything Ross Sinclair had managed.

He led us all the way to the entrance hall and extracted his coat and a pair of boots from a well-concealed wardrobe beside the door. Bella looked reluctant to head out into the cold, but there was a cashmere coat for her to borrow and so she slipped it over her shoulders and chose some fur-lined boots to go with it. There was nothing in my size of shoe or outerwear, and so I took a woolly hat and several scarves to wrap around me.

Once we'd crossed the front courtyard, Gilbert was determined to walk through the snow as fast as he could. The path upon which I'd driven to the house was no longer visible, but the flakes were not coming down as rapidly as they had before. Each white crystal floated to the earth like a feather. I watched my black dinner jacket turn spotty, as though I were a Dalmatian that had been turned inside out and back to front.

"It's not on, do you hear me?" Gilbert was safe to make such a remark now that we were well away from the Viking of a man he'd previously upset. "Everyone knows that I was very fond of Cecil. I wouldn't have spent so much time with him otherwise."

"You wouldn't have spent so much time with him if he wasn't rich, you mean." I sometimes suffer from the same disease as Gilbert and, though I'd attempted to mutter this under my breath, he evidently caught my meaning.

"Oh, and that makes me a killer, does it?" He stepped around Bella to address me as the three of us circled the perimeter of the building. "I happen to be a banker."

Bella slowed down to glare at me. It was clear she expected me to treat the abscess that was growing on her with something approaching civility, but that was no easy feat.

"You're twisting my words," I petulantly responded. "Bella, did I say, at any point, even in private, that Gilbert was the killer?"

"No, you didn't," she conceded with a tired sigh. "But that doesn't change the fact that you men have been acting like snakes in a pit since we discovered poor Cecil's body."

She had once again provoked a begrudging silence. The only sound was the crunch of snow beneath our feet. I really should have looked around for some boots as my socks were already sodden and my toes were turning to stone from the cold that was now working its way up my body. The hat and scarves had done little except make me look a fool.

"That being said," Bella soon continued, "I think it's in everyone's best interest if Marius and I ask you some questions, my love."

Perhaps words affect writers more than normal humans – and yes, I would make a distinction between the two. Her affection for that odious man sent a fizz of fury through me, and I once more had to ask, *What in Heaven's name does she see in him?*

"I know nothing about Cecil's murder." He didn't look at us as he said this but kept his eyes on the brightening sky. The moon had succeeded in slicing a small hole through the clouds for a single beam of light to break through.

"You may not think that you do," his softly spoken sweetheart began, "but who's to say what secret some seemingly insignificant detail could unlock? Perhaps there is something you've seen or overheard that could help us apprehend the killer."

Gilbert moved his jaw from one side of his mouth to the other as he considered the possibility. "I suppose there's logic to what you say." He wafted his hand through the air in a magnanimous yet simultaneously arrogant gesture. "Ask away, dear Belly. Ask away."

"First, where were you when Cecil was killed?" she asked with an angelically innocent countenance so as not to upset the brute.

Gilbert answered in his usual superior tone. "I was on the telephone in the office. Far from the front of the house."

"How convenient," I replied, and I'm sure that Bella would have kicked me in the shin if she could have reached.

Instead, she placed one hand on her boyfriend's folded arms and continued in a gentle tone. "You know all about Cecil's financial arrangements. Do you think his money could be a motivation for someone murdering him?"

"Of course it could!" This idea made Gilbert quite jubilant just as I took a wrong step and found myself up to the knees in snow.

"I don't mean in general," Bella persisted, as I returned to shallower folds. "I mean, is there anything in particular that you know about him that could explain his death?"

Gilbert's cheeks wobbled indignantly. "As I was just saying to our supposed friends in the sitting room, Cecil had a talent for stepping on toes. Take this house, for example. He charmed the old couple who lived here, bought the place for well below its value and the family were not happy at all. The heirs took the story to the papers, and there was a big rumpus about it, but there were far more dastardly things he got up to which few people ever discovered."

He peered behind us in case we were being followed. It was overly dramatic, and he looked a fool. "Hortensia Alcott is a case in point." He really was very fond of himself and grinned from cheek to cheek.

"What about Hortensia Alcott?" Bella asked. "That was before my time, remember. I never had the chance to meet her."

"Oh, yes, of course. Well, the inordinately wealthy woman Cecil married was off her rocker. She might have enjoyed her final years on this earth with him at her side, but there's no question that he took advantage of her. Think of all that money. Most people couldn't afford to dream of buying a place like this."

He stopped and looked up at the impressive façade of Everham Hall. We were on the eastern side of the property and could look into the dining room and various bedrooms on the floor above. The peculiarity of the architecture caught my imagination once more. There was something fantastical about the place, and I knew exactly what Gilbert meant about the murdered actor's good fortune.

"Are you suggesting that someone killed him because of the way he treated his dead wife?" I had to ask.

He did not respond but continued studying the building from one end to the other, as though expecting something to happen. "I beg your pardon?" he blustered, but my words must have been echoing about his brain somewhere, as he eventually managed to respond. "Oh, well... yes. I think that's quite possible. Put yourself in the place of the old coot's niece or cousin or what have you. I imagine you'd be rather upset to have a fortune taken from you."

Bella did not respond directly, but another thought occurred to her. "Do you know how she made her money?"

Gilbert released three staccato notes of laughter. "Yes, I do, and there's a rather ironic similitude to it. Just like Cecil, she married a much older suitor and, when he died, she inherited everything. If I'm not mistaken, he was an aristocrat who had interests in Ireland. Hortensia liquidated the fellow's assets and rollicked and roistered for forty years before Cecil met her." An arch look appeared on his face for a moment before fading in the shifting moonlight. "He certainly did well out of the arrangement. He was not the soft touch he appeared to be."

"So you're saying that your dead client was not so easy to manipulate as you would have wished?"

"Ahh, now. I wouldn't... umm..."

He was clearly prevaricating, and Bella would not let him get away with it. "Answer the question, Gilly."

"Now, now, Belly." He was such a haughty beast. Every word he uttered sounded as though it were designed to patronise. "You know you only call me that when you're angry."

"Exactly, *Gilly*." She gave as good as she got! "And I will be very angry with you if you don't answer the question."

We had reached the far end of the house by now. Even from

the outside, I could tell that this wing was not as well preserved as the rest of the building. The windows were dingy. The brickwork was covered in moss and, as Cecil hadn't lacked for money, he'd evidently run out of time or interest to finish renovating Everham Hall.

"Fine, Marius is correct. I might once have believed that Cecil would provide me with seven years of plentiful harvests, but, in the end, it was feast and famine every day with him. He would allow me to forge ahead with one raft of investments, only to baulk at the next. He didn't seem to care that I was making him a fortune on top of the one he already had."

It occurred to me then that I didn't know the first thing about Gilbert's background. He had a plummy voice but, judging from his gainful employment, he was no aristocrat. Something in the way he spoke told me that he needed Cecil Sinclair more than he was willing to say.

"There's another part of the story you haven't mentioned, isn't there?" This was not me speaking but my graceful companion. "The pair of you argued the last time we were here, and you wouldn't tell me what it concerned."

Gilbert pretended to be hurt. "My darling, what do you think of me? Do you take me for some charlatan, defrauding our friend? Are you really suggesting that I killed him to hide a discrepancy in our financial dealings?"

Thankfully, Bella would not be taken in by such poor acting. "I suggested nothing of the sort, though the fact that you would defend a charge that has yet to be laid against you hardly bodes well for your innocence."

Before he could say anything more, we skirted a dilapidated conservatory and followed a long, dark path that was sheltered from the snow by overhanging trees. Where snow had not broken through the thick pines, there were piles of mildewed needles and a row of untended flowerbeds which might once have contained pretty displays. Just as he'd applied make-up to hide the wrinkles around his eyes, Cecil had done what was required to create a luxurious façade to his home. I thought it rather fitting that there should be a secret, crumbling side to the property that was only visible on closer inspection.

"Come, come, dear." That puffball Gilbert was fond of repeating himself. "There's no need for such suspicion. You know what Cecil was like; he could have represented Great Britain in the World Arguing Championships." He laughed at this turn of phrase, but Bella wouldn't let him off the hook so readily.

"You're avoiding my question." I loved seeing her so angry, not just because it was directed at such an inferior character, but because it provided another glimpse of the fire that still burnt within her. "I heard him when we visited over Christmas. He said that you had a week to sort out the problem, or you'd be in trouble. That week just finished and now Cecil's dead. So prove to me that the two facts are unrelated."

This explained why she'd acted so hesitantly for much of the evening. As soon as we learnt of the killing, her usually bright personality had dimmed; she was clearly afraid that her boyfriend was to blame.

Gilbert seemed to have taken the air he required, as his vermilion cheeks had returned to their normal pinkish hue. That didn't prevent a spot of embarrassed crimson from rising as we once more emerged into the moonlight. "That was merely a misunderstanding."

"Tell me the truth." This was the formidable woman I admired, not the trembling ingenue who had been at Everham Hall for much of the night. "Tell me what he wanted you to do?"

The toad finally croaked out an answer. "As I said, my dear, it was all a misunderstanding. Just before Christmas, Cecil managed to stop drinking for some days. He evidently took advantage of that lucidity to look into his finances and noticed that some of the money from a recent dividend hadn't reached him."

If this had been any other suspect, I would have had something to say on the matter. It being Gilbert, I was happy to watch him squirm.

Bella had a further demand to put to him. "Tell me you didn't do something dishonest."

"My darling, are you really asking such a thing?" He stopped again to take her hand and look her in the eyes. "The money was somehow diverted to the wrong account. It was a case of human error and had nothing to do with me. If it hadn't been for the bank closing for Christmas, it would already have been transferred to Cecil."

To my horror, she seemed to believe this tripe. "At the very least, you should have told me. I would have understood, but instead I've spent this evening imagining that you were not only a criminal, but a murderer."

I shouldn't have taken such pleasure in seeing Gilbert's predicament, as things were about to get a lot worse for me. I had to stand there as he pulled her into an embrace and whispered the sweetest of sentiments into her ear.

"My dear Bella. I am so sorry that I didn't tell you before. I just hope you can believe me when I say that I was only thinking of you. It's not as if you don't have enough on your plate as things stand with your father's ill health and the rest of the demands that your family place upon you."

I looked about for some bushes in case my stomach were to take a funny turn.

"Oh, Gilbert, I knew deep down that you could never have done those things."

They stopped talking and held one another for frankly far too long. I was back to silently cursing them – Gilbert for being an irremovable boil, and Bella for loving him.

"If you didn't do it," I interrupted to cut this precious

moment short, "then what other reason might there be for Cecil's death?"

Perhaps it was too open a question. After all, detectives don't just go about asking who committed the crime. To emulate my fictional detective, Inspector Rupert L'Estrange, I would require cunning, brio and the most refined skills of deduction. It was my first day on the job, though, and for the moment, this would have to do.

"I'm sure you have your theories." Gilbert placed his arm around Bella, and the three of us walked past the sitting room windows without the other suspects catching sight of us.

"That's not what I asked." I tried not to be short with him, but it wasn't easy. "I want to know your thoughts on the case."

Bella gave him an encouraging look, and he presumably decided to do what it took to keep her happy. "All I can say is that, while the pair of you have been off and about, the whole lot of them have been behaving strangely. I've always liked Wilson, but he's been as restless as a lost homing pigeon for the last few hours. He can't sit still and hovers about the place as though he doesn't know where he is. It's quite disconcerting."

"Leave the poor boy alone, Gilbert." Bella was quick to come to the young man's defence. "He must be the loneliest of the lot of us. Everyone except him has someone for company. You may be able to tolerate a man's murder in the middle of a party, but he clearly cannot."

"Well, I wouldn't have let him come if I'd known what a coward he was. Honestly, you think you know a person, and then he turns into a jabbering wreck at the first dead body he encounters." Gilbert really was full to the brim with the milk of human kindness.

Bella was having none of it. "I told you to leave him alone. What is wrong with you tonight?"

As much as I enjoyed hearing him told off, I tried to keep us focused on the crime we were supposed to be solving. "Fine, Wilson is fidgety. What else did you observe?"

He had a quick think as we looped around to the front entrance. "I don't trust Ross Sinclair, or his young wench. They are forever whispering to one another. She's clearly nervous about something, and I think the logical conclusion is that she murdered Cecil because he couldn't accept his father marrying a much younger woman. He and Ross had a number of bitter rows on the telephone over the last few weeks about Cecil's refusal to meet Edith. And if you consider how sensitive Sinclair senior has been tonight, I think the logical conclusion is that he's the killer."

He'd presented two logical conclusions in the space of a few sentences. At this rate, the only possible solution was that every last one of us had played a part in murdering the victim.

"Is there anyone else?" I asked without much hope.

"Yes, the Cavendishes."

"Of course." Even Bella sounded sceptical.

"That's right, they haven't spoken a word to one another for some time. I think they know something." He clicked his fingers together. "Either that, or they were involved themselves. It really is the only logical conclusion."

"Wait one second. Are you suggesting that Ross and Edith are up to something because they keep whispering to one another, and Alma and Anton are likely culprits because they're oddly quiet?"

"Precisely." He was ever so pleased with his skills of deduction. "I wouldn't trust any of them as far as I can roll them down a hill."

"Thank you, Gilbert. You've been of enormous assistance." I surprised myself with just how little sarcasm I used to pronounce this lie.

"You're very welcome, and I'm ever so glad we've put the

past behind us and can talk matters over like the two civilised men that we are."

"Absolutely." I mounted the steps to the front porch and was relieved that the conversation was almost over. I might have had to throw a snowball at him otherwise.

"You know, that's what I told Cecil to do with Anton after the misunderstanding with Alma." He puffed out his cheeks and a little cloud of steam escaped his lips. "I said, 'You kissed the man's wife. The best thing you can do is get it out in the open and talk it over like civilised gentlemen.' In my experience, that's always the best option."

Like figures made of ice, Bella and I were stuck in place on the steps before the porch.

"Would you believe it? It's almost midnight." Gilbert beat me affectionately about the shoulder. "We'd better make a move if we want to ring in the new year."

EIGHTEEN

We should probably have followed him inside, but we were still making sense of what we'd just heard. It wasn't simply the revelation that Cecil and Alma had been romantically involved in some way; it was hard to comprehend how Gilbert could have prattled for so long without mentioning this essential fact.

The man was a pure, unadulterated buffoon.

"Did you know about this?" I asked Bella once her boyfriend was halfway down the hall, whistling a soft melody as he went.

"No, of course I didn't. As far as I know, Alma and Anton are very much in love. They always seem so suited to one another."

"I see." We were only a few feet apart, but I took a step closer to impress upon her the importance of what I had to say. "But before we go any further, there's something which has been weighing on my mind."

She became more serious. "Very well. "

I breathed in to prepare myself. "I simply can't concentrate on the case because I keep questioning what attracts you to that odious little banker. Is he really the person with whom you wish to spend your life? I've met earthworms with more charisma than Gilbert Baines. In fact, there's a glum basset hound in the sitting room whom I can recommend as a boyfriend ahead of your current pick."

Her expression barely changed as she moved away. "Don't be petty, Marius. It doesn't suit you."

"Petty? You're calling me petty?" I thought this was a fair response until I realised that petty was exactly what I was being. It wasn't Bella's fault that she couldn't see what a moron the man was... Actually, hang on one second. Yes, it was! "I've never known such a petty chap as Gilbert Baines."

"I've already told you." She sat on a bench to remove the borrowed coat and boots. "You haven't seen the best side of him, but Gilbert provided the support I needed at the darkest time in my life." Her stare grew harder. "And you're not so innocent yourself, Marius Quin. I loved you with all my heart when we were young. I went up to our tree house on the night before you left for France, believing that you would ask me to be your wife, but instead you—"

This was all that she could manage before the memories of that night overwhelmed her. That night when, with flowers scattered around us, I looked her in the eyes and had every intention of proposing. But instead of asking that eternal question, I saw an image of my corpse lying battered in some anonymous French field and couldn't go through with it.

"It's almost as if you've forgotten." In all the time we'd known one another, I'd never seen her look so hurt. "This whole night, you've acted like I did something wrong, but it wasn't me, Marius. It was you."

"I was trying to protect you," I told her, but I was no longer sure that this was true.

I doubt she even heard me as the words streamed out of her. "I'm sorry that Gilbert doesn't meet your high standards. But, as it happens, I don't need your permission to decide whom to love. Gilbert isn't the most confident person. He gets nervous and says the wrong thing sometimes, but that's his biggest failing. More importantly, though, he has kept me sane through my father's illness. He has loved me when no one else made the effort. Maybe one day you'll see just how good a person he really is. Until then, I'd appreciate it if you could keep your opinions to yourself."

She had slipped her Spanish heels back on and was ready to flame off down the hall to the sitting room. I should have stopped her. I should have apologised for every mistake I'd made, but, instead, I just watched her go. I watched her as she shot along the corridor like the bullets that lodged themselves in Cecil's brain.

Have you ever had one of those moments when you realise that you've been living your life in entirely the wrong way? Well this was my second in a little over a week.

She was right, of course. Since I'd failed to ask her to marry me for fear of the pain I would cause should I die abroad, I'd done nothing but feel sorry for myself. She hadn't rejected me; I'd ruined everything. And rather than return to England to beg for forgiveness, I'd stayed away to avoid the shame that seeing her again would bring. I told myself I was trying to be a better man. That I would build myself up to be worthy of Lady Isabella Montague at last, but the truth was far less noble. I'd been a coward.

And when she had disappeared into the sitting room, I did the only thing that hapless fools like me can do at such a moment; I punched the wall.

It hurt much more than I was expecting. I thought that getting knocked off my feet by a German bomb at Amiens was painful, but this was five times worse. For a minute or two, I really believed that I'd broken my fingers. I had to flex them to see if they were all still capable of movement.

I would like to be able to tell you that the wall came off

worse than I did, but it was an uneven fight and there wasn't a scratch on him. Aware that I had just personified an inanimate structure supporting an entrance hall, I decided to seek out human company as quickly as possible.

By the time I made it back to the sitting room, the tension had only grown. Ross Sinclair was sitting at a card table away from most of the others. Despite the fact that his pretty companion was stroking his hair, the look on his face suggested he was about to eat someone. He shot such furious looks across the room that I imagined his eyes popping from their sockets to launch themselves at his most recent enemy. Gilbert was clearly aware of the ire he'd provoked and had taken a seat as far as possible from his deceased client's father.

Poppy was on the floor before the Christmas tree, stroking Percy's belly. My dog, meanwhile, was doing his best to make me feel jealous by peering soulfully across the room. It didn't work. I was far too busy to worry about him. Bella had taken a seat on the sofa and glared at me as I entered. I would never tell Percy, but such a look from a beautiful woman will always beat his puppy-dog eyes.

I noticed that Alma and Anton were sitting together but, much as Gilbert had said, could not bring themselves to look at one another. As nervous as ever, Wilson peered into the middle distance and, as far as I know, that's all the looking, staring and glaring that was going on in the sitting room at that moment.

To break the silence that had settled over us, Anton decided that it was his job to entertain everyone. He walked over to an upright piano in the corner of the room and began to run his fingers across the ivories. "Alma, my dear. I think it's time for a song."

His wife evidently had no wish to fulfil his request. Her expression was so hard that it could have been used to cut granite.

Gilbert decided to put another name forward. "Bella has a beautiful voice. Why don't you sing something, my darling?"

His darling was still busy being angry with me and seemed surprised to be addressed. I'd expected her to issue a polite refusal, but she floated across to the piano as if in a daze. Anton whispered a suggestion for a song before she nodded and turned to face her audience. With all the flair he usually possessed, he played a few tinkling, jazz-infused notes, and she began to sing.

"I'm feeling so strange,
I'm feeling alone now.
Darling, who should I blame?
When I'm all on my own now.
I've done all that I can,
But I'm just not myself without my man."

She truly did have a beautiful voice, and yet I had no memory of ever hearing it before. Not like that, at least. I remembered shouting along to raucous nursery rhymes together as children, but this was totally different.

"You should never have left,
I should never have pushed you.
You left me feeling bereft,
I do nothing but miss you.
I've tried all that I can,
But I can't stop dreaming about my man."

She arrived at the chorus, and I saw her forget about the problems of that weekend as she was swept up in the emotion of the song. She turned to me for the briefest of moments, and it felt as though there was no one else in the room with us.

"He may not be a duke or an earl,

But all I want is to be his girl.
My heart is breaking, I'm aching,
I don't think I can take it without my man."

She sang another verse then, but the words didn't settle in my brain. I'd been staring directly – unapologetically – at her for two minutes without interruption and found myself in some state of reverie with which I was quite unfamiliar. I believe she sang the chorus again, but it was only as the last notes faded out and Anton applauded that I returned to reality.

Gilbert rushed forward to kiss her, and I felt more distant from Bella than I had since the war. In a few seconds, I'd gone from romantic stargazing to crashing back down to Earth in a thousand pieces. That song wasn't *for* me, it was about me. I was the one who couldn't take the heartache and suffering any longer. The only difference was that Bella wasn't my girl and never would be because I'd missed my chance.

Despite this incredible performance, the song did nothing to resolve the frosty atmosphere, and we returned to the awkwardness we'd previously endured.

"It's one minute to midnight," Alma informed us to break that horrendous silence.

Nobody was particularly excited about the possibility of welcoming in the new year. To be quite frank, we largely hated one another by this point. Edith seemed to still be in love with the old man to whom she was betrothed, but the rest of us wished for nothing more than to escape from Everham Hall and never cross paths again. It was simply that kind of party.

This wasn't our only problem, either. There was a feeling I couldn't ignore that something catastrophic was about to happen. As the seconds ticked by, the staring became a little more nervous. Eyes flicked about in search of reassurance rather than to apportion blame. Bella no longer looked as though she wanted to stab me, and her expression was one sad plea for help.

"Ten, nine, eight..." Alma began, but I wasn't ready.

"...seven, six..." This was the moment when the night would really go to the devil, and there was nothing I could do to stop it.

"...five, four..." I looked at each of our suspects in turn to determine who would be the one to flick off the light switch and raise a knife to a rival's throat, but it could have been any of them and there was no time left.

"...three, two, one!"

NINETEEN

No one dared breathe. No one said a word, and I knew that we'd all been having the same dark thought. I tensed every muscle in my body, waiting for blood to pour or a gun to fire, and it was only when Gilbert loudly announced, "Well, that was anticlimactic," that I could see I'd been mistaken.

"Happy New Year," Anton said to no one in particular. "Let's hope it's better than the last one."

"Hear, hear!" Wilson raised his glass to celebrate, and I realised that they all had champagne. How had I missed that? I'd been so busy thinking about people's eyes, the argument with Bella, and a second murder that never happened that I'd failed to notice this basic fact. That wasn't all I'd missed, either. There were assorted hors d'oeuvres on the tables and Christmas crackers left about the place for our amusement. The staff had persisted with their jobs even as we investigated their employer's murder.

With midnight over and the new year in full swing, there was nothing to keep us there but propriety. No one wanted to be the first person to say, *well, that was a washout. I'm off to bed.*

We sipped our drinks, nibbled morsels of food and returned to gnashing our teeth. To interrupt the stasis in which we found ourselves, Alma suddenly gripped her throat.

"What is it, darling?" Anton approached his wife, but she couldn't speak.

"She's been poisoned!" Poppy declared from the carpet. Percy was up on his feet like a lightning bolt, though, beyond that, there was nothing he could do to help.

Alma had two hands wrapped around her throat, as though she were trying to strangle herself. Her husband stared desperately into her eyes, while the rest of us stood in helpless passivity.

It was Edith who came to understand what had happened.

"The peanuts," she said, pointing to the bowl on the table where Alma had been sitting.

"The peanuts were poisoned!" Poppy tried once more.

Ross Sinclair was the first to react and shot forward to slap the poor woman on the back with one enormous hand. A few moments later, the nut shot free, and she was breathing again.

"Another anticlimax," Gilbert said, and I had to wonder how many deaths he required for one evening's entertainment. He would surely have loved the ancient Romans' idea of a good night out at the Colosseum.

Though Poppy's claim of poison had proven incorrect, she was not one to forget such non-existent dangers and began to cry. "I asked Matthew for those peanuts. It could have been me!" Percy waddled over to offer some more affection, so at least there was one man who could stand her.

"That's enough," Anton declared on behalf of the group. "That's all I can take for tonight, and I will see you in the morning." He escorted his wife from the room and, clearly relieved to be alive, Alma nodded her thanks to Ross and Edith as she went.

"I feel just the same," her saviour replied as he put his arm around his fiancée, and they walked to the door.

"Looks like it's you and me, pup." Still tearful, Poppy picked up the heavy beast and followed the others into the hall.

Despite our recent disagreement, it was clear that Bella was reluctant to be parted from me, which put Gilbert's nose out of joint.

"I was rather tired anyway," he declared and blustered off ahead of us.

"I shouldn't have spoken to you in that way," Bella told me when even poor lonely Wilson had wandered from the room. "I know you've only got my best interests at heart, but I promise that I wouldn't have anything to do with Gilbert if he weren't a truly good person. I'm certain that, if you met in other circumstances, the two of you could even be friends."

I would have snorted in derision, but I could see that she was trying to make peace, and I didn't have it in me to upset her again.

"Then I should probably apologise, too," I conceded.

The gloom faded, and a mischievous smile appeared on her lips. "Go on then."

"I beg your pardon?"

"If you think you should apologise, go ahead."

I had to laugh as we exited the festive sitting room and trailed behind the group towards the main staircase. "Very well, I'm sorry, Bella. I am truly sorry for thinking the worst of Gilbert and doubting your capacity to judge a person's character for yourself. I regret any offence I may have caused."

"See, that wasn't so difficult." She elbowed me in the ribs, and so I gently returned the gesture. Even platonic affection from Bella was better than the prospect of losing her again.

I was also greatly relieved that the number of casualties had stayed at one. I was so used to detective novels where one death is followed by another (and perhaps a few more to boot) that it was hard not to expect the worst at every moment. As we climbed the stairs to go to bed, the world seemed a little less dreadful than before. Cecil was dead – murdered in his own bedroom – but he was no saint; whoever had killed him presumably had a good reason and, though we still hadn't uncovered what that was, there was nothing to say the culprit would kill again.

When we got to the guest bedrooms in the upstairs corridor, Poppy was making a fuss of Percy, and the others were saying goodnight. I was relieved to see that Bella and Gilbert had separate rooms. I took this as a small, deserved recompense for having to admit that her boyfriend might not be the pig for which I'd taken him.

"I'm sorry, my love," Ross told his paramour. "I left my glasses in the car. You know I can't fall asleep without something to read. But don't let that stop you. Go to bed, and I'll see you in the morning." He kissed her on the forehead, and I remarked once again that their relationship seemed more paternal than romantic.

He walked past us, back along the corridor to descend the staircase once more.

A thought occurred to me, and I addressed his fiancée who had the room across the hall from my own. "Actually, Edith, if you're not too tired, may I have a word?"

She nodded in that coy manner of hers, then said goodnight to Anton, Wilson and Gilbert before they all disappeared through their respective doors. I silently signalled to Bella that I would need her assistance, and Edith opened her door for us to walk in ahead of her. The room was not so different from my own but, somewhat ridiculously, appeared to have been designed for the exclusive use of female guests. The walls were covered in pink, cherry blossom wallpaper and there were matching curtains covering the two tall windows – not to mention the pink upholstery, bedding, cushions and even two rose-marble nightstands. It was as though whoever had decorated the place believed that women were allergic to any other colour.

"I don't believe I've offered my congratulations on your engagement," I began as she sat down in an armchair and Bella went to stand beside the window. I could tell that neither of them knew quite what I was thinking, but I didn't mind that one bit.

"That's very kind of you," Edith replied in an uncertain tone. To be perfectly honest, I doubt that she possessed any other kind. "My life has changed entirely since I met Ross. He has made me happy in ways that I never imagined possible."

She sounded rather like a radio announcer. There was something not quite authentic about the way she spoke of her gnarly old suitor, as though she had been paid to say such nice things about him. This was the first time I'd seen them apart, and it was too good an opportunity not to quiz her.

"What was your life like before your paths crossed?"

She looked at Bella for support, and my generous friend nodded her encouragement.

"I had a fairly normal childhood. Comfortable, you know, but nothing out of the ordinary. When I reached adulthood, my family couldn't afford to have me hanging around the house anymore, and so I did a secretarial course and took work in an admiralty law office to help ease the financial burden. That's where I met Ross."

"He's a lawyer?"

She smiled a little at this. "No, far from it. He was a sailor and had dealings with the company, but he's retired now."

Ah ha! So the old dog really was a seadog. Perhaps I wasn't such a bad detective after all.

"I see. And it was love at first sight, I presume?"

Out of the corner of my eye, I saw Bella's face crumple in

disapproval at this question, and I decided that it was time she took over the discussion.

"Not at all," Edith confessed. "I was there for a couple of months before we said more than good morning to one another. We found ourselves on the same train one day and started talking."

"I've always thought that trains are very romantic," Bella intervened without my prompting. "And where do you call home, my dear?"

"Not very far from here, actually. A small, out-of-the-way place that most people will never notice on a map." She cast her mind back to that hazy afternoon when her planet had collided with Ross Sinclair's. "We chatted away together all the way from St Pancras until we crossed the border into Hampshire. He was on his way to see Cecil, and I was going home to my family. I'd rarely felt so at ease talking to a relative stranger. He was really very charming."

"You are so young." Bella spoke in a vaguely patronising tone, and it was my turn to cast her a judgemental glance.

"I'm already twenty." Edith responded in the manner of a small child – which did nothing to strengthen her case. "Twenty-one in June, in fact."

"By which I mean..." Bella attempted to smooth things over. "I mean that you are so young and pretty. I'm sure that most men would be frightened to go anywhere near you."

Edith blushed before showing a more worldly side to her personality. "You'd be surprised."

"Were you hurt by Cecil's refusal to meet you?" I asked, to disrupt the overly comfortable mood we'd adopted.

My question had the desired effect. Edith looked once more to Bella for help but would have to answer for herself. "It saddened me. Yes, of course it did. I wish to marry Ross and spend as much of our lives together as we can. I didn't see how that would be possible if one of his sons refused to accept my existence."

"Were you angry?" I pushed, as this was the key point. In fact, it was really the only point that might suggest she had gone there to kill her future stepson.

"I've already told you. I was sad... upset. I wanted my life with Ross to start joyfully, not mired in antagonism."

I considered this interesting woman for a moment. She was something of a contradiction, and surely out of place there at Everham Hall. She was well-spoken enough to fit in – with nice manners and just the right level of sophistication not to stand out – but among the glamorous group of actors, a director, the daughter of a duke and, dare I say, a briefly successful author, the girl who had gone to work in a legal office to help her struggling family pay the bills was an outsider.

"And how did Ross feel about the matter?" Bella was a good partner in this strange endeavour. It was not simply that she had a more intuitive connection with our suspects than I did. She knew what we needed to know before such thoughts formed in my head.

"You'd have to ask him, but I imagine that he felt much the same." Edith showed a degree of defiance for the first time. It did not last long, and she soon offered a more accommodating response. "He tried to explain to Cecil that I wasn't just a money-grubber. In fact, I didn't know anything about Ross's son when we started seeing one another socially. I've never been one for the cinema and don't read the sort of newspapers that discuss the lives of actors like Cecil Sinclair."

I couldn't fault her for this. As far as I'm concerned, the world pays far too much attention to a group of prancing, pouting celebrities who have nothing to recommend them except their silent gurning on the cinema screen.

"Give me a good book any day." The girl fished the words straight from my head!

Bella smiled at the sentiment and couldn't resist a brief look in my direction to see that I was doing the same.

"Ross told me that he had arranged a dinner to announce your engagement and that Cecil didn't attend," I said to halt all that unnecessary grinning. "When was that, exactly?"

Her naïveté shone through once more. "The fifth of December. I'll never forget that date. It was such a wonderful night, even without Cecil there to share it with us. Ross's other sons came, and there were lots of his friends from his days at sea. It was a real celebration."

"Your family weren't there?" I told you I was rude. "Didn't you invite them?"

Edith didn't look at me but kept her eyes on my partner. "I'm afraid not. You see, they don't approve of my marrying Ross. They think that he's unsuitable for me."

Bella didn't press her on the exact reason he was unsuitable – as I surely would have – but moved on to another question. "How did your fiancé react when his youngest son failed to make an appearance?"

The fingers on Edith's right hand sought out the cuff below her left and she tugged on it until it was pulled taut. "He didn't show his disappointment at the party."

Bella knew what this meant as well as I did. "And after, when all your friends had gone home, what happened then?"

It was obvious that she didn't want to tell us. I suppose she was weighing up what would make her fiancé look more guilty – the murky truth or her failure to provide an answer.

"Ross was furious," she eventually explained. "He said that he'd done everything he could to make up for his mistakes, but it would never be enough for Cecil."

"Take your time, dear," Bella said to reassure her. It was lucky that she had taken charge. I would have probably said something like, *It's gone midnight. Could you hurry things along?*

Edith seemed to chew over the impact of her words before continuing. "I suggested we have a drink in the American Bar at the Savoy to finish the night, but when we got there, he hardly spoke a word. We ordered cocktails, and he tipped his down his throat and hurled the glass to the floor. The barman told us to leave, but Ross was already on his feet and on his way home before anyone could throw him out."

Bella evidently considered this a key piece of evidence. She took her time to form the question she would put to our witness. "I don't know how to ask this... Do you believe that Ross wished his son any harm?"

Edith moved as though to shake her head but didn't quite have the conviction to go through with it. Instead, she got to her feet and went to stand next to Bella beside the window. As a pretend detective myself, I found it interesting to examine such behaviour. Was she trying to hide the fact that she considered her fiancé a potential killer? Or did she need to summon the courage to admit this very thing?

"No..." she began, just as cautiously as ever. "I really don't see that Ross could—"

"Look there!" Bella interrupted in a brittle tone, and I shot to my feet to see what she'd spotted through the window.

"But..." Edith's eyes traced a path through the snow. "Why would anyone be alone out there so late at night?"

Bella pointed to the courtyard we had crossed with Gilbert. "Do you see him, Marius?"

Down in the snow, following the route we had taken around the perimeter of the building, was a figure in a long black coat and winter hat. As he approached the far end of the T-shaped building, there was something unsteady about his movement. His hand was extended unnaturally in front of him, and it took me a moment to realise what he was holding. *The moonlight caught the jagged edge of a lustful knife in the hand of the cloaked figure*, and I finally understood something that had been playing on my mind for months.

"Oh my goodness," I said as the shadowy outline ducked through a door into the house. "I know how to finish my book!"

"Marius!" Bella did not look happy with me. "I think some-one's about to be killed."

I tried to hide just how happy I was. "Yes, well... that too."

TWENTY

"Marius, move!"

I must admit that I was in something of a daze, as I'd just had the most brilliant idea for my unwritten novel. Sometimes, when I'm thinking about my books, it's as if I've travelled to another plane of existence. I see myself in a long hallway, filled with doors to other worlds. I was just about to turn one of the handles when Bella spoke again, and it pulled me back to Everham Hall.

"Marius, did you hear me?"

"Right... yes. Where exactly should I go?"

She was pushing me through the door. "Downstairs, of course, you bufflehead. We just saw the killer. Maybe we can trap him before he murders anyone else."

Out in the hallway, she ran right, so I turned left to trap the blighter as she'd suggested. The cool corridor enlivened my senses and cleared my head.

I ran along that half-lit space as Bella issued a final instruction. "I'll follow the path through the snow and meet you in the oldest part of the house. That's where he must have been going."

"Understood," I called back over my shoulder, though what I should actually have said was, *No! Don't do that! It's insanely dangerous and you could get killed.* As I've already pointed out, I really wasn't myself just then and blindly followed her ill-thought-out plan.

Lining the hallway, there were old photographs of the original owners – their grandchildren sitting on a beach somewhere, their grandchildren putting on a play in the theatre, their grandchildren... In fact, there were a lot of photographs of the grandchildren, but that's not all there was. As I moved beyond the newer part of that floor and came to the dilapidated section in my search for a staircase down, I discovered yet another haul of weapons on the wall.

There were maces, spears, those balls on chains of which medieval types were so enamoured, and swords by the armful. The selection was so extensive it was hard to make a choice, but I grabbed a rather fierce broadsword and continued on my way. I got to the end of the hall and realised that I must have missed the stairs. They were evidently concealed behind one of the doors, but I had passed about thirty of the things and, having tried a few at the end with no luck, I gave up and ran back towards the front entrance.

My clattering on the stairs must have alerted a sleeping footman as the now bleary-eyed Matthew poked his head through a door that led off the parlour.

I yelled at him to look alive. "Come with me, man. We may have sighted the killer."

That certainly woke him up, and he sped along behind me as I tried not to think about how little exercise I'd done over the last couple of years whilst sitting at a desk not writing. There was no sign of anyone at first but, as I approached the office, Gilbert stepped into my path with several paper files in his hand.

"Ahhh! What are you doing with that sword?" He was more

frightened than a child lost in a forest. "Please don't hurt me."

"I wouldn't dream of it; Bella would never forgive me." It was tempting to lop a hand off as I rocketed past, but I managed to restrain myself. "Nice dressing gown, by the way."

He produced no retort, and Matthew and I soon made it to the dingiest part of the house. There were far fewer candles burning here, and I had to assume these rooms were used for housing staff and general storage. We reached the far, perpendicular wing, and I thought about the plan of the house as I'd seen it from outside.

"This way," I told my companion, who had seized a candlestick with which to defend himself.

"Whatever you say, sir." If anything, the footman sounded more impressed than frightened and followed this comment with another. "I'm fine so long as you lead the way with your sword aloft."

I'd been issued a bayonet in the army but, happily, never had to use it. Matthew's confidence in me was certainly heartening, though what good I'd be with a sword was anyone's guess.

Perhaps it was this trust he showed, or the darkness that surrounded us, but I found myself thinking of a trench raid I'd been on in the last few months of the war. I was one of the few men in my division who spoke German and so they cleared a path through no-man's-land, gave us our rum rations and sent us over the top.

It was a cold, moonless night, and it was my job to sit in a hole in the darkness just yards from a German trench to listen in case they gave away their plans. I expected the sound of gunfire or a lobbed hand grenade to echo in my ears at any moment. I can honestly say I've never been so frightened in my life, but our journey through Everham Hall that night came close.

The further we went from the main wing, the grimier it got.

We crossed an unused lounge where the chairs and tables were covered in dustsheets; they looked like the ghosts of furniture that had long since died. There were cobwebs in every corner and the moonlight lent an eerie greyness to everything as an unnerving sound echoed about the place.

"What was that?" Matthew had a ghostly visage himself just then. He was a gaunt, pallid chap at the best of times, but whatever he'd heard really put the wind up him.

"I heard it too." I ran through the gallery a little faster. "It sounded like crying. Someone must be in here with us."

The third room we reached was deathly silent. It was a large conservatory with a glass ceiling and three walls supported by a white wooden frame. It reminded me of a miniature Crystal Palace, and I remembered a happy visit to that singular edifice with my parents when I was a child. Of course, chasing after a killer with sword in hand really isn't the time for such sweet recollections, but it was better than thinking about that night on the front line.

I signalled to Matthew to cover the other side of the room and we swept across it with our weapons raised. My heart was playing an oom-pah-pah rhythm at an unhealthy tempo and, when my companion stumbled into a sideboard and nearly tipped over a vase, my every muscle vibrated as though they'd been plucked like the strings of a violin.

We had reached the end of the wing, and I could see the door where the figure in black must have entered. We took smaller steps now, for no other reason than the fear that ran through us. There was a grand piano covered in a pool of darkness and, if the killer was in the room with us, he had to be hiding there.

We both slowed down, aware that we had passed the point of no return. Matthew looked at me as if to say, *I'm not paid enough to go running at a killer, and you're the one with the sword.* There wasn't much I could say to that, especially as we were trying to remain silent. I could hear a faint noise coming from the other side of the piano, and I continued inching forward, praying that the culprit wouldn't jump out at me before I had the chance to strike him.

I came to a complete standstill and held the glistening silver blade over my shoulder. It was all very well being heroic in theory; the practice is a totally different thing. With every nerve in my body tingling, I was about to rush forward and swing my sword when a terrible screech emanated from the other side of the room. I dived for cover, fearing that the killer had tricked us, and we were actually moving towards a piano with a few mice living in it.

"What are you doing there?" Bella asked as she stepped through the unoiled door and out of the snow.

Matthew could take it no more and released the scream he'd been holding ever since we left the main wing.

I stood up from behind the packing crate where I'd bravely hidden. "Ah, Bella. I'm glad you could join us. Did you see anyone outside?"

"Not a soul." She looked between the two of us but showed no sign of amusement. "The footprints led in this direction. Whoever we saw coming in here can't have left through the garden."

As though we had struck on the same thought at the exact same moment, we turned to the corner to look at the piano and its potential family of mice. I didn't want to appear a coward in front of the woman I had spent most of my childhood trying to impress, so I strode forward, and that same faint sound started up once more.

"I..." a voice most definitely pronounced as I passed an upturned piano stool to reach the last possible place our target could be hiding. "I'm..." it said again and, when I prodded the bundle that I found there with my sword, Poppy managed to finish that sentence. "I'm hurt. He stabbed me."

TWENTY-ONE

That was all she said before the pain got too much for her, and she collapsed in a pile.

"There's not too much blood." Bella had shown no fear as she rushed around the other side of the piano to come to our second victim's aid. "I know how to dress wounds. We must get her somewhere clean, warm and comfortable."

"Should we take the knife out?" Matthew looked a little green as he pointed to what I took to be a hunting dagger that was sticking out of her left shoulder.

"No," Bella and I replied as one. She knew the answer because of her medical training, and I knew the answer because I'd seen far too many wounds first hand at the front.

"It's best to leave the dagger in for the moment so that she doesn't lose any more blood." Bella stood back so that the neatly dressed servant could take her place. "You two will have to support her all the way back to the sitting room. I'll do what I can for her there."

"Cook is a dab hand with a needle, if that helps," Matthew revealed as he kneeled down to put one shoulder under our patient's arm, and I did the same. "The gamekeeper shot himself in the foot once and she fixed him up nicely."

Poppy wasn't fully unconscious. She groaned as we lifted her up and moved slowly across the room.

There was a question I simply had to ask the footman. "I'm sorry, but do you mean that literally?"

Matthew responded as though I'd said something terribly rude. "I beg your pardon?"

"That the gamekeeper shot himself in the foot. Do you mean that literally?"

"Do I!?" he replied. "He unloaded his shotgun right through his shoe. When the doctor got here sometime later, he was very impressed with what our Gladys had achieved. She'd got the shot out with the end of a sterilised teaspoon and then sutured the wound with a needle and thread."

Bella was walking ahead of us to open doors as we passed back through the house. Even in the dark, I could see that she was not convinced by the servant's suggestion. "Let's hope it doesn't come to that, shall we?"

Poppy was still in the sleeveless dress she'd been wearing all evening and so we could see the damage quite clearly. It bled a little as we carried her through the house, but the knife was doing a good job of plugging the wound, and I had to hope she would recover. We got her back to the most festive room in the house – nothing says Christmastime like a stabbing victim – and then laid her down on the reddest sofa there.

There was a drawer in one of the bookcases where, if I'd learnt anything about Cecil Sinclair, I suspected I might find some cigars. Sure enough, there was a wooden box with several gold crests, a few words in Spanish on the cover, and an elaborate drawing of Romeo and Juliet. I pulled it out and handed it to Matthew, who still looked concerned as he stood beside the would-be corpse.

"You were incredibly brave tonight and I think you should have these."

"But they're Mr Sinclair's." He seemed aghast at the very idea of taking from his master's supply.

"Well, he's not going to need them where he is."

"I'm really not so sure, Mr Quin."

I tried to insert them into the pocket of his waistcoat, but that was too small, so I prised open his fingers and pushed the box into his hand instead.

"A very Happy New Year, Matthew."

His reluctance melted away after that and he left the room, muttering, "Wait till my wife sees what I've got. It'll make up for that Christmas present I bought 'er."

What I wanted most of all was to fire a few questions at Poppy, but she was in no state for an interview. Admittedly, she had been through any amount of terror, but until we caught the fiend who'd been terrorising us, all our lives were in danger.

There were so many things we didn't know – not least among them was what the woman with a knife currently sticking out of her shoulder had been doing in the most dilapidated part of the house past midnight on New Year's night. Where the killer had slipped off to would have been my subsequent enquiry. And if she could tell us what he looked like and perhaps his name, that would have been good to know, too.

I rang the local doctor on the off-chance he owned a horse and sleigh, but this being southern England, such things were uncommon and there was no way he would trek through the snow at such an hour, even if the victim hadn't been in a stable condition. To be honest, I didn't blame him. My feet were still cold from our walk with Gilbert.

Poppy suddenly sat up, startling Bella. "There was..."

I ran over in the hope of deciphering her words, but this was all she managed before the pain overwhelmed her and she collapsed backwards. We waited for a minute to see whether she would revive again, but she was gone for the night.

"I'll stay with her," Bella told me in a whisper, though I doubted that raised voices would have disturbed the patient.

"Are you sure we shouldn't do something to the wound?"

She kept her eyes on Poppy, who seemed happily distant from the haunted house we were occupying. "I'll wrap some gauze around it and make sure that it's as clean as possible. She's lucky. The knife clearly hasn't hit an artery or there'd be blood everywhere and she might not have made it until morning."

"As lucky as a woman with a knife sticking out of her can be, I suppose."

Bella held my gaze for a moment, and I realised just how much she had been through since our parting. She had spent years caring for her sickly father and lost cousins and uncles in the war but kept doing her bit for others, no matter what. I wanted to take her hand and tell her that, if there was any service I could do for her in the future, I would. Instead, I gave her a respectful nod and left the pretty sitting room to search for my bed.

I walked back to the front of the house and was about to ascend to the first floor when Edith came down the stairs. "Have you seen Ross?" she asked with the panic back in her voice.

"I can't say I have. We went to the old part of the house and found Poppy half dead, but I've seen no sign of your fiancé."

"That poor woman," she said absent-mindedly, though I could tell it was the old man who most concerned her. "I hope she's all right, but Ross hasn't returned since he went out to his car."

It seemed that my bed was not calling quite so loudly as I had thought, and so I accompanied her outside – grabbing the scarves and silly hat once more and offering the big coat to

Edith. There was no sign of the spare men's boots, so that oaf Gilbert must not have put them back in the right place.

It didn't take us long to find Cecil's father. It seemed he'd been rummaging in his car when the killer got him. He was laid out across the front seat of his grey Austin 40 and Edith immediately burst out in piercing cries.

"It can't be. Not Ross." If she'd been one of the actresses in the house, I might have doubted her distress, but even for an experienced thespian, such grief would be hard to fake. "Please tell me he's all right."

Instead of trying to comfort her, I ran around the car to check on the third victim – they really were piling up by this point. Upon opening the driver's door, I had a sense that, fortunately, the death toll was stuck at one. Beyond a swollen lump where he'd been clobbered on the back of his head, I could see no sign of damage. Sure enough, when I felt the pulse on his neck, it was as regular as the rhythm section of a polka band.

"He's alive," I put my head out of the car to tell her, just as the old sailor began to stir.

"What happened? What am I doing here?" He manoeuvred himself onto his side to look at me.

"Don't worry, Ross," I told him, though I doubted he would take the advice. "If you can stand, we'll get you inside and find some salve for that bruise. It looks as if you took a nasty bash."

He blinked a few times to make sense of this. "I don't remember a thing about it." He looked down at his right hand then and showed me the item for which he'd been searching. "I just came to fetch my glasses. I must have slipped on the ice."

"That must be it." I didn't like to contradict him when he was in such a state and moved around to the other side of the car. "Now, if you give me your hand, we'll go back to the house."

His legs were out of the door, and it didn't take much to get him on his feet.

"Ross, are you badly hurt?" Edith had calmed down a little, but her voice remained as fragile as a cocktail glass.

Ross put his hand to the back of his head to check the bruise, and it instantly stung. "Well, a whisky wouldn't go amiss, but I'm sure I'll live." His usual toughness was back, and I imagine that he had guessed by now exactly what had happened.

Edith and I each took one of his arms and, much as I had for Poppy, we guided him back through the house.

"Do you have any idea who could have hurt you, my darling?" Edith asked, and he shook his head and let out a brief, bemused whistle.

"No, but I'm fine now," he insisted, clearly not wanting us to make a fuss. "I can walk on my own, thank you."

Ross Sinclair was not the kind of man with whom I had much hope of reasoning. He pulled his arm away, and I decided I should talk to his fiancée instead. "If you take him along to the sitting room, Bella will look after him. She's set up something of an infirmary, and I'm certain she won't mind another patient." Even as I said this, I could see that Ross didn't like to be thought of as infirm in any way, and so I offered him a few words of consolation. "I've no doubt you'll find a bottle of something strong in the drinks cabinet to help with any pain."

He grunted an unimpressed response. Edith mouthed her thanks, and then I was finally free to go to bed. Well, I paused at the bottom of the stairs for a moment to make sure there were no faint voices calling for help. To be quite honest, if anyone else was attacked, there'd be so few suspects remaining that I'd have to think I was the likely culprit.

As I bumbled along the corridor and back to my room, all I had in my head were question marks. The case before me was beyond perplexing, and yet this should have been my strong suit. Even though I've no head for technical subjects, I've always been amazed by the idea of unsolvable mathematical theorems and unknown quantities in science. Discovering something which you've been told is beyond human understanding has to be the most rewarding experience imaginable, and I find there's a sense of that in mystifying crimes. And so, while this really should have been my moment to shine, I still only had fleeting theories for why Cecil had been killed.

I lit a fire, got changed into my excessively expensive silk pyjamas – which no one but my family had seen me wear – and climbed ever so wearily into bed. I selected a clean page in my writer's notebook and was about to scribble down my thoughts on that strange night when I remembered that Percy would be shut up in Poppy's bedroom. I threw back the bedsheets and wandered back along the hall to find my dog. It was freezing in there and he seemed happy to see me, his sabre-like tail wagging as we returned to my room.

He went to sleep on the ottoman at the end of the bed, and I opened my notebook once more. I should probably have written down the fantastic idea I'd had for my next book, but Cecil's murder and the attacks on Poppy and Ross were more urgent matters just then. I wrote the names and professions of the suspects, and what I took to be their respective ages.

Anton Cavendish – film director – 40
Alma Cavendish – actress – 35
Ross Sinclair – former shell-back / father of the victim – 65
going on 21
Edith Havelock – his fiancée and a receptionist at a legal
firm – 20
Gilbert Baines – banker-cum-toad-hybrid – 28
Carl Wilson – clerk in the swine's office – 22
"Just" Poppy – aspiring actress – 30

Carl had been far from the scene of the crime when Cecil was murdered. Poppy and Ross had both been assaulted, and we were interviewing Edith when it happened, which really only left Gilbert and the Cavendishes. Oh, how I wished that Gilbert was to blame! My life would be so much sweeter if he was packed off to prison. I'm not a monster, I'd spare him the gallows if I could help it. But of all the suspects (based on the principle of whom I found most distasteful) he would surely be my first choice.

I stared at the list for a few minutes before realising this would not magically solve the case for me. I decided to note down potential solutions to the crime but, as almost everyone had a reason to kill the puffed-up actor, this was approximately as helpful as writing the list of their names.

And so, as neither of these stratagems had worked, I tried to think of the gaps in my knowledge and all the fascinating little contradictions we'd discovered. I'd long been aware that a good mystery is built upon contradictions. And so, instead of thinking like a police officer, which I had no claim to being, I decided to consider the case from a writer's perspective.

It is not a writer's job to imagine the most likely culprit, but the suspect who is best placed to get away with murder. That is why contradictions are so important. An intelligent killer strives to make us think he could not possibly be to blame. Confusing the time of the murder is one way of achieving this, but as we all saw Cecil alive mere minutes before the shots rang out, this did not appear to be relevant. Two killers working together might have ensured that the true facts were obscured, but I was struggling to pin down one likely suspect and dreaded to think how long it would take me if there was a team of them.

The murder was carried out in such a manner that anything less than perfect timing would have swiftly revealed the culprit's identity and scuppered the whole plan. However, the attacks on Ross and Poppy seemed more haphazard. I had to assume that the first had been out of necessity. Ross had left the house at the wrong moment and was clobbered accordingly.

After that, the killer made his way to the conservatory to stab Poppy, who he must have known would be there waiting for him... somehow.

But it was all so unnecessarily risky. For one thing, taking a path through the snow to get to the victim not only exposed the killer to detection – anyone on the eastern side of the building could have spotted him on his slow trek – it also made his escape more difficult. But escape he had.

It was at this point on my path of frustrated musing that my eyes grew heavy, my head began to nod, and I fell fast asleep. Except for the moment when Percy came to snuggle up next to me in the middle of the night, I slept soundly through to the morning and, I'm sure you'll be glad to know, no one else was murdered, stabbed or knocked unconscious as I rested my weary bones.

TWENTY-TWO

When I awoke nice and early the next morning, the whole world looked brighter. This was no mere metaphor; the sun shone through my curtains and the snow was already melting by the time I pushed my dog off me and rolled out of bed. It was time to find some answers, so I threw on a more casual outfit than the one I'd been wearing the night before and, after taking Percy for his morning constitutional and depositing him in the kitchen with the cheery cook, I sallied forth into the bowels of Everham Hall.

The first thing I had to find was the killer's escape route from the scene of Poppy's attack. There had to be a staircase on that side of the house; the basic rules of architecture dictated it. And so I returned to the far end of the corridor, where I had spectacularly failed to locate it the night before. I found plenty of dusty old rooms this time, but my search was once more in vain. I was about to give up – believing that the creation of a single staircase to the upper floor of such an enormous house had been the quirk of the eccentric who had designed the building – when the very last door opened. There were the stairs which led down to the abandoned wing of the house. That door had been locked when I'd tried it the previous night, and so I finally knew something for (fairly) certain.

This was progress; this was good. The killer had entered the conservatory to attack Poppy and then made his way back through the old part of the house to the stairs that went up to the bedrooms. He either had a key with him to enable this, or there was one in the door, and he had been lucky. There were marks on the dusty stairs, so it was clear that someone had been there, but I couldn't make out any definite footprints.

Just imagine if I'd spent all that time puzzling over this crime and then identified the killer from the size of his shoe. I would never have concluded a mystery novel in such a mundane fashion, and I was frankly relieved that this would not be the case in real life.

I left the old wing of the house behind and peeked into the makeshift infirmary, where the two patients and their attendant nurses were sleeping. Poppy was on one of the sofas, and I was happy to see that the knife in her shoulder was still holding in the blood. I did wonder for a moment whether she was at risk of tetanus or some such nastiness, but I could only conclude that Bella would have worried about that for me. If the good weather held, a doctor would show up before too long and, with the sun shining through every east-facing window, I was confident that everything would turn out fine.

I've noticed a tendency in me for optimism on sunny days, and I do not approve of it one bit. I could have done with a healthy dose of my usual negativity as I investigated the wicked deeds of man. Instead, I strolled along to the breakfast room whilst humming a cheery waltz.

It turned out that I was not the first to rise. Alma was already at table, enjoying some dainty French pastries.

"Good morning," I practically sang.

Alma could do little but sigh. "If you say so, dear."

This at least put my good mood into some perspective, and

so I helped myself to some bread and jam and considered what to say next.

"We haven't had the chance to discuss what happened last night," I began, and I was about to explore this really very serious topic when the snooty butler appeared in the doorway.

"Would sir care for a hot drink?"

"Yes, sir would." I considered testing the range of beverages on offer – would hot toddies and mulled wine be available at such an hour? – but I plumped for tea instead. "Assam with milk and two lumps of sugar, please," I told him, and he glumly glided away to fulfil the task.

The interruption had thrown me a touch, but I soon retraced my thinking. "In fact, Alma, I've barely spoken to you since you arrived last night." She looked apprehensive, and so I hoped a little flattery would help. "Of all the people here, I've found you and Anton to be the most level-headed and welcoming. To be perfectly honest, I was relieved when we met in the entrance hall and you brought me to see the rest of the group."

She had a sweet nature and couldn't help but respond in kind. "We were very happy to meet you, too, Marius." She paused then, as though deciding on the best response to deploy. "Cecil's parties don't always have the most respectable guests, which was why we asked him to keep this one small."

"I concluded that you'd both been here before. Anton seemed to be quite at home from the moment he stepped on the premises."

Her smile grew at the mention of her husband. "It's true that we've spent a little time here since Cecil bought the place, but Anton's like that wherever he goes. He's just one of those people who is always comfortable in his surroundings."

I could tell that there was truth in what she was saying, and yet it did not capture the whole picture. Perhaps it was unfair to judge so soon after their friend had been murdered, but the pair of them had appeared far from relaxed for much of the previous night.

"What an admirable quality. The world would be a better place if more people realised how lucky they already are," I said and then realised I could have been talking about myself so changed the topic. "He mentioned the problems that Cecil had caused on set. It must have been difficult working with such a colourful person."

She turned to look out of the window at the sparkling snow. The light of the morning sun caught her deep brown eyes, and I think I saw something of that special quality Anton had identified when he first found her working in that department store. "He wasn't the most conceited actor with whom I've appeared, but neither was he easy-going. The saddest thing about Cecil was that he truly was talented and, when he was himself, he could act most other people off the screen."

I was hoping she might spontaneously tell me about the time the pair had kissed, but it was hardly a point I could broach without coming across as a terrible Nosey Parker. "From what I understand, he had various issues with alcohol and suchlike." This was far too much of a euphemism, even by the standards of polite society. "Anton said it caused problems on the set of your productions. I noticed on the posters in his bedroom that you and Cecil had appeared opposite one another in several films over the years."

"Yes, we've worked together often since Anton discovered me. It was fun at first, but things deteriorated after he inherited so much from his wife. It makes me wonder whether being rich is all it's cracked up to be. I mean, we all strive to have as much money as the Marquess of Edgington, but if we end up like Cecil, is it actually worth the effort?"

"I've no doubt you're right." Unable to ask anything too personal, I continued asking questions to which I already knew the answers in the hope she might tell me something new.

"What about the films you made last year? Did Cecil's behaviour interfere with their production?"

She took a glass of orange juice from the other side of her plate and sipped it before answering. "I can't say he helped, but the British public continued to adore him, and so we continued to work together. The biggest issue was simply the time it took. In the past, we could record a five-reel film in the space of a month. But as we never knew which version of Cecil would appear, *The Devil Dances in Darkness* took nearly ten weeks to complete. That meant more expense, more people waiting around for him, and more stress for Anton."

Ah ha! This was more like it. I could build a story around an over-worked film director who is driven to despair by his leading man and resolves the issue with a few bullets to the actor's brain. Whether the police could build a case around such an idea was another matter.

"It must have been hard for you both. Not only do you work together, but you live together, too. You must have borne the brunt of Anton's frustration more than anyone."

She wrapped a lock of hair around one finger. Her husband had told me she was an incredible actress, but she was certainly no expert at hiding her feelings. "Every marriage has its difficulties. I don't know what more I can say than that."

I wouldn't let her be so coy and pressed for something more substantial. "I'm not asking you to tell me your every secret, but I'd like to know how the three of you rubbed along together." Obviously, that wasn't all I was hoping to discover, and my ploy was so obvious that I found myself telling the truth after all. "Or rather, I'd like to know how Anton was affected by Cecil's lack of professionalism."

Her answer came swiftly and with a hint of irritation. "It didn't change anything. Anton is a wonderful director. He treats all his actors the same way. Whether it's me or—"

As she was speaking, someone appeared in the doorway.

We both must have assumed it was Perkins returning with the tea, as it was only when a voice interrupted her that we turned to see the director himself.

"What my dear wife is too polite to tell you, dear chap, is that I have been a despicable wretch for some time."

Alma couldn't say anything just then. She had been outspoken for much of the previous evening but was now quite mute. I thought she might at least dismiss his comment in order to keep up appearances, but she could only glance down at her empty plate.

Anton came into the room and pulled over a chair so he could sit between us. I had to wonder what this said about his intentions. "With all his vices and woes, Cecil was determined to play up to the stereotype of the capricious actor, and so I played the part of a domineering director. It was all very melodramatic and, at some point, I forgot that it was just an act. His behaviour became more abhorrent on set and so did mine. It was poor Alma here who suffered most."

This was interesting, but it still didn't explain a kiss between two stars who apparently didn't like one another. I really should have waited until Bella was with me. She'd have known what to say to get the truth from them. Sadly, she was still asleep, and so I clumsily asked, "Well then? How did everything come to a head?"

They looked at one another, and I think Alma was quite relieved when her husband answered for her. "A kiss."

Hurray! I thought but didn't say, as I was about to get the information I needed after all.

"You know it was nothing," Alma interrupted and leaned across the table to put her hand on her husband's. She offered a tentative smile, and I had to believe that whatever fault lines had appeared in their relationship would soon be fixed.

"I know that now." He looked down at her dainty fingers, and I'm sure he was considering his foolish actions. Well, it was either that or he was a terribly good actor, and this whole scene had been staged for my benefit. "I should have trusted you from the beginning but, to coin a phrase, I couldn't see the fog for the mist. Nothing felt permanent because we'd built our lives on the back of a man who cared little for the needs of those around him."

This was a very different picture from the one that most people had painted of their darling friend, Cecil. Even Bella had been unwilling to criticise the shambolic character. It also spoke once more to just how reliant Anton Cavendish had become on his leading man.

"I think we should explain what happened." Alma squeezed his hand a fraction, and her husband nodded his agreement.

"It really was foolish of me, but *The Devil Dances in Darkness* was weeks behind schedule and, when we got to the final scene – with the killer in the story punished, and the loving couple united at last – I had to film my wife kissing the man who had made my life such torture. I suppose it was down to the pressure but, when I watched that scene over and over again until it was perfect, something just snapped."

He could no longer look at his wife but peered across the long room with its medieval portraiture and twin chandeliers.

"I was certain that the two of them were in love and that Alma was about to leave me." He needed a moment to compose his thoughts. "I was not proud of myself, even then, but I made a terrible scene. I knocked over the camera and screamed some excuse about their acting not being up to the superlative Anton Cavendish's high standards. I stormed off the set in Ealing and took the tube home to London Bridge. I refused to finish the film, and so my assistant had to take over for the last few days."

Perhaps I was soft-headed, or at least soft-hearted, but I felt sorry for the fellow. I can't imagine it would be easy to go through such an experience, and I didn't blame him for getting his dander up.

At this moment, Bella would have thought of an ever so affectionate way of sympathising with his plight while simultaneously persuading him to reveal what happened next. As we have already established, I possess no such delicacy, so I simply asked, "What happened next?"

The man was still distressed, and it fell to his wife to answer. "I went home that night and did what I could to console Anton, but he wouldn't talk to me. In fact, we haven't really spoken about it in the months since then."

In a sudden rush of action, the director lunged from his chair to kneel at his leading lady's feet. "My darling, can you ever forgive me? I've been such a fool. I shouldn't have blamed you for doing your job. Perhaps it was Cecil's murder, or maybe I just needed time to see the error of my ways, but I know now that you would never have betrayed me – especially not with Cecil. Please tell me you believe me."

A rush of romantic sentiment surged from within her, and she stroked her beloved's hair. "I believe you, my darling. I never doubted you for one moment. I'm just so glad that you can trust me again." She fell to the floor in front of him and the pair embraced.

This would have been a beautiful ending to a love story. Of course, if I'd been writing the script, I wouldn't have placed a practical stranger just a yard or two from the grand scene of reconciliation.

I cleared my throat to remind them that I was there. "That's wonderful." I tried my best to sound sincere. "Truly moving, in fact. But would you mind finishing your account for me? Did you resolve the situation with Cecil?"

A little reluctantly, they released one another and returned to their chairs. It was very awkward, and I really wished I hadn't been there, but... well, there was a murder to solve.

"Yes, we spoke to him." Alma pronounced the words as though they were a grave confession.

"Or rather, he came to me to apologise for his behaviour," her husband clarified. "The fact is that I don't believe he knew why I was upset. Gilbert was the only one who understood my true feelings, and that was only because he'd been at the set that day and guessed what was wrong. I never told Cecil, and he assumed that it was his intoxication that had so unnerved me."

"He was actually very sorry for his behaviour." Alma tapped the table nervously as she spoke. "He promised us both separately that he would be sober by the time the next project began filming, and that was when he invited us here for the party."

"So there was no ill will left between you?" This was the message I had extracted from the discussion. Perhaps I was naïve, but it was hard to think badly of the pleasant pair.

"As far as Cecil was concerned, yes," the director began, "but I couldn't just forget what had happened, and so I continued to treat my dear wife unkindly. I don't understand why, but it was only recently that I could be myself again. I'd held on to that pain with all my strength, and it took me until today to be able to let go."

They were holding hands again, and I could tell that they wished to be off somewhere private, wrapped up in one another's arms. Sadly for them, there was one thing that still didn't make sense.

"Yet, despite all that, when you arrived at the house last night, you seemed to be getting on perfectly well. It was only when Cecil was murdered that you began to act out of character." They exchanged a curious look as I spoke, and I was hard pushed to say what it meant. "So I'm going to ask you a question that you've already answered, but I'd like you to think very carefully this time before replying. Where were you both when Cecil was murdered?"

Alma did not take my advice and immediately spat out the same alibi she had previously given. "We were together in our room, changing for dinner. Why would you doubt us?"

Her indignation was enough to stifle any belligerent reply I might have offered and so I tried a different question. "And what about last night? After you went upstairs to go to bed, did either of you come back out again?"

It was Anton's turn to issue a denial. "No, of course we didn't. Alma lay straight down and fell asleep, and I followed her soon afterwards. Why? What's happened now?"

I watched them for a moment to see whether they would betray any fear of discovery. "Both Poppy and Ross were attacked. Luckily, neither was killed."

And then, to my great surprise, they looked at one another and began to cry. It was quite alarming, and I couldn't make sense of it. Alma got up from her chair to sit in her husband's lap and, a moment later, they were holding one another tightly.

"I'm so sorry, Anton," the actress whimpered. "I love you more than I can say. I really do."

"I know, my angel. I know," Anton pulled away to mumble, but then he buried his head in her shoulder once more.

Instead of pushing them to explain what any of this meant, I felt very out of place and hurried from the room. "Umm... Right... It was awfully good of you to talk to me. I won't take up any more of your time." I didn't even get to drink my tea.

TWENTY-THREE

I made a promise to myself not to interview anyone else without Bella. It's not that I don't know how to talk to people. I actually think I'm quite charming when I have to be. It was more about those clever angles that the detective in my book manages to identify. I was far too direct, too honest, and it let the suspects off the hook. I'd believed every word that nice couple had told me, and I could do nothing to prove them wrong.

Fearing a repeat performance with whomever I quizzed next, I sought out my childhood friend in the sitting room. She gave me a friendly smile.

"It's about time you made an appearance." This was not Bella speaking but her patient. "I was beginning to wonder whether the doctor would get here before you did."

I must say, it was rather comical to see her lying on the sofa, chattering away indignantly with the knife handle still sticking out of her. I could only imagine that one of the footmen had found her some remarkably strong medicine to deal with the pain.

"Why were you waiting for me?" I felt compelled to enquire.

"Because you haven't heard what happened last night." She was clearly excited to tell me, but I needed a moment to recover from my encounter in the breakfast room.

I soon realised that, though Bella looked pleased to see me, Ross and Edith had disappeared. "Where did your other patient go?" I asked.

"Edith just went upstairs to get changed, and Ross insisted that he felt fine and went with her. There was nothing I could do for him anyway except keep a cold flannel on his head. I managed to convince them both to stay here last night just in case he had a concussion. There was no sign of a problem this morning except the bump on his head, and I think he's safe to be alone."

"That's good," I replied. Bella's confidence and competence have always set me at ease.

"No, it's not good. It's not good at all." Poppy immediately disturbed my peace of mind. "You do realise that the killer almost crossed me off his list? I told you all last night that I'd be next. Somebody tried to murder me, and yet you've got more sympathy for that gruff sailor's bruised ego than my very real stab wound."

I could only imagine that being anywhere but the absolute centre of attention was a woman like Poppy's greatest fear.

"Very well. Why don't I sit down and you can tell me everything?"

Before she could answer, my dog appeared in the doorway. He had evidently left the kitchen in search of his new favourite person and looked between me and Poppy before going to sit beside her. So much for man's best friend.

I sat down on the sofa opposite and, thankfully, Bella took charge of the interview. "Start by telling us everything you remember. Take all the time you need and don't feel any pressure if you've forgotten something or it's a strain." Her solicitous manner immediately put our suspect-cum-witness-cum-victim at ease.

"Well, I was down in the old conservatory having a cigarette – to which you both know I'm partial – when I heard someone behind me."

We also both knew that there was a smoking room nearby. Her story already sounded implausible, but I didn't interrupt.

"I turned to see a figure dressed in dark clothes moving towards me with a knife in his hand. I backed into the corner and thought for sure that I was about to die but, when he lunged, I crashed into the piano stool. I must have turned a fraction, as the blade hit my shoulder instead of my heart."

"And then what happened?"

"He tried to pull it out, but I assume it caught the bone or something as he didn't succeed – it was quite excruciating, I can tell you. He was clearly most put out by the development and groaned a deep, mournful groan. You know, I almost felt sorry for him. Imagine going to all that trouble to try to murder me and not managing it. He should really have brought a second weapon."

"And then he ran away?" Bella fought to suppress her laughter at this matter-of-fact assessment, whereas I didn't quite manage it.

"That's right." Poppy did her best to look serious, whilst lazily stroking Percy's velveteen ears. "He darted out of the conservatory to the old wing of the house and, just as his footsteps died away, I heard another sound. I cried out, then became terrified that he was coming back to finish the job. I don't think I've ever been so frightened in my life. When I saw that it was you, it was the relief more than the pain that made me pass out."

It was quite a story, and I took a moment to consider whether any of it was true. Bella was quicker once more and asked a pertinent question.

"How could you not have seen his face if he was so close to you?"

"You were there. You know how dark it was. The only light was from the moon and that was directly overhead as he came inside. All I could see was blackness."

"He may have been wearing some kind of mask," I suggested. "Or one of those woollen protectors that soldiers wore in the Crimean war."

She considered the possibility. "Yes, that would make sense. Though, to be quite honest, my first concern was not to identify my assailant but survive the attack."

She was by far the *second* most objectionable house guest, after Gilbert of course, and I was not inclined to believe her. However, she was resolute in her statement, and she showed no signs of nerves. What I couldn't understand was why she was so keen to talk to me. I already knew that she'd been attacked in that draughty old conservatory, but it was as though she took pride in the fact and wished us to celebrate her part in the case.

I looked at Bella, who appeared just as perplexed as I was. When she spoke, it was in a tentative, almost exploratory tone. "Poppy, if we accept that the killer targeted you in particular, then we must ask why that was."

"I would say that was obvious." She certainly didn't lack for confidence. "That maniac killed Cecil and wanted to punish him further by murdering his love."

"Well, that is one theory." Bella's perplexity only grew.

"I have another," I tried, as new paths appeared before me. "Perhaps you saw something that could lead us to the killer. Perhaps he's afraid that you'll be able to reveal his identity, and so he tried to silence you."

"What do *I* know?" She apparently did not like the idea, and her voice came out in a dry rasp. "If I'd seen anything significant, I would have told you. In which case, the killer wouldn't have bothered chasing after me with a knife."

"The problem is that we still don't know why Cecil was murdered," Bella reminded us, and I got to my feet to think over the matter.

"There are certainly plenty of motives to consider. With Cecil at his worst, his father had a tumultuous existence over the last year. Anton and Alma haven't had it much easier, and as for Gilbert, Wilson and Edith, they all have factors which could speak against them."

"It doesn't sound as though you've got very far." Poppy glanced down at her brightly polished nails as she dismissed our work in one sharp sentence.

I stood in my favourite spot beside the mantelpiece and realised that there was nothing I could say to prove her wrong. I had not solved the mystery of Cecil's death. I hadn't even worked out whether anyone except my friend actually liked the fellow.

"Let's start from the beginning," Bella said to make things simpler. "Everyone retired to their rooms, while Marius and I talked to Edith alone."

"And Ross went outside to get his glasses," I added.

"That's right." Bella stood up to stroll in front of the Christmas tree as she remembered the steps we'd taken. "While we were in Edith's room, we saw the killer moving through the snow towards the conservatory." She clicked her fingers then as she realised we'd been ignoring a hugely important point. "But if you were only in that lonely old part of the house to smoke a cigarette, how would the killer have known where to find you?"

Poppy didn't seem so sure of herself for once. I could see that she was debating how much to reveal, but then she shrugged her uninjured shoulder and answered the question. "Didn't I tell you about the note? I was certain I had." She wasn't a very good actress after all. I really couldn't imagine her ascending to the heights that Cecil or Alma had scaled. "I went to perform my toilet and, when I came back out, there was a note waiting for me. Someone had evidently slipped it under my bedroom door."

"What did it say?"

She shook her head as though the answer was obvious. "It said that I should go to the conservatory, obviously."

"But why did you comply?" Bella launched another question at her.

"Because..." She didn't have a good answer and searched for an escape route. "Because it told me to go there, and so I did. What would you have done?"

"Not gone?" Bella put one hand to her cheek, apparently unable to make sense of our contradictory witness. "Or at least told someone about it to be safe."

"That's easy to say now, but how should I know which one of you to trust?"

"What did you do with the letter?" I asked in case this was all just a story – which was exactly how it sounded.

"Well, I burnt it, didn't I."

Bella came to stand next to me, and we stared at this odd character, unable to make sense of her truly unique perspective on the world.

"It was a horrible note, and so I destroyed it."

I crouched down so that my eyes were almost at the same level as Poppy's. "It was a horrible note that told you to go to the conservatory, and so you destroyed it and went to the conservatory?"

"That's exactly it."

Bella discovered some urgency, and her voice became more insistent. "That's not the whole truth, is it, Poppy? Anyone can see that you're hiding something. So why don't you tell us what the note really said?"

Our suspect looked quite irate and, though she couldn't march off in a huff with a knife lodged in her shoulder, she turned her head away. She didn't say anything for a moment but stared at a golden bauble on the Christmas tree. It was hard to know whether she was appreciating its shimmering beauty or trying to catch her own reflection.

"Fine, it didn't just tell me to go to the conservatory. It said that, if I didn't go there, whoever wrote it would reveal my secret."

This word seemed to bounce off me and back to her. "Your secret?"

"That's right. He said he would expose me."

"What's your secret?" It was probably a stupid question, but then this whole discussion had been quite bizarre from the start.

"I don't know exactly what he meant by it but, to be on the safe side, I decided to see what he wanted."

I'm glad that it was Bella who reacted to this and not me. I might have shouted something rude. "Poppy, are you out of your mind?" Well, ruder. "Your boyfriend was murdered and yet you wandered off to meet a killer in the most secluded part of the house because you were worried about your reputation."

"Oh, please. As a lady yourself, you must know that reputation is one thing that can never be repaired. It was *because* Cecil had been murdered that I went to the conservatory. I thought someone had got the wrong idea about me and concluded that I was to blame. If that was the case, I could have nipped it in the bud and called for some cocoa before bed."

Bella could no longer look at the frivolous creature, but wandered back and forth on the hearth rug, trying to put the nonsense we had heard into some kind of order. "So then, you don't have a secret?"

Poppy let out a piercing laugh until her shoulder began to hurt and she had to quieten down. "Of course I have secrets. We all do, don't we? If one of you discovered something about me that I wouldn't want anyone to discover, then it only stands to reason that I would do whatever was necessary to—"

I could hold it in no longer. "You could have been

murdered. As it is, you've got a knife sticking out of you and, had you not been born under such a lucky star, you could have bled to death by now."

Even as she winced at the pain in her shoulder, she remained immune to such logic. "There you are then. I was born under a lucky star and had no reason to fear a killer's blade."

I turned to Bella in disbelief. She looked just as flabbergasted as I was, and so it was lucky that Matthew arrived to interrupt the proceedings. "I beg your pardon, sir, madams. We've just had a call from Scotland Yard. They were informed of Mr Sinclair's murder and the subsequent attacks. They've sent a detective inspector who's on holiday nearby. They hope he'll be able to get through the snow before lunchtime."

"And what about the doctor?" Poppy demanded.

Matthew eyed his dead master's girlfriend with little affection. "He's on his way on foot from the village. He called half an hour ago and should be here at any moment."

Poppy looked inordinately pleased with herself. "You see, Marius. There was no need to worry after all."

TWENTY-FOUR

I pulled Bella into the corridor and, when that wasn't far enough, I kept going until I reached the first suitable room I could find. The library at Everham Hall had everything you could wish for in such a space. Immense bookcases stretched up to the ceilings and there were several ladders for accessing the higher books. From the look of things, people rarely did and, much like the house itself, this less-visited area appeared terribly unloved. There were cobwebs and dust all over. The armchairs in the centre of the room had stuffing coming out of them and yet it was still easily my favourite room in the house.

I could only conclude that the majority of the titles in there had come with the property. Easily distracted as I am, I had a quick look at the selection on the nearest shelf and decided that seventeenth-century political journals and scientific treatises on mould would not have been to Cecil's taste. To be quite frank, they weren't to mine, either, but I couldn't help feeling a thrill as I stepped inside the grand old space. Books just have that effect on me.

Aside from the literature that the room housed, there was a

red Chinese carpet on the floor with a huge dragon across it that was probably put there a century earlier to protect the green, blue and golden-spined volumes on the shelves.

Bella was apparently less excited than I was. "Marius, will you please stop marvelling at a lot of dusty old tomes and tell me what you're thinking?"

"I'm thinking that I should buy more books," I replied without considering my tone and received a tut in response.

"Please concentrate. The police will be here soon and what have we got to tell them? There's a killer on the loose. We don't know what he's been up to or why anyone would want to hurt the victims, but we're terribly pleased that the dead man had such a fine library?"

I mused on this for a moment. "We could. It's more certain than most of what we've uncovered so far."

She sighed at me. I didn't like it.

An even bigger dose of frustration entered her voice. "Surely you garnered something from Poppy's account."

"I did. I garnered that she's lying."

"You mean that she was involved in the murder?" Her mind raced to connect the myriad pieces of evidence we'd discovered. "Yes, that's how it seemed from the beginning. Perhaps she helped the killer do away with Cecil, and then the swine attempted to kill her in order to cover his trail. I can just imagine Cecil's rival, Alec Pemberton, hiding away in the old wing somewhere. Perhaps she smuggled him here in the back of her car. That would explain all that rubbish she was telling us about the note that never existed. She went to that part of the house because she knew her accomplice would be there!"

I was tempted to point out just how good she was at divining theories for the murder without any input from me. I felt a little guilty that I'd led her on, though, and so I clarified the situation as she continued to pace the room, which smelled just beautifully of leather and old paper.

"No, I'm sorry to disappoint you, Bella. I can't say for certain that Poppy's to blame. I just know that she's lying. I don't understand her motives but, for the moment, she's as much the killer as Alma or Ross... or Gilbert, for that matter."

"Ross must still be a suspect." She showed no sign of being disheartened but ploughed on with another idea. "The obvious assumption is that the killer knocked him out before going on to stab Poppy. But what if Ross stabbed Poppy, then ran back through the house and gave himself a bang on the head to make it look as though he'd been there the whole time? There really wasn't much of a wound to speak of and he could have feigned his dizzy spell quite easily."

"You're incredible. By which I meant to say..." I didn't quite know what I'd meant to say, so, blushing like an idiot, I left it at that.

"Do you have any theories you haven't yet revealed?" She was so very much alive as she contemplated the different solutions before us that it was impossible not to feel a little inspired by her.

I occasionally receive correspondence from readers who get excited trying to solve the murders in my book before Inspector Rupert L'Estrange can. Just as I do to those letters, I replied to Bella with as much enthusiasm as I could summon. "The Cavendishes have been acting strangely since the killing was announced. They claimed it was down to trouble they'd had with Cecil on a recent film, and the jealousy that Anton felt over a kiss on screen, but there's more that they aren't saying."

"I see." Her high spirits descended a fraction. We were no longer talking about characters in a thrilling story but the possibility that two of her best friends were murderers. "Objectively, I completely understand why you would consider their involvement. Cecil was extremely difficult last year and, despite his best efforts to rein in his behaviour, as soon as he started spending time with Poppy, he returned to his bad ways. It was awful for his director and co-star."

"And what about subjectively?" I asked, as she apparently wasn't going to tell me without prompting. "What do you feel in your heart?"

Her enthusiasm increased once more. "Subjectively, I would tell you that Anton and Alma would never do anything so evil, and there's no possible way they could be the killers."

"Excellent. I'll cross them off the list then." I winked in case it wasn't clear that I was joking. "Who does that leave?"

She performed a few brief calculations and returned an accurate answer. "Edith couldn't have attacked Poppy or her boyfriend, but she was alone when Cecil was killed and might have been involved."

"Very true. And fitting with your previous supposition that Ross attacked Poppy and then feigned an assault on himself, we cannot rule out the possibility that he and Edith were working together. You never know, Ross may have killed his son to prevent him from changing his will. Perhaps Cecil was murdered so that his father could live here with his new wife."

She paced about in front of me as I remained perfectly still. Her sheer force of character was enough to make me believe that we could actually solve the murder.

"Which means we've been through everyone but Carl—"

"—Wilson," a voice from the other side of the room called, and the man himself jumped up from a high-backed armchair that was facing the fireplace. "I'm terribly sorry. I had no intention of listening to your conversation, but you were nattering together at such a rate that I never had the chance to tell you I was here."

He was gripping his hard-cover book and looked just as apologetic as ever. I thought he had more to say but, when nothing came, I tried to soothe his nerves.

"There's no need to worry." I was clearly still infected by Bella's good mood. "It's not your fault we didn't check that the room was empty. What have you been doing in here?"

He tapped his book a few times and held up *The Secret of Bewley Place* by Carmine Fortescue. I shared a publisher with Fortescue and was not a fan of his work... or his personality... or his habit of completing several manuscripts a year. And now that I come to think of it, I couldn't stand the clothes he wore, his voice, the way he spoke to waiters or— Actually, I couldn't abide the man in any sense.

"Have you read it?" Before I could tell him that I very much hadn't, he kept talking. "It's absolute claptrap from beginning to end. It's sold so many copies that I thought it had to have something going for it, but I've never read such a poorly conceived mystery. The killer was obvious from the first page, but I had to keep reading just to make sure I was right."

"And were you?" Bella perched on the back of a chair to await his response.

"Sadly, yes. I really believed there would be some last-minute revelation to salvage the novel, but I've reached the final chapter and it's just not going to happen."

I considered walking over and shaking the young fellow's hand. I somehow found the willpower to resist and pointed to the chairs around the hearth for us all to have a seat.

"So, have you worked out that I'm the killer?" he asked quite casually as the three of us took our places, and he poured some water from the jug beside his chair. Bella and I must have shown how surprised this question made us as he immediately became nervous again and tipped the jug of water over his book – which is the lightest punishment that any Carmine Fortescue novel deserves. "I'm sorry. I didn't mean to suggest that I actually am the killer. I was trying to ask whether you had any theory that placed me at the scene of the crime."

Bella was there to reassure him. "Carl, dear, you needn't be so anxious. Unless you have the capacity to be in two places at once or a device for travelling through time, it seems unlikely you're responsible for Cecil's death."

"But it's not just Cecil who was hurt, is it? Ross told me that he and Poppy were attacked, too, and I haven't the shred of an alibi for last night. To tell the truth, I heard you both shouting outside my room. I knew there was something amiss, but I was already in my pyjamas and didn't have the courage to see what the matter was." His already sincere expression became a touch more earnest, and his voice cracked. "If I'd known that anyone was in danger, I would... I would... Well, I would probably have locked my door and hidden from the killer. I'm a real chicken-heart at such moments, but you could have counted on me if you'd knocked."

He truly was a wet sheet of paper, but likeable in his own way. In fact, he rather reminded me of Percy, who's all barks and growls whenever the postman is outside, but as soft as goose down when we open the door to receive a parcel. I chastised myself for going so lightly on a suspect, but you try interviewing a puppy dog and see how you fare.

"Don't worry about it. I was fairly nervous myself when scrabbling around in the dark in search of a killer. Bella here has always been the brave one between the two of us."

She shook her head in that, *Oh Marius, you are incorrigible* manner of hers. "Don't listen to him, Carl. He loves to tease me."

"No, I do not," I said before realising that he really had no need to hear us bickering. "That being said, I do have to correct my old friend on one point. I don't know how much of our conversation you heard, but there was one suspect she over-looked." The pair of them showed some alarm at this, and I imagine they were skimming the list of potential culprits to spot the missing name. "Wilson, is it fair to say you've become a close acquaintance of Gilbert's recently?"

Lady Isabella was not amused. "Marius, is this really necessary?"

"Oh, come along, Bella. I'm not doing this to hurt your feelings; I have no desire to be cruel. But we must consider every suspect, and your boyfriend had just as much reason to want Cecil dead as anyone else did."

She considered my point for a few moments before nodding. "Fine. As I know that Gilbert can't be the killer, go ahead, Carl. Answer the question."

Wilson looked even less eager to have this conversation than Bella. "Mr Baines has been very kind to me at work. He's taken me under his wing, so to speak, and I was very happy to be invited here this weekend."

Bella showed her appreciation for this formal answer and added an extra detail in support of the man's good character. "Gilbert is often generous to younger members of staff. You're not the first apprentice in whom he's shown interest, and several of them have become successful at Hargreaves Bank." This was hardly the most impartial reference.

"How interesting." A wry smile appeared on my face as I addressed Wilson once more. "Do you know anything of his relationship with Cecil Sinclair?"

He looked at Bella in case she expected him to give a similarly favourable answer. "I... I know that Mr Sinclair is... or rather, was, one of the bank's most valuable clients. Gilbert allowed me to look over the files of his account to help me learn more about the way our company works."

"Fascinating, fascinating." Fine, I was less than objective myself. "In which case, you may have noticed some small discrepancies recently."

It was Bella who reacted to this in little more than a whisper. "Oh, the discrepancies." I wondered if she had blocked out the memory of what Gilbert had told us the night before.

"That's right. Money that should have been in Cecil Sinclair's account that, for some reason, went missing."

Wilson kept his eyes trained on me this time and had to gulp down a breath before replying. "I don't think... I mean to say... Well, yes, actually. I did."

"I'm sure you did. A bright man like you would have spotted such a mistake. But you weren't the only one. Did you realise that Cecil himself had challenged your superior about the money?"

"I had no idea." There was suddenly no reason to hesitate. He might have been a twitchy sort of fellow, but at the mention of any wrongdoing, he was evidently keen to tell the truth. "When I noticed that Mr Sinclair's investments hadn't been paying any interest or dividends into his account over the last month, I spoke directly to Mr Baines, who told me that he would solve the problem." He looked at Bella as he uttered this final statement. I felt he wanted her to know that, whatever he had done, he had followed the protocol of his position to the letter.

"And can I just confirm that you had never seen Cecil before you arrived at the house last night?"

That jerkiness was back in his muscles and his tongue seemed to trip and tangle. "That's not quite true." He kept us in suspense for a few moments, and I came to question whether he was as innocent as he seemed. "I've watched every film he's made at the cinema." No. The man was even more scrupulous than I'd imagined.

"Very good, Wilson. I appreciate your candour. Now, I have one last question for you. Aside from Gilbert and Bella, had you met anyone in this house before you came here last night?"

"No one, sir." It feels wrong to be called *sir* outside of a schoolroom or an expensive shop, but this wasn't the time to complain about such things and Carl continued. "I wouldn't have come here at all unless Mr Baines had invited me."

That wasn't the impression I'd got when we'd spoken to Gilbert on the matter, and I had to consider why the slippery eel would have lied. There was still nothing to suggest that nice but boring Carl Wilson could be the killer. Far more interestingly, however, I would now have another chance to be rude to Bella's dreadful boyfriend.

TWENTY-FIVE

"What was all that about, Marius?" Bella asked once we'd left poor nerve-shaken Wilson in the library. "Gilbert explained that the problem with Cecil's account was a clerical error. There was nothing untoward on his part, as you well know."

I answered her as best I could whilst darting from door to door in search of Baines the Banker. "I know that's what he told you, but I also know that the illegal withdrawal of funds from his company would be an offence that could at best lose Gilbert his job and, at worst, land him in gaol. Can you really say, with all your heart, that he had no reason to murder Cecil?"

Her jet-black hair whipped through space as she shook her head. "That's not the point. Of course Gilbert had a reason to kill Cecil, but I'm sure that you could attribute one to me if you tried hard enough."

"You killed him in order to protect your thieving boyfriend?"

"Ah... that was easier than I'd imagined." She was apparently surprised by this. "But whatever you think of Gilbert, I know that he wasn't stealing money, just as I know that he wouldn't kill another man. You've got it all wrong."

"Good."

There was no sign of him in any of the state rooms, though I did come across an elegant ballroom that I hadn't entered before. It really was a very large house.

"I beg your pardon?" my companion asked as I ducked back out to the long unlit hallway where I seemed to spend half my time.

"I said, good. I don't want Gilbert to be guilty if it breaks your heart." This was at least half true. "But we still have to talk to him. If only I could find the fellow."

"Are you looking for Gilbert?" There was a note of surprise in Bella's voice that took me aback.

I came to a complete stop in front of the door to the dining room. "Of course I am."

"Why didn't you say so? He'll be in his room. He always gets up late after a party. He's like a three-month-old baby when it comes to sleeping. If he goes to bed after midnight, he often loses the whole next day."

"What did you think I was doing in this corridor if not looking for Gilbert?"

She folded her arms across the golden dress she was still wearing from the night before. "I thought you'd lost your mind. Though, in all honesty, I came to that conclusion when I found you laid on your back on the pavement in the middle of Bloomsbury."

"So that's why you invited me here, is it?" Why did so many of our conversations end up as arguments?

She took a step closer, as though looking for a fight. "That's exactly why." Her eyes were on fire, and it gave me an odd thrill to remember just how passionate she could be. "Actually, I'm lying."

"I beg your pardon?"

She was not about to mince her words for my sake. "You heard me, I lied. Your publisher is a friend of my uncle's.

Bertrand Price-Lewis was worried about you, and so he called Uncle Basil. Basil called me and asked me to check that you weren't going out of your mind. When I found you on the pavement, I decided that a night away from the city might do you good."

I turned to look at the light spilling in from the entrance hall. It was tempting to go running outside in the hope that my car would make it back to London. For the amount I'd paid, I would hope it would make it through the English Channel, let alone a foot or two of melting snow.

"I'm sorry, Marius. I didn't mean to..."

She wasn't the one who'd upset me. Bertie had gone behind my back. He was one of the few people I'd told about my history with Bella, but his only concern was the money he would make from my next book.

I finally settled on what I wanted to say. "What did my publisher tell you?"

She exhaled a noisy breath and looked sympathetic. That was much worse than having to suffer her anger. "All I know is that you've been having trouble writing your new novel. He thought that seeing a friendly face might make you feel better. I knew that you were meeting on Christmas Eve, and we arranged for me to bump into you when you'd finished. It was my idea; I doubted that you would have talked to me if I'd called by your house."

I'd heard enough and walked away from her. I couldn't stomach the idea that two people who were supposed to be my friends had conspired against me. Even if they'd been trying to help, that didn't change the underhanded way they'd gone about it. I was clearly just a simpleton to them – a dote to be treated with kid gloves.

I wandered up the stairs, and Bella trailed lazily behind, looking really quite defeated.

"There were other reasons too," she continued, but I didn't turn back to her. "I wanted you here for moral support and because I knew that Cecil had started drinking again." She really wasn't winning me over. "And I wanted to see you again, Marius. I really did. You were my best friend for years. I've never found someone to replace you, and I doubt I ever will."

I should have forgiven her and told her how meeting her again had made me feel. Instead, I pressed on along the corridor and knocked on Gilbert's door before she could catch up with me.

"I'm asleep. Go away," the prickly chap murmured, and so I ignored him and marched inside.

The room was dark, and the air was musty with sleep. It was as though every morsel of oxygen in there had cycled through Gilbert's red-wine-and-whisky-infused lungs.

"Do you mind?" he asked most pompously and, obviously, I answered, "Not at all."

I made myself comfortable in a Rococo chair that was already in position a few feet from his bed. "I'd like to ask you some questions."

He propped himself up against the headboard and reached for a pair of horn-rimmed glasses that I hadn't seen him wear before. "Please, feel free to write to my secretary at Hargreaves Bank in the City. She will respond to any enquiries within the week."

"To be quite frank, old man, I don't think that you'd like innocent young Dorothy at your office to get wind of anything that I have to say."

"How did you know my secretary's name was Dorothy?"

It was a lucky guess and, as this had already broken the flow of my assault on him, I ignored the question and pressed on with what I wanted to say. "The point is," I told him quite masterfully considering that I was only half confident what my point would be, "we've been speaking to your colleague, Wilson."

"And?" I'd rarely met a man who could inject such disdain into a single word.

"And I'd like to know why you invited him to Cecil Sinclair's party."

Gilbert pulled his neck in so that his face was flat against his body. "I didn't invite him. He practically begged me to come."

Bella stood limply beside the door. It was clear that she would have liked to answer each question for him, but she must have realised that it was down to Gilbert to scramble out of the hole in which he found himself.

"Don't talk rot. You're not the sort of man who could be convinced to do anything against your will." I ploughed on even as he opened his mouth to object. "So tell me the truth. Did you invite him here to take the blame for what happened to Cecil?"

"How dare you, Quin?" His rage was burning bright. He would no longer lie in his bed to be insulted, and so he hopped to his feet instead.

"What lovely pyjamas." I will never get tired of ribbing Gilbert Baines. "I had no idea you could buy clothes with Union Jacks all over them."

"I'll have you know that my mother embroidered these for me by hand!" He grew yet more incandescent, changing from a candle flame to a thousand-watt bulb. "Now listen here, you jumped-up hack. I will not be intimidated by your petty games. If you've a problem with me, that's fine, but Bella needn't hear any of this."

I was quite comfortable in my antique chair. He could wear himself out puffing and pacing about as much as he liked.

As I said nothing, his girlfriend spoke up in a quiet voice. "You should answer his questions, Gilbert. I think it would be better for everyone."

He looked at her for a moment before emitting another

burst of bluster in my direction. "I have no interest in whatever spurious claims you wish to—"

"But perhaps the inspector from Scotland Yard does." I may have mentioned that, at my best, I like to consider myself a smooth sort of fellow. Well, this line was like pure silk.

"Scotland Yard?"

I luxuriated in his reaction because I am a very cruel person. "That's right. He's in the area on holiday. He may already be here by now."

Gilbert stopped his pacing and turned to his sweetheart for assistance. Bella was smart – not to mention painfully beautiful, funny, adventurous, caring... I'll stop there, as that list could go on for some time. Her intelligence was her foremost quality, and she knew not to offer him an escape until he'd explained himself.

"Just tell us the whole story, Gilbert. If you've done nothing wrong, then you won't be in any trouble."

When he made no effort to do so, I repeated the most interesting point that Wilson had revealed. "I'm sure that the inspector would love to hear of how you shared the financial dealings of your influential client with an underling at the bank. The same underling who went on to discover evidence of your misdeeds. The same underling, in fact, who you decided to invite to an intimate soiree at that client's stately home where that same client..." I have no idea why I kept saying the word "same". "...was murdered. Did you show Wilson Cecil's files and bring him here as a scapegoat for your crime?"

He had no wish to look at me but kept his eyes on Bella. "This is all wrong, my darling. You must see that he's twisting what happened. I wouldn't kill someone over a simple misunderstanding. I don't know how this man's brain works, but I fear he may be insane."

She looked from her suitor to me and back again. It was clear that she didn't know what to think, and I didn't want to push her, so I gave Gilbert a chance. "She can't help you, old boy. But if you're innocent, simply explain what really happened and everything will be fine. Start with Wilson. Why did you invite him?"

He puffed up both cheeks and his eyes darted about nervously. "I told you, he wanted to come. I don't see why I'm being lambasted for what I thought was a good deed. The poor boy's parents are dead, and he has no family in London. As he didn't go home for Christmas, I thought he might enjoy a good old-fashioned whoopee. Tell him, Bella. Please tell him."

She appeared torn over the best course of action but uttered a carefully worded response. "That all matches what I know of Carl."

"Then why show him the files relating to Cecil's account before he came here? Surely that's not standard practice in a secretive business like yours?"

He stopped moving altogether and, despite the fact he was wearing those ridiculous pyjamas, made his best attempt to look respectable. "For that very same reason; I was trying to give the boy a head start in a fiercely competitive industry. There is nothing stopping me from sharing the details of an account I oversee with a colleague. I believed it would give him a better understanding of the world in which we work." He pulled on his flannel top rather triumphantly. "And let me ask you this, Marius Quin, if I'd been stealing from Cecil, would I have handed an apprentice the details of my crime?"

Oh, botheration! He'd got me there and, for a moment, I didn't know what to think. "Perhaps not," I conceded and then my wonderful old brain saw a gap in the story and filled it. "But that doesn't explain why the money wasn't returned. It's been at least a week since you learnt of the problem. Cecil himself realised there was a discrepancy, and yet it still hasn't been resolved."

"I'm afraid that's how money works, dear boy." That smug

banker was grinning like the sun in a child's drawing. "It moves ever so slowly. That's why I was still on the telephone at a party on New Year's Eve. I was chasing up the people who were supposed to have sent thousands of pounds to Cecil and had failed to do so."

I wanted to groan... No. I wanted to scream. Not that it would have done me much good. I'd been defeated by a man with the wits of a woodlouse.

"Don't feel so hard done by, Marius." He came to place one patronising hand on my shoulder. "No one was expecting you to solve the case. Why don't you leave it to the gentleman from Scotland Yard? You need a professional for this sort of thing."

Bella still looked apprehensive, but it appeared that the inspector would not be carting Gilbert away in a police van after all.

There must have been some good in him, as he sighed and offered a consolation prize. "Listen here, chum. You've been going about this all wrong. I know it's your job to tick off the suspects one by one, go through every possible scrap of evidence, and examine different angles, but it's best to keep things simple. You should have started with those who would benefit most from Cecil's death."

"And who would that be?"

"Well, I can't tell you for certain, but he changed his will a few weeks ago. If I were you, I'd look for that and work out who the killer is from there."

I couldn't believe what I was hearing. "He changed his will?"

"That's right. I was a witness, along with his cook."

"He changed his will, and you didn't tell me?"

His fleshy jaw fell open. "Ahh, when you put it like that, I can imagine it sounds rather—"

"Where would it be, Gilbert?" Bella demanded, in just as much of a hurry as I was.

"He didn't store it with the rest of his papers in my office, so I suspect it must be in the tower with his personal belongings."

Bella had left the room before I could get to my feet.

"You may not be a murderer, Gilbert. But you're as witless as a sleeping donkey!"

TWENTY-SIX

I ran after my old playmate, just like I had when we were younger. As a child, I'd been small for my age and hated the fact she was faster than me. Then, one summer when I was about ten, I suddenly got taller. I remember the first time I could outrun her, and the feeling as I whistled through the trees in the forest around Hurtwood House. I remember how hard we both tried to outpace one another, our muscles and limbs pumping and our hearts beating as fast as a hummingbird's wings.

I had that same feeling as we bolted along the corridor and down the stairs to the entrance hall. There was a man in a black gabardine mackintosh just arriving at the front door and Matthew was on hand to take his coat.

"Hello, I'm Detective Inspector Lovebrook," the young officer called, but we would not be distracted from our task.

"We'll be with you in just one moment," I explained as Bella unlocked the door and we thundered up the stairs to Cecil's tower. "I think we might be about to solve a murder."

We stopped in the dressing room and peered about the place. There were still piles of clothes all over the furniture, and the floor was covered in empty bottles and cigarette stubs from whatever private party Cecil and Poppy had enjoyed up there before he died. What I couldn't see was any sign of files or papers, or even an obvious place where they might be kept. There were no bookshelves, as the walls were covered with framed posters from his career. I spotted his most recent role in *The Devil Dances in Darkness* directed by the great Anton Cavendish and starring his wife Alma, but I didn't see how this could help us.

Bella had poked about in the wardrobe, too, but to no avail.

"Upstairs," we said at the same time, though who would take the lead was another matter.

As we walked over to the spiralling staircase, the inspector we had seen arriving poked his head into the room behind us. "Is this where the body is?" He seemed a jolly chap, but we were a bit busy just then, and I took the first step up to the next floor.

"It must be here somewhere," Bella said as we began the search of the dead man's bedroom. It was clear that she had no desire to look at his body again. As her eyes swept the room, they skipped the bed entirely. I couldn't help looking at him, but there was no out-of-body flashback this time. I just felt thoroughly sad to see Cecil's lifeless form there. His face had a strangely waxy look to it. It was more than just pale; pallor mortis had long since set in and turned his previously tanned skin white.

Lovebrook mounted the stairs to stand next to me. "I'm sorry to interrupt, but could you—"

I held my hand up to stop him and went to inspect a bookshelf on the right-hand side of the room.

"Now, listen," Lovebrook continued. "I was only going to ask you to cover your hands if you plan to keep touching everything." He rummaged in his pocket and produced two pairs of white cotton gloves which, smiling apologetically, Bella and I both donned before continuing our search.

"I always carry spares." He continued chattering as we searched. "It's a trick I learnt from the great—"

"Nothing over here," Bella muttered, and the handsome young inspector looked a little disappointed. She'd been going through a box beside a poster for a Western called *The Dark Frontier* but now dropped to the floor to peer under the bed.

Apparently uncomfortable with silence, Lovebrook babbled once more. "I drove as close as I could, then parked at the end of the drive. The snow was too thick to come any further. It's turning to slush now, though, and I should think you'll be able to drive out of here by this afternoon. I've got an auntie in these parts, and she says that, though it sometimes snows in Everham, it rarely sticks for long." Apparently frustrated by our failure to respond, he walked over to me and demanded, "Tell me what it is you're hoping to find, and I can help you look."

"Cecil Sinclair's will," I finally told him.

He nodded and frowned at the same time. "That's a very good thing to look for. Where should I start?"

With the inspector's help, we ransacked the place. Not a book or paper was left undisturbed, and Bella even rifled the pockets of a few coats hanging by the stairs. It was no good, and so I stood right where I was to consider other possibilities.

I held my hand up as an idea occurred to me. "Inspector, you'll have to lend me a hand." I pointed him over to the other side of the room, where Bella was poking through a pile of what looked like receipts.

The biggest poster of all was on the wall above the bed. It was the kind they have on the outside of cinemas and was for an American pirate film that I remembered my mother enjoying. Cecil had not been the main star of *The Wicked Sailor's Lament*. His character only appeared in the lower corner of the poster, but it must have pushed him on to greater things, and he evidently considered it worthy of a prime spot on the wall.

"Are you ready?" I asked as we placed our hands on the side

of the heavy frame and Bella stopped to see what we were doing.

"Ready!" Lovebrook confirmed, and we lifted it up and off the wall.

Of course, we were doing all this over the corpse of the dead actor and couldn't just put the thing down on the bed. We had to stagger towards the stairs to place it on a free patch of carpet. But, sure enough, the poster revealed its secrets.

"How could you possibly have known?" Bella was impressed and Lovebrook gave me a pat on the back as he saw what we'd discovered.

Attached with adhesive tape to the back of the frame was a large Manila envelope, along with a few other treasures. There was a photograph of Cecil and his elderly bride on their wedding day, a very old cinema ticket, which I conjectured may have been the first he'd bought as a child, and his passport – there for safekeeping. I looked at the photograph for a moment – and compared it to the one we'd found on the bed – but it was the envelope that most interested me.

"It was simple," I replied, though uncertain that my explanation would make much sense. "Cecil Sinclair was a haunted man. He had demons to fight and losses to mourn, so I thought he might have associated himself with the poster that he woke up to each morning. *The Wicked Sailor's Lament* just about sums him up. He may not have been a pirate, but he was painted as wicked by several of those closest to him. I have no doubt that he lamented many of his choices in life. Both you and Ross talked of Cecil's guilty feelings, so I thought that looking behind this poster was worth a try."

"I can see that the case has been in good hands in my absence." The inspector ran the side of his thumb over his lightly stubbled chin.

"And besides," Bella added with her usual mischievous

bent, "the back of a painting is the kind of place people hide things in mystery novels, isn't it?"

"That too," I confessed before pointing to another of the posters. "And I thought it was a better bet than *Betty's Broken Heart.*"

"That's smart thinking." Lovebrook was surprisingly well spoken for a police officer, and I found him intriguing.

"I'm sorry to have been so mysterious, Inspector." In my line of work, I rarely had to make such an apology.

He was shaking his head in wonder at the treasure before us. "That's all right. The footman below told me that the pair of you have been doing a good job investigating. I didn't like to cut you off in the middle of things."

"We've done what we could," I insisted, but Bella disagreed.

"My friend Marius Quin has been connecting up all the different pieces of evidence, which is what brought us full circle back to the scene of the crime."

"But what my friend Lady Isabella Montague isn't telling you is that she has done most of the work herself."

"I'm sure you've both played your parts." Detective Inspector Lovebrook interrupted before we could waste the morning gleefully bickering. "I'm terribly grateful that you were here to get to the bottom of things. Now, perhaps we should have a look at what you've uncovered."

"I believe that Cecil Sinclair's will was changed mere weeks before he was murdered." My eyes flicked over to the body, as it felt a little strange to be talking in such a manner so close to his resting place. "If you'd like to do the honours, Inspector, we'll find out whether I'm right."

Lovebrook knelt down to do as I'd suggested. He was ever so careful with it and opened the envelope with the delicate tips of his gloved fingers and then extracted the document inside in much the same manner.

"You are correct, Mr Quin." He stood up with his find, and

we gathered around him. "The will's dated the twelfth of December and witnessed by a Mr Gilbert Baines and a Mrs Gladys Mitchell."

The inspector moved from one page to the next, handling the document as though it were a precious artefact from some ancient civilisation.

"There," I said, stabbing my finger at the document and instantly regretting my clumsiness. "Oops, sorry. But look there." We all scanned the passage and, as I got to the key line, I read it aloud. "I hereby give, devise, and bequeath all my estate, both real and personal property, of whatsoever kind and wherever situated, to Miss Penelope Alcott."

Bella gasped. I cursed Gilbert for not giving us the vital piece of evidence that could have solved the case for us before anyone else was attacked, and Lovebrook asked, "Who's Penelope Alcott?"

TWENTY-SEVEN

I'm a cheat. I'm sorry, but there's no other word for it.

We did all that work to track down the guilty party and then found her name on a piece of paper. It's hardly the stuff of great mystery novels. I doubt that Mrs Christie will ever tire of writing a book three-quarters of the way through and have Hercule Poirot declare to his assistant, *Hastings, forget everything we've considered and all the evidence we have acquired throughout our investigation. The will of the deceased should tell us the name of the killer.* Of course, it was only my first case, so I hope you'll make some allowances.

Miss Penelope Alcott had clearly murdered Cecil Sinclair in order to inherit the Everham Hall estate and his substantial monetary fortune. All we had to do now was figure out who Penelope Alcott actually was.

"What a complete waste of time." I couldn't stop shaking my head and cursing Gilbert's stupidity as we trailed downstairs. I barely noticed whether Bella and the inspector were following me; I was busy reading that last sentence over and over again in my head.

"Just to be clear," I asked my friend as we reached the second staircase. "Cecil's wife's name was Hortensia Alcott?"

"Yes. And so Penelope must be her estranged daughter."

I shook my head a few more times for good measure.

"Will you be informing the police of the details of what happened here, or would you rather keep it a secret?" he asked in his typical cheerful tone, with just a hint of sarcasm thrown in for good measure.

"You'll have the full story just as soon as I've put all the pieces together," I replied. "I take it you have a pair or two of handcuffs with you?"

This perked him up, I can tell you. "I certainly have, Mr Quin. And I am always happy to use them on the right person." He cleared his throat then, as he'd identified a flaw in this plan. "Though, now that I come to think of it, they are back in my car."

"Jolly good. Well, I think you'd better fetch them. We will need them before long. And, if you're lucky, the snow will have melted, and you can drive a bit closer." Even as we spoke, the sun was streaming in through open doors along the corridor.

"Excellent. I'll be back forthwith." Though his message was chirpy enough, the expression he wore was less sanguine. He had presumably realised that he would have to get his trousers, socks and shoes wet in the snow once more.

"Do you really know who the killer is?" Bella asked when we were alone. She put her hand on my arm, and it sent that same electric shock through me as the last time.

"Well, we can't be far from the truth." I'd been waiting to say this to her since Cecil was killed. "Assuming that Penelope isn't the very poorly chosen name of a man, we can reduce our list of suspects to just three people, and I know who my money's on."

In a moment, her serious aspect disappeared, and that radiant expression emerged. She was a sunbeam: my sunbeam.

And, if we never met again after we left Everham Hall, this was how I wanted to remember her – not sitting in our treehouse with tears on her face after I broke her heart. From now on, this would be what I saw whenever I thought of her; the picture of a girl with a golden dress glinting in the morning sunlight. An exquisite woman with doe-eyes, porcelain skin and silky black hair.

"What can I do to help?" I wondered how many times she'd asked this question in her life. She always put others before herself, and I was tempted to tell her to find a sitting room somewhere and have a quiet rest, but our job was not quite finished.

"Could you round up everyone that you can find? All the suspects and Philip and Matthew too, just in case Inspector Lovebrook isn't quick enough with his cuffs."

"Of course." She was off before I'd finished speaking. "And perhaps I'll get changed when that's done. I do love this dress, but it's more suitable for a special evening rather than a whole night and the following day."

"Ask everyone to meet in the ballroom in half an hour," I shouted after her.

She didn't turn around but waved one hand over her shoulder to show that she'd heard. Bella was not one for looking back. She had her gaze fixed ahead of her. Unlike me, she was concentrating on the future, not the past.

The house was briefly silent, and it felt as though I had that elegant old palace to myself. It was only a minute before I heard feet pounding on the floorboards of the hallway above, but this brief stillness did me a world of good, and I wondered whether Cecil had enjoyed that unique sensation when he'd first moved into such an immense building all on his own.

As I descended the hallway, I noticed the original features of the house once more. Not just the Cornwallis crest, but the beautiful moulding on the ceiling and the sculpted alcoves that displayed old stone figures of cherubs, angels and strange, half-recognisable mythical creatures. Just like Cecil Sinclair, Penelope Alcott and Marius Quin, the house had a story to tell, and I wondered when it had started and how it might one day end.

I stepped into the ballroom that I'd discovered that morning. It was so grand and glossy that it reminded me of the one in Blackpool Tower. The ceiling was rounded, like a railway arch that had been stuccoed with soft romantic images of women in flouncing dresses riding about on clouds for some reason. The last rays of morning sunlight rebounded off the snow and onto the gold leaf that had been applied to practically every wooden surface bar the polished floor. It was so bright that I shielded my eyes as I walked to the centre of that luxurious room to assemble the fragments of a solution that were scattered about my brain.

You see, I don't think in quite same way as most people. I can't say exactly why but, when I'm writing, I picture myself in a hallway with many doors, and a world to explore behind each one. I travel to the different realms, get to know the inhabitants and study the flora and fauna as best I can. When I close my eyes, I am there in that stately home in the moonlight or, if I go through the next door along, I can visit a London theatre on the opening night of a play just as an actor is shot on the stage.

I have a special way of looking at things, but I hadn't created a door for Everham Hall until I stood on my own in the middle of the glittering ballroom and closed my eyes to think of everything Bella and I had discovered.

I put my hand on the doorknob and pushed.

I don't know how long I stood there but, when Lovebrook turned up, leaving a trail of wet footprints behind him, I understood how the pieces fitted together and could see the links between any number of seemingly disparate facts.

"I'm glad you're here, Lovebrook," I told him and walked over to shake his hand as I should have when he first introduced himself. "I have a story to tell you."

He stood there listening attentively as I unfurled the tale

and, when I'd finished, he remained silent for a few seconds longer and bit his bottom lip as he took it all in. "Do you know what, Marius?"

I waited for him to tell me.

"That was a fascinating story, and I think you deserve to tell it again."

He signalled to Anton and Alma who, their hands entwined, had just entered the room. Bella and Wilson were just behind them and, within a minute or two, all the suspects and a few other assorted guests had arrived.

Lovebrook took a seat in one corner and pointed at me to take the floor. To be quite honest, that was the last thing I wanted to do, but there was a finality to telling everyone at once that appealed to me. With my eyes on Bella as I returned to the centre of the room, I opened my mouth to tell Cecil's story once more.

"At the end of most mystery novels, the detective goes into excruciating detail about why each suspect could or couldn't have killed the victim. You'll be happy to know I'm not going to waste your time with any of that. I'd prefer to tell you straight out that Poppy is the killer."

TWENTY-EIGHT

The local doctor had removed the knife from Poppy's shoulder and presumably sutured the wound. He had secured a bandage and was giving his patient one last check as she began to scream.

"This is just the kind of thing I've had to put up with my whole life." The blood rushed to her cheeks so that they matched the colour of her lipstick. "Blame the hedonist, blame the loose woman. You close-minded prude. You'd condemn me as a killer just because of the length of my skirt."

Her outburst would not dissuade me from my task. "That's right. I spoke to Detective Inspector Lovebrook, and he's agreed to put you on trial based solely on the dress you're wearing."

Seated in a simple, high-backed chair, she was still fuming like a cauldron. The frightened-looking doctor beat a retreat, muttering a short recommendation as he went to, "Go to a hospital as soon as possible to have the wound checked for infection. And try not to get stabbed again."

With Poppy's treatment completed, Lovebrook walked over to put one hand on her unwounded shoulder, but he didn't cuff her just yet. She was silenced, for now at least, so I allowed myself one last look at the suspects before revealing any more secrets. Alma had taken a seat in a throne-like golden chair and sat regally in front of her husband. The two footmen were on guard duty on either side of the door, and the others were spaced out in a long line beside the wall.

Ross appeared to have made a full recovery and had one arm around Edith, though I assumed this was out of affection rather than any need for physical support. Bella offered encouraging smiles whenever I needed them. Wilson was there, book and all, and my dog apparently didn't realise he was sitting on the feet of a murderer.

It seemed unfair to speak only of the killer and ignore the victim, so I began my explanation with the person who had brought us all there. "Cecil Sinclair was a complicated figure. He could be kind and cruel, honourable and calamitous. He not only had demons to fight, but he was haunted by guilt. He felt guilty over his relationship with his family, the way he treated his friends and, perhaps more than anything, the marriage of convenience between himself and an elderly widow by the name of Hortensia Alcott.

"It wasn't Cecil's films that made him rich and enabled him to buy this house. Hortensia left her every last penny to him and, with his inheritance, he bought the Everham estate from the impoverished Cornwallis family for a scandalously low sum. The money he had simply created more money, and he was able to fund the production of his own films. But wealth and fame can attract the wrong kind of people just as flies are drawn to honey."

This was hardly the most original metaphor, but not every writer can be as quick off the cuff as Oscar Wilde. I hope I would have done better if I'd written this speech down and gone through countless rounds of editing.

I'd been slowly moving forward until I was only a few feet away from the killer. From the way she looked at me then, I was afraid I would be her second victim. I didn't have much hope that she would change her bad opinion of me any time soon.

"Poppy..." I began. "Actually, you never did tell me your surname."

"Just Poppy," she replied with a bat of her eyelids, as though her theatrical agent had told her how important it was to look coquettish when she introduced herself.

"Oh, of course. 'Just Poppy' came into Cecil's life when he was already battling drink and addiction. She had spent some time loitering on film sets before catching the eye of Cecil's rival, Alec Pemberton. At one point, I considered the possibility that Pemberton had despatched his minion to kill Cecil, but I don't think that was the case. It seems far more likely that Poppy was merely using a lesser star to get to a more successful one."

She was still at her belligerent best. "How typical of a man to see things so simply. It couldn't be that I met Cecil and fell in love? Oh, no. I'm the Jezebel who used my looks to get what I desired. It's the same old story going back to the Bible."

I wouldn't be discouraged from what I had to say. "You keep saying that you're not to blame, but you have no alibi for the time at which Cecil was murdered. You know the house well and could have planned his killing down to the second, and you had plenty of opportunities to practise the scheme whenever Cecil was inebriated."

"I'm not a killer!" she wailed. "If anything, I'm the one who's suffered most here."

Her words bounced off me now, and I pushed on with the revelations. "We all used Cecil in different ways as we hung from his expensively tailored coattails. Some of you wanted his money, some his fame, and we all enjoyed the free food and drink here at his house. But it was only by chance that I discovered why one of you took a gun from the armoury, filled it with bullets, and shot him three times in the head.

"I'd considered every motive for his death from embezzled

money to family feuds, romantic rivalry to bitter jealousy. But, in the end, the reason was far simpler. It was only this morning that one of you thought to reveal the key piece of information that your excessively wealthy friend changed his will last month. After his father upset him by asking for the hand of a much younger woman, Cecil decided to leave this house and all his money to the daughter of the widow who had made him so rich in the first place. He left everything to Penelope Alcott, or Poppy for short."

TWENTY-NINE

To my surprise, the hush this announcement inspired actually held for a few seconds. The only sound was a yawn from Percy, who looked deeply unimpressed by my work so far.

"Are you trying to torment me?" The killer pushed her chair back, and her screeching voice was even louder than the scrape of the legs on the glossy wooden dance floor. "You can't blame me for his death just because he left me some money."

"So then you don't deny that you're Penelope Alcott?"

"Why would I? I've done nothing wrong."

It was hardly a surprise that she wouldn't confess, so I laid out the evidence against her. "I've given you several opportunities to reveal your true name, but you've been 'Just Poppy' ever since you got here. Even after your boyfriend was murdered and you knew you were a suspect, you didn't come to me and explain the difficult position in which you found yourself. You continued to lie, knowing that the will would leave you everything."

I thought she might deny this, but it was one thing she accepted without challenge.

"I'm right, aren't I? You knew about the will because you

convinced Cecil to change it. Did you tell him who you really were? Or did you persuade him that the only way to assuage his guilt was to leave his estate to Hortensia Alcott's estranged daughter?"

She said, "This is absurd," but she meant, *Yes!*

"You wormed your way into Cecil's world, first courting his fading rival when he got a part on Cecil's last film and then jumping ship and seducing the man who stole your birthright."

A few of the others had come closer to get a good look at the killer. Edith was clearly horrified and hid her face in Ross's shoulder, but the others couldn't help but stare, perhaps trying to make sense of the beautiful woman who had resorted to murder. For her part, Poppy looked lost. She searched for something – anything – to prove her innocence.

"But I'm a victim, too!" She tapped her bandaged shoulder with an open hand, and the crowd waited to see how I could explain the attack she had suffered.

"No, you made it look as though you were. You paraded past the east side of the house with the knife visible, then stabbed yourself in quite the least dangerous part of the body. You were lucky that you missed any major arteries."

If I hadn't known just how much there was to incriminate her, I might have believed that the desperate expression on her face was genuine. "Why would I have stabbed myself?" She turned to address the inspector in the hope that the man with any actual authority could help her. "Please believe me. I'm not a monster. I was very fond of Cecil, and I had no reason to kill him."

Lovebrook looked uncertain, but I wouldn't let her sway him. "You had hundreds of thousands of reasons to kill him, but you knew you would be the likely suspect and so you devised a scheme to distance yourself from your crime. You saw that Bella and I had gone into Edith's room to talk to her last night, and you made the most of it. You covered yourself with heavy clothing and big boots to disguise your figure and footprints, then ran outside where you noticed your dead boyfriend's father heading to his car. You didn't want him spotting you, so you knocked him out with the knife handle or whatever else came to hand, then tramped around the building."

I had moved away from her to deliver the last of the evidence and stood once more in the centre of the room under perhaps the biggest crystal chandelier that Everham Hall possessed.

"You stabbed yourself to make it look as if the killer had bungled his attack on you. You claimed that he'd slipped a note under your door to summon you to the conservatory and that you'd burnt it immediately, but when I fetched my dog from your room last night, it was cold and there was no fire lit. By the time we reached you, I assumed the culprit was long gone. In reality, she was right there in front of us with a knife in her shoulder."

"You've got this all wrong." Poppy looked from face to face, but she'd done nothing to win the good opinion of the other guests, and they stared back with little sympathy. "I never said that I burnt the note in my room. I used the fire in the entrance hall on my way past. And as for stabbing myself, I simply couldn't do such a thing. I'm not nearly brave or stupid enough."

I stopped for a moment to let the silence gather around me, and it was soon replaced by the chatter of the other suspects as they came to realise that, despite Poppy's denials, she really was to blame.

"You told us all that you would be a great actress one day, but I believe that you already are. You convinced Alec Pemberton and Cecil Sinclair that you were in love with them. You made us all believe that you were an empty-headed fool desperate for fame, but it was money that you came to Everham

Hall to obtain: the money your mother had so selfishly left to her petticoat-pensioner."

She dropped back down into her seat and looked fit to cry, but no tears would come. Her hand fell to stroke Percy's coat, but he was no longer there. He had wandered off to stand in the corner of the room for... whatever reason dogs do such things.

I nodded to Lovebrook, and he pulled the heavy cuffs from his pocket. I had to hope that he'd managed to bring his car closer to the house or it would be a long walk for Penelope Alcott to endure. I'm sure the cold would cut straight through her bandages and into the wound, reminding her of the path she'd walked and the wicked deeds she'd undertaken.

As Detective Inspector Lovebrook informed the murderer of her rights, my dear friend Bella looked at me with something approaching pride. I thought I'd made a perfect mess of everything, but as our eyes met, I felt rather wonderful. No matter the errors we'd committed along the way, the most important thing was that the right person would be punished for the crime. I may not have taken the smoothest path to get there, but given ten or twenty more opportunities, I might even make a passable sleuth.

THIRTY

Before we could leave Everham Hall, there were statements to make to the police and tea to be enjoyed in the sitting room. Everyone seemed impressed by the work that Bella and I had done. As a reader of mystery novels, Wilson, in particular, had any number of questions for us.

"It's incredible!" he insisted. "Just incredible, but there's so much I don't understand. Did you suspect Poppy from the beginning?"

The remaining... well, they weren't suspects anymore, so let's just call them guests. The remaining guests, the inspector and I were sitting on the red velvet sofas as Perkins the butler served us drinks and tiny, crustless sandwiches.

"I don't think so. Though you must remember I'm an outsider here, like you. My only contact with Cecil was when he made a scene in the games room. I remember watching as he stormed about the place and thinking that it was amazing any of you had accepted his invitation. I saw the sadness he'd inspired in you, Carl, a genuine fan, as he berated you for even looking at him. I saw Bella's apprehension as she realised that he had already broken his promise before any of us arrived. I saw the

Cavendishes recoil at the monster in our midst, and Gilbert largely ignore everything as he was busy on the telephone."

Gilbert's smile unfurled on his face at this moment, though I'm not certain that he was listening. He was sitting in a comfy chair with Percy on his lap, scratching my fickle hound under the chin.

"In fact," I continued, "when we found Cecil's body, I truly believed that any one of you could be to blame."

"Yes, yes," Wilson persisted, "but what about Poppy? When did you really cotton on to her guilt?"

I thought for a moment before replying. "I never wanted to believe it was her. But I think she was relying on that very fact." The writer in me can't tolerate gaps in a narrative, and so I did my best to fill them in. "She told us a number of times how unfair it was to suspect her just because she was a young, independent woman."

"In other words," Bella spoke up to poke fun at me, "you fell for her charms and didn't want to think badly of her because she was pretty."

I laughed at this and moved on to a confession. "The truth is that it was all just as difficult as I imagined it would be. It's easy enough to solve a murder when I choose the killer from the beginning, but writing books didn't prepare me for the real thing."

The inspector nodded, and I got the impression he approved of this sentiment. He knew better than the rest of us what a thankless task being a police officer was; I wouldn't have swapped places with him for the world. There were several neatly dressed bobbies marching about the house by now, and I had to assume that one of them had been put in charge of the prisoner until she could be taken to a cell.

"No matter how hard Bella and I worked to establish the motive for Cecil's murder, the ground kept shifting beneath our feet. His killer could have been any one of you."

"Very well then," Anton began. "You said that we all had reasons to murder the man. I know my own. Cecil was intolerable to direct, and I lost my temper with him. But what about—"

"That isn't all, though, is it, darling?" Alma had lost the cautiousness she'd had for most of the weekend, and now seemed quite relaxed, even when it came to the discussion of their motives for the crime. "We've been behaving like loons ever since Cecil died."

That suave chap furrowed his brow pensively and then kissed his wife on the top of her head.

As Anton had initiated the conversation, I didn't think he'd mind my explaining further. "I must admit, I did find your reticence rather alarming, and it was only this morning that I understood why you'd been acting in such a manner."

"It's probably best if I admit my own mistakes." The director straightened his back, and I could see he was taking this seriously. "I've acted like a fool. You see, I suspected my own wife of being the murderer." He paused then and I doubted he would be able to continue, but Alma held her hand out to him and it gave him the strength he required. "We'd had an argument just before the fatal shots were fired and Alma stormed off. I hadn't a clue where she'd gone, and when I learnt that Cecil had been murdered, I lied to make sure she had an alibi. I genuinely believed she had killed Cecil in order to put an end to my jealousy."

There were two perfectly parallel tears running down Alma's cheek as she squeezed her husband's hand a little more tightly. "If you were a fool, my love, then that goes double for me. When you lied, I thought the worst." The words caught in her throat and, for a moment, it looked as though she would break down entirely. "I thought that you were so angry over everything that had happened that you'd killed Cecil as I hid in one of the spare guest rooms, crying my eyes out."

"Oh, darling." He leaned over to put his cheek against hers

and ruffle the hair at the back of her head with his free hand. "I'm so sorry for everything I've done."

"I don't think anyone can blame you for being cautious," our fair and forgiving inspector contributed. "From what Marius has told me, your financial reliance on Cecil and the recent, very public disagreements you'd had made you likely suspects. The fact is, though, you should have told the truth from the beginning... at the very least to one another."

"Please don't judge us too harshly," Alma pleaded. "We had no way to prove where we were at the time Cecil was killed and every reason to want him dead. Anton was merely worried that the police would jump to conclusions and arrest us."

"Easy there!" Lovebrook clearly objected to this characterisation. "The majority of officers are good at what we do. It was only a few months ago that I was complimented on my police work by the great—"

"Of course, I would have had to be a raving lunatic to kill him," Anton said, presumably without realising that the inspector was still speaking. "I had a new film with Cecil slated to start this spring. *Mrs Clayborne's Secret* was going to be our biggest production yet..." He turned to look out of the window with a wistful look in his eyes. "It's a tragedy really, as he truly was an incredible actor."

Bella looked particularly gloomy just then. I think it was a strange moment for everyone there. Cecil's friends were happy that his killer had been brought to justice, but that wouldn't bring him back to life.

It fell to the film star's fan to change the subject.

"What about me, Marius? Was I ever a likely suspect?" Wilson leaned in closer to hear what I had to say. I imagine he would have taken notes if he'd had a pen and paper.

"You were in the room next to Bella and me when we heard the gun shots, but we couldn't rule you out immediately." I felt a touch guilty detailing such considerations against an innocent man, but he did ask. "It would have been impossible for you to be in two places at once – but what if you didn't need to be? As Alma suggested, we couldn't be sure that the three explosions we heard were not the shots that killed Cecil. It wouldn't have been difficult to set some fireworks on a long fuse. You could have run from the games room to the tower to kill Cecil and then sprinted back to the main part of the house before they went off. Simple."

"That doesn't sound simple to me," Wilson replied in a matter-of-fact tone, and I could only agree with him.

"Well, quite. And for another thing, you wouldn't have had time to murder Cecil between the moment he was deposited in his room and the explosions. And you would have had to find a way to silence the gunshots that did kill him. Furthermore, except for the brief, rude conversation you had to endure with the future victim, you had no obvious reason to kill him in the first place."

Now that he'd heard all the evidence against him, Wilson seemed to relax a touch. "I'm very happy to hear that I am not a killer, or even an accomplice to one. I must say, this whole situation has been thoroughly nerve-wracking, even as an outsider."

Bella had been listening intently and sat forward to reassure him. "Don't worry, Carl. You were never high on our list. I told Marius that you weren't the type."

He nodded appreciatively, and I realised at this moment that I had a confession to make. "The truth is, I made a number of beginner's errors. In fact, there was one suspect whose potential involvement barely crossed my mind."

"That's quite understandable, old boy," Gilbert naively responded. "Some people are simply beyond suspicion." He smoothed his tie at this moment as though he were very proud of himself.

"That's true, Gilbert. But I was talking about Bella, not you." There was a small amount of snickering around the circle as we witnessed the arrogant fellow's surprise, and I explained my thinking. "It was perhaps lazy of me not to suspect my partner on the investigation of being the killer – especially as that is always a wonderful twist in a detective novel. After all, she could have invited me here this weekend to be her alibi and fixed up some sort of mechanism to kill her supposed friend in the tower as we were mid colloquy." Edith gasped at the very thought of this, and I rushed to rule out the possibility. "This solution was hugely improbable and, as I was with her for most of last night and have known Bella since we were practically toddlers, I think I can be certain of her good character."

"Wait just one moment," Gilbert was quick to demand. "What possible reason could you have for suspecting me of murder?"

I was glad he'd asked, and so I said, "I'm glad you asked. Although I am now willing to accept you had no criminal intentions, a substantial sum of money went missing from Cecil's account and still hasn't been returned days later. Furthermore, you took us out of the house last night in the freezing weather, which could well have been your attempt to locate a secluded place to meet and attack Poppy. Ultimately, if you had feared for your job, your freedom and perhaps your courtship with the irreproachable Lady Isabella Montague, I could imagine you murdering your client to keep your misdeeds a secret."

"Fair enough, but I didn't steal anything or murder anyone, so that's that." He would not deny the sense of my claim, but continued to stroke Percy as though nothing I'd said was of the slightest consequence. I really was beginning to question that dog's taste in people.

"Yes, Gilbert," I pronounced with a weary breath. "It appears that you are innocent. But Cecil was still angry about the money last night when he appeared at the party. You were on the telephone attempting to solve the problem, even as your colleagues were enjoying their festive celebrations. Despite the fact you're not the killer, a night in the cells might make up for your being such a slave driver to your subordinates on New Year's Eve."

I thought this was a wonderful idea, but Detective Inspector Lovebrook would never have gone along with it. Indeed, he crossed his arms and gave a fractional shake of the head to dismiss the suggestion.

Bella spoke up at this moment with an observation of her own. "You may not have committed a crime, Gilly, but you were less than helpful when it came to our investigation."

Her boyfriend looked surprised once more. "My darling, how could you think such a thing? I would go to the ends of the earth to aid you in whatever way you required."

The pair were sitting on armchairs opposite one another, and Bella looked down her nose at him. "I was referring to Cecil's will, which you failed to mention until this morning. I don't suppose there was any reason behind your forgetfulness?" She looked quite innocent as she put the question to him, which was fitting as he looked perfectly guilty.

"I don't know what you're suggesting."

It took me a moment, but I soon caught her meaning. "Baines, you conniving so-and-so! You thought you'd solve the case yourself. That's why you didn't tell us about the will." I searched my memories to back up this claim. "That's what you were doing last night in the office when I ran past. You were searching for the will so that you could impress everyone with your detective skills."

Gilbert opened his mouth to explain himself, but there was nothing left to say. Luckily for him, Ross Sinclair spoke up before Bella could tell him off again. Wrapped around Edith on a love seat, he'd been practically silent since we'd entered the room.

"If you don't mind, I think I'd prefer not to hear about any of the problems I had with my son. Those things are best left in the past." His mouth barely moved, so it looked as if his curly beard had produced these words. "To be frank, I'd rather think of the happier times we had together."

"Of course," I replied, and I gave him a comprehending nod. There was an awkward moment as I considered whether this appeal should apply to his fiancée too, but seeing just how nervous Edith looked even when there wasn't a killer on the loose, I decided it was best to abandon the discussion entirely. To be perfectly honest, except for the fact she hadn't changed for dinner and Cecil's disapproval of his young stepmother, we'd found very little evidence against her anyway.

"So Poppy was always the likely culprit, then," Wilson concluded, and I felt a mite less clever than before.

"I wouldn't say that exactly." I tried to think of a reason why not, but Bella beat me to it.

"On the face of things, she didn't stand to gain anything from Cecil's murder. We assumed Ross would inherit this estate in the event of his son's death. Whereas Poppy appeared to have lost everything when her rich suitor died."

"But then we discovered the will and the whole story changed," I added, and we relaxed back in our chairs to think about the strange case in which we had all played a part.

"She could have chosen a better pseudonym than Poppy," Wilson stated after a few moments' silence. "Penelope and Poppy are hardly a million miles apart and we were bound to wonder what her real surname was."

"It would have all come out in the reading of the will," Lovebrook pointed out. "It amazes me that she thought she could get away with it."

He had a point, and this sparked more possibilities in my head. "It raises the question of how much Cecil actually knew."

"You don't think he—" Bella cut the words short, but I answered all the same.

"He was the only one of us who knew that his dead wife's

daughter's name was Penelope. It's more than possible that he had realised who she was. After we realised her identity, I did detect a likeness between Poppy and the photographs of her mother in Cecil's room."

"To think, he invited his own killer into his home." The inspector shook his head in wonder. "It shows you can never really know people until it's too late."

Despite this truly terrifying conclusion, there was a sense of peace that we hadn't enjoyed in Everham Hall until this moment. Silence swirled about the festive room as we sipped our tea and nibbled our sandwiches.

After all we'd been through, I was looking forward to heading home.

THIRTY-ONE

No one was desperate to stay on Cecil's estate after the night we'd had. The sun was burning brightly, and the icy covering outside turned to slush, then mush and, by the evening, would disappear altogether. Once we'd all packed our bags and the police had finished talking to us, we were free to leave.

"That must have given you enough ideas for your next ten novels," Bella told me as we waited in the entrance hall to say goodbye to everyone.

"I should say. But first of all, I know exactly how to continue my second book."

"You know, we should make a regular go of it." Her smile – the real one that was just so perfectly hers – was shining on her face and it was hard not to respond in kind.

"You mean hunting your friends' killers?"

"No, silly. I mean solving mysteries."

I had to laugh a little under my breath, as it was just the kind of thing she would have suggested when we were nine years old. "And how does one go about finding mysteries to solve?"

"How does anyone do anything in this world? Through

family connections, of course." She was deadly serious. "Just think about it. How many aristocrats have been murdered in the last couple of years? There was the Duke of Chandos up in the Lake District, the Earl of Croydon at Cranley Hall, and didn't I hear that the Duchess of Hinwick was stabbed to death not so long ago?"

"Your point being what, exactly?"

Those two large dimples appeared on her cheeks. It came back to me now that, as a child, I used to poke my fingers in them to annoy her. Don't worry; I resisted on this occasion.

"My point is that members of the aristocracy are always murdering one another. The more money someone has, the higher the chance they'll be croaked. There's bound to be the need for two intrepid detectives like us."

"Haven't Lord Edgington and that other chap... what's his name? Heathcliff Lennox! Haven't they got the world of private investigation all sewed up?"

Inspector Lovebrook appeared at this moment with his prisoner. The pair stood listening to our conversation, and Poppy clearly still hadn't forgiven me.

Bella answered my question, nonetheless. "Those crime-solving wizards can't be in all places at all times. There are bound to be enough crimes to go around and, besides, we'll be different. We're younger, willing to take on any adventures, and we'll have more fun doing it."

To be perfectly honest, I didn't need persuading. If Bella had suggested working in a fishmonger's together, I would have strapped on an apron and set to work with a filleting knife.

Nevertheless, she turned to the real detective for support. "Inspector, tell Marius that the world would be missing out if he didn't try his hand at amateur sleuthing."

"It is not my job as an officer of the law to encourage members of the public to nose about in police business," he said very formally, before changing to his usual relaxed tone. "How-

ever, from what I've seen this morning, it's clear that the pair of
you have done a fantastic job." He winked then, before trying to
impress us with a claim of his own. "Did you know that I had a
hand in investigating the murder of the Duchess of Hinwick?
That was where I got the chance to work with the great Lord—"

"They haven't done a good job at all." Poppy tried to rub her
wrists as she spoke, but the handcuffs made it quite impossible.
"You're arresting the wrong person."

"Of course I am." Lovebrook just laughed and ushered her
outside. "Come along, madam."

"You know, I still have questions about exactly how Poppy
pulled off such a daring plan," Bella told me in a moment of
calm between the other guests leaving. "You said that the door
on the first floor was locked when you tried it last night but not
this morning. Did she run up there and open it before we found
her in the conservatory? And what about—"

I'm sure she had found any number of points that needed
explaining, but the Cavendishes came to say goodbye at that
moment and our conversation would have to wait. The director
and his muse were both quite effusive as they shook my hand,
and Anton talked again of getting my book onto the silver
screen. I'd come to realise, however, that people involved in
film-making say a lot without necessarily meaning it. It was
probably a good idea not to rely on any money from him until
the cameras started rolling.

Ross and Edith followed close behind but were understandably more withdrawn. I could see the pressure that the weekend
had put on the wind-whipped sailor. He nodded and clapped
me about the shoulder but was not in a talkative mood as he
shuffled out of the entrance hall and through the front door.
One good thing about Poppy being the killer was that Ross
Sinclair would presumably now inherit his son's estate. After
everything the poor man had gone through, he deserved some
happiness.

Carl Wilson came by next and, with his shy smile, he quickly lightened the mood.

"I have to tell you what a marvellous weekend it's been." He immediately regretted this and stuttered for a clarification. "I mean... well, I think you know what I mean. Not the murder and violence, but the mystery of it all. I've always adored puzzles and wordplay, so to see the pair of you in action was a thrill beyond anything I've experienced."

Bella gave the nervous fellow a hug for his troubles. "I'm glad you could find something positive in your time here," she replied with diplomatic restraint. "You'll have to visit my family estate in Hurtwood sometime."

He was clearly ecstatic at the thought of this and produced a jubilant squeal as he hurried off to his car. Gilbert appeared then to talk about some dull concern with Bella, but I didn't pay attention because I was busy considering something she'd said. Without really thinking about it, I pushed the front door open and there, carved into the wood, I caught another glimpse of the Cornwallis crest. The former owners must have been very proud of their family to mark their stamp in so many places across the house.

In the courtyard where the guests were preparing themselves for the journey home, it was a truly splendid winter's day. The snow still lay heavy on the trees and lawn, but the sun was bright overhead and did its best to warm me. None of that was important, of course, as I was working out a puzzle of my own.

"Cornwallis," I whispered, unaware that Bella had drawn alongside me.

"I beg your pardon?"

"Cornwallis." In the hallway in my head, I spotted an imaginary door to Everham Hall and launched myself through it. "Cornwallis!" I shouted as I made my way down the steps towards the line of cars that the footmen had already cleared of snow. "Carl Wilson: Cornwallis. It's the same."

That curious young man was getting into a dinky little Talbot 10/23 that was the furthest car from the house. He pretended not to hear me, but I caught a furtive look in his eye as he pulled the door shut behind him.

"It's an anagram," I shouted to Lovebrook, who looked quite bemused and remained where he stood. "Carl Wilson is Cornwallis. It's an anagram." I should have reminded him of the significance of Cornwallis if I was to have any hope of making him chase the blighter. Wilson was already reversing out of his space, and so I devised an alternate plan. "Ross, stop that car. Block his path before he gets away."

The tough old sailor caught on quickly and raced across the courtyard to block the exit. Wilson had navigated the circular fountain in the centre of the oval space and was headed straight at Ross Sinclair. It really wasn't a perfect plan, as the toe-rag behind the wheel shot straight at Cecil's father. If Ross hadn't been light on his feet, the Talbot would have ploughed straight into him.

Instead of stopping to gawk, I ran to my car, feeling rather pleased that I owned such a sporty model. The other guests had evidently worked out what was happening and cleared the way for me to pursue the escaping vehicle. The engine of my Invicta started first time, despite the cold it had suffered overnight, and I'd never felt so excited to drive that unbeatable machine. I reached the driveway in seconds and could see Wilson navigating the bumpy path a hundred yards ahead of me.

Admittedly, my driving wasn't as smooth as I would have liked, and the slippery surface did me no favours, but I soon made up the ground on him. His car was without mirrors, and I doubt he knew he was being followed until he heard the roar of my engine and looked back over his shoulder. By then, it was too late. I shot forwards and found the angle I needed to pull alongside him and nudge the Talbot into the ditch.

I blocked the drive off the Everham estate and pulled the

car to a screeching halt, throwing up mud and ice as I did so. Wilson was already proclaiming his innocence as I jumped from my vehicle, pulled open his door and yanked him out.

"Arrogant swine," I barked and pushed him into the passenger seat of my car before climbing back inside. I reversed towards the gatehouse, and then we shot past the abandoned automobile and back along the path to the hall.

"You fool, you absolute fool. You used an anagram!?" I could hardly believe it, but it was the only thing that made sense. "How could I have been so blind?"

He didn't say anything at first but pushed himself against his door to stay as far away from me as possible. I imagine he considered jumping from the vehicle, but I would have caught him, and I might not have been so gentle a second time.

"It never truly felt right that Poppy could have killed Cecil," I uttered to myself more than to him. "I'm not saying she didn't have the capacity, and she was certainly here to get his money, but it's one thing to conceal her surname from us and quite another for the police not to find it out. If she was relying on the fact that no one knew her true identity, it just wouldn't have worked."

"I really don't know what's got into you, Marius," he mumbled, but it would do no good. "What's this nonsense about an anagram?"

My response kept him pinned to the door. "You tell me, Cornwallis! Weren't you just saying how much you love word-play? I knew that Carl was a rare name in Britain, but there are always exceptions. Cornwallis has been in front of me all week-end, though, and I just didn't see it." We had reached the court-yard once more, and I returned the car to its original position. "I take it that your family owned this place until Cecil swindled it from your grandparents?"

I didn't wait for an answer but threw my door open and called to the inspector once more. "Lovebrook, I was mistaken. I got it all wrong and the real killer is in my car. The chap we know as Carl Wilson is the one we need."

Bella was standing on the steps to watch the bizarre scene unfold. "But that doesn't make sense. We saw him. He was there in the room next to us when the shots were fired."

Young Mr Cornwallis sheepishly exited the car just as two uniformed bobbies emerged from the house.

"You're right, Bella," I replied. "You're absolutely right. He couldn't have been the one to fire the shots that killed Cecil, but I bet that he stabbed Poppy and knocked out Ross. He wasn't working alone, you see." I gazed about the array of guests to locate his murderous partner. "His accomplice was Edith Havelock... or Cornwallis, or whatever her name is."

THIRTY-TWO

This was how it was supposed to feel when you unmasked a killer. I enjoyed a brief rush of confidence and, though it would require some work to fill in the gaps, I was determined to prove that Wilson and Edith were the real culprits.

"They're the descendants of the family who owned this estate. Their surname is all over the house." It only took me a second to find what I needed. "'Cornwallis' – you can see it up there in the family crest above the porch. I found it on windows, shields and countless other places, including on the gun which killed Cecil." I was shaking my head again as I realised how foolish I'd been. "Can you believe the arrogance of a pair of killers using a murder weapon with their name stamped upon it?"

Edith looked as frightened as ever, but I was surprised to see that Wilson was not the tearful wreck I'd expected him to be. There was a self-assurance about him that he had not previously conveyed and, when he spoke, he sounded a great deal more refined.

"You certainly took your time, old bean."

"As I said before, arrogant is just the word for you," I told him across the roof of the car. "You killed a man without the slightest doubt that you would be able to get away with it. From the gun you used, to the smile on your face when we saw you in the games room after your sister carried out the deed."

"She's my cousin, actually," he replied without fear. "But you weren't far off otherwise."

Edith looked more afraid than her glib accomplice, but then she was the one who'd actually murdered someone. I watched as the truth settled in her fake fiancé's brain. Poor Ross Sinclair had been through enough, and I hated to see him suffer, but there was no way around it.

"Right. She's your cousin. What a despicable family you must be."

"Despicable?" The Cornwallis boy's anger flared. "I'll tell you who's despicable. It's that man up in the tower who deserved a hundred bullets through him for what he did to us. He poured honey into our grandparents' ears, convinced them to sell this place for a pittance, and then destroyed us with his fancy barristers when we took him to court. My parents were penniless. They..." He couldn't bring himself to say it on the first attempt and needed another try. "My parents killed themselves rather than live in squalor and shame. The whole thing was criminal, but your friend went unpunished. Coming here was the only way to secure justice for them."

"You came here to kill," I replied to correct his weaselly choice of words.

"Cecil Sinclair was an internationally adored scoundrel. My family had nothing without this place, and he ruined us."

"Don't misunderstand me," I continued in a stern voice. "I can appreciate that you had every reason to want revenge. I just happen to be one of those pernickety people who don't agree with murder. Whatever you think of your noble deeds, that's what you did; you murdered a man in cold blood. You plotted for months to get close to his friends and then wangled an invitation to his party in order to end his life."

I was tired of looking at him and moved on to Edith on the other side of the courtyard. Though she was taller and slimmer than her cousin, they had the same dark eyes and pallid skin. In fact, I'd had a sense of it when I'd first seen them together. She'd introduced herself to him so that we would think they'd never met before, and I remember noticing that they matched somehow. It wasn't because Wilson found Edith attractive that he'd looked so distraught to see Ross's affection towards her. It was because he couldn't bear to witness his enemy's father pawing his cousin.

"You worked just as hard of course, Miss Cornwallis." It felt wrong to call them by their assumed names and so this would have to do. "You took a job in an office where the father of the man you wished to kill had regular business and made sure that he noticed you. Except for your cousin, you were the only person here who didn't already know Cecil through his work. Once I'd identified your accomplice, I only had to pick the other outsider in the group to be sure of the part you played. You were also the only two people with perfect alibis – your cousin couldn't have killed Cecil and you couldn't have stabbed Poppy."

The others remained silent as I explained the devious plan that had stolen a man's life. "In many respects, you stayed close to the truth. You said that your family were from this area, which helped explain why you and Ross would have taken the same train on the day you became better acquainted. You even told us that they hadn't attended your engagement dinner and didn't approve of your choice of fiancé. I suppose that makes sense considering that you were passing yourself off under a false identity and were due to marry the father of the man every Cornwallis must despise."

I doubt that the old sailor could take in much of what I said.

He was sitting on the bonnet of his ageing Crossley tourer, and his eyes were fixed on the trickling fountain. It seemed that fake Edith retained something approaching pity for the man. She moved as though to comfort him but stopped herself and attempted to defend her actions.

"We're not bad people. We set out to right a wrong when no one else would." She scanned the scene in search of support, but there was none to be found. The others looked on in shock, unable to comprehend how anyone could dream of justifying such an act. "We never wanted to hurt anyone else. This was just about Sinclair and what he did to our poor grandparents and—"

She'd had her chance to speak. I cut her off before she could utter another word. "You went up to your room last night, claimed to your companion that you needed to get ready for dinner, then sneaked off to the tower to kill his son. You were quick about your work, and Cecil's inebriation meant that he couldn't put up a fight. You hid in his wardrobe until Bella and I had reached the body then returned to your bedroom as though nothing had happened."

Even as I told this tale, new pieces of evidence slotted into place. "The one mistake was that you came back down to the dining room in the same clothes as when you arrived. You clearly didn't have time to kill a man and get changed, but it was a minor detail in the scheme of things."

The two bobbies had reached the Cornwallis boy. I thought he would make it difficult for them but, far from it, he smiled as they clicked the metal bracelets around his wrists.

"More telling was the pistol that killed Cecil," I continued. "I assumed at the time that the crest on the grip was evidence of the killer's opportunism rather than a connection to your family. Finding a gun to use here lessened the possibility that the murder was planned in advance. However, that would mean it was kept loaded, which seemed unlikely, or that the killer had been able to find the right bullets for such a particular weapon, which would have been a difficult task in an enormous place like Everham Hall."

"Actually, Mr Quin," Poppy's attacker shouted across the courtyard in that same patronising tone, "the correct name is Cornwallis House. This estate has been in our family for centuries, and I'd appreciate it if you could use the proper title."

I ignored him and finished describing his cousin's part in the affair. "Unlike many of the suspects, your motive appeared weak. Your fiancé's son may have treated you cruelly, but you'd never even met until last night. It seemed unlikely that your first act would be to murder him. I could imagine you inciting a screaming argument, but such a swift resort to violence would have been hasty, to say the least."

She looked straight at me – her dark, alluring eyes full of fear and her jaw trembling – but I would not flinch now.

"Not every killer can conceive of such a clever plan. You killed Cecil while your accomplice was somewhere that witnesses could attest to seeing him. And then, when we came to interview you in your bedroom, your cousin went outside to be seen with the knife, thus ruling you out of the equation. You even walked over to the window in case we failed to catch sight of him. I really was a fool not to suspect you."

"Come, come, Marius. I thought I was the fool." Fake Carl was still desperate for attention. "And arrogant with it, didn't you say?"

I wasn't about to give him what he wanted. "The difference between Edith and her chattering cousin over there is that she actually went through with her murder, whereas he made a mess of his."

This really upset him. "I didn't make a mess of it, you simpleton. I chose not to murder Poppy in order to make you think exactly what you did. You swallowed everything like the fish that you are. If I'd killed the hussy and the idiot sailor, there wouldn't have been many suspects left and you would have considered the pair of us more carefully. Poppy was the real decoy, though. That's why we put her mother's photo beside Cecil's body. You were supposed to see the similarity and work out the rest from there. It only took me a few days of research into Sinclair to realise who Poppy was. Any woman who deigned to touch that odious actor deserved whatever she got."

He said all this to my back, and I didn't give him the satisfaction of turning to face him. Once Poppy had thrown a few insults his way, I addressed the rest of the story to the relative innocents among us.

"The note Poppy received was real. It said that she should go to the conservatory and wait, or the sender would disclose her secret. Fearing that her identity would be revealed, she did as she was told, and fake Carl provided fake Edith with her alibi. It also presented a situation with which any avid reader of mystery fiction is familiar; it was theoretically plausible that Poppy had staged her attack in order to suggest she was not the killer."

I looked at the Cavendishes and once more felt happy that they'd had nothing to do with the crime. "I knew early on that the killer was familiar with the house. This seemingly ruled out Wilson and Edith, but it turned out they knew the place better than anyone. They must have spent their childhoods visiting their grandparents here and would have known the location of every room and staircase, especially in the old part of the house which Cecil hadn't changed. But they made another mistake there, which Bella noticed before me. You see, the door to the stairs in the first-floor corridor was locked last night but open this morning. Poppy wouldn't have had the time to unlock it, especially with a knife sticking out of her."

"You're absolutely right... for once." Poppy couldn't resist the chance to draw attention to my failings. I thought she might be happy now that the handcuffs had come off, and she was free to pat Percy again, but it would take some time to forget the humiliation (and the wound to her shoulder).

"May I say, Mr Quin, this is another impressive piece of detective work," Lovebrook proclaimed before realising that this was not the most opportune moment to compliment me. "Of course, Miss Alcott, we're terribly sorry for the mistake. The most important thing is that we got the right culprit in the end."

I doubted that Poppy would agree, but she didn't have time to respond as the Cornwallis boy hadn't finished complaining. "Passing myself off as someone I wasn't – getting a job in a bank with forged documents – that's what I call impressive! Actors blither on about the skills of their trade, but I could have acted Cecil Sinclair off the screen." His confident tone suddenly absent, he adopted Carl Wilson's nervous delivery one last time. "You... you all believed that I was some snivelling little mouse of a man when I am far, far from it. I am a Cornwallis. Do you know what that means? Cornwallis!"

Lovebrook clicked his fingers at the two bobbies, and they manhandled the furious criminal into their car. He continued raging, but I didn't mind as, once he was behind glass, I couldn't hear a word he said.

I turned back to his co-conspirator as the constables approached her. She was still just as pretty and just as retiring as when she'd arrived the night before. I almost pitied her as she was cuffed and cautioned, but she was not the shy, uncertain creature we had come to know that weekend. She was a killer and would be sentenced accordingly.

"Really, Marius." Bella came to congratulate me as the chaos settled. "That was astonishing stuff. I knew you had it in you."

Gilbert looked on grumpily as his girlfriend made a fuss of me, and I'm sure that my typically dark cheeks were not their usual colour.

"Well I got there on the second go. Of course, I couldn't have done it alone, old friend."

We were smiling at one another like happy babies when Poppy walked up to me and set Percy down on the floor.

"Mr Quin, I'd like a moment of your time." She expertly delivered the end of her shoe to the most sensitive part of my shin. "That's for all the bad things you said about me. I'm not a killer. I'd never planned to murder Cecil, and I didn't do anything illegal. I may have helped him to assuage his guilt by suggesting that he change his will in Penelope Alcott's favour, but I deserve every penny that's coming to me."

"I'm sorry, Poppy," I began quite sincerely, though I felt like yelling out in agony. "I'm very much an amateur detective, and I made a mistake. Perhaps in future I should ask Percy what he thinks of any suspects; he appears to be a better judge of character than his master." I might have smiled humbly at this moment, but I was busy rubbing my leg. "What I can say is that I genuinely never wished to cause you any pain, and I—" This was as far as I got before she kicked me again.

"You certainly were mistaken." Her cheeks had turned the colour of her lipstick by this point. "And just so you know, I had no need to kill Cecil because he would have drunk himself to death in no time, anyway. So here's one more for luck."

I suffered a third blow and, with both my shinbones throbbing, I collapsed back onto the running board of Bella's Sunbeam. I'd had enough punishment by this point and decided that it was best not to mention the possibility that Ross would challenge the will in court and leave her with nothing.

"Thank you, Poppy. You really are too generous."

THIRTY-THREE

I went back to the entrance hall to collect my belongings and watch the various attendees of Cecil Sinclair's glittering New Year's gathering get into their vehicles and leave. The two Cornwallis cousins were driven off the estate in separate police cars, and Lovebrook gave us a fond farewell and promised he was only a telephone call away if we should happen across any other adventures. So then it was my turn.

In spite of everything that had transpired, I couldn't bear to step through the front door.

"You know, Marius, I should most likely apologise." Actually, Gilbert's continuing presence was almost enough to send me running back to my car, but I listened to what he had to say, nonetheless. "I must admit to feeling rather jealous – considering the past you share with dear Belly. I can't say that I've been on my best behaviour, but I am truly sorry for being such a stinker."

I tried (and failed) to sound magnanimous. "I'd expect nothing more."

He put his hand on my shoulder to help me towards the

door. "I mean it. You've seen the very worst of me, and I promise to high heaven that I am not normally so rude."

"Of course you're not."

"And speaking of stinkers, it occurs to me that Carl Wilson, or whatever his real name was, may have removed the money from Cecil's account so that I would be grateful for his pointing out the discrepancy." He cleared his throat then, as if embarrassed to have to address such a point. "Think about it; he informed me that the funds were missing and, mere minutes later, mentioned that he would be alone on New Year's Eve. I think he even told me that he was a fan of Cecil's films. I fell for his manipulations, but I'm certainly no thief."

He held his hand out to me, and I still didn't know what kind of person he was. On the surface he was a prime candidate for lackwit of the year, and yet Bella evidently had her reasons for loving him. So, much against my better judgement, I held out an olive branch... of sorts.

"We haven't seen the last of each other, Baines," I told him as I crushed his hand in mine.

Perhaps he was smarter than I'd realised, as he evidently caught my meaning. "That's undoubtedly true, old boy."

"I mean it. I'll be watching you."

"Stupendous. I can't wait to see you again." He continued to shake my hand even as his own disintegrated beneath my grip.

"Marius, dear." Bella's voice carried down the corridor to us from where she'd been talking to the Everham Hall staff. "Are you leaving?"

"Yes, my dear. I'm afraid I am." I made sure to catch Gilbert's reaction as I embraced the woman who meant so much to me. "I can't tell you what it meant to have this time together."

She had a melancholy look about her as I pulled away. "I can promise that it won't be another decade before we see each other again." Her smile was brighter than the North Star. "Don't forget my proposal."

"I won't," I told her and, for approximately the fiftieth time that weekend, I just about managed to stop myself from placing my hand against her cheek and planting a kiss on her perfect lips.

"What proposal?" hog-head Gilbert asked, but his girlfriend wasn't listening.

Percy trotted up to me with his tail wagging, and we wandered down the steps to where my exquisite red car was waiting. I climbed into the driver's seat without a look back. Fine. I watched Bella in my wing mirror and kept my eyes on her for as long as she remained in view, but she didn't know that.

"Bella, my sweet," I heard that bloated pig's bladder railing as I started the engine and the Invicta purred. "I demand to know what proposal you made to Marius."

I put the car in gear and moved off around the fountain. It was hardly the start to the year I'd been expecting, but it was a weekend I'd never forget. I rolled down the driveway to pass various landmarks that instantly stirred up memories. There was Bella's Sunbeam, glinting in the afternoon sunshine. Further along, the culprit's Talbot was still in the ditch and, when I passed the gatehouse, the cantankerous guard gave me a glum nod as I pulled onto the country lane beyond.

"I hope you had a lovely time, Percy," I told my hairy chum and, perhaps unsurprisingly, he said nothing. He curled up to go to sleep beside the signed photo of Cecil Sinclair that I had swiped for my mother when no one was looking. For some reason, it made me think of my missing father.

I could only hope that, wherever he was in this world or the next, my dear dad would be proud of my achievements. Well, perhaps not the petty larceny, but I'd made sure that the right people had been punished for a truly evil act, and that was definitely something he would have admired.

As I drove back to London, I turned the case over in my head. It takes a certain kind of maniac to believe that you have the right to deprive another person of his life. Cecil was not a good man. He had hurt those around him and, if what the killers said was true, he should have been punished for his misdeeds. But he did not deserve the sorry fate he met, and the image of pretty young Edith holding the gun to his head would take some time to leave me.

I had to wonder how different I really was from Cecil Sinclair. We'd both made mistakes – both fallen prey to the lure of too much money and found ourselves chained to a house that, in almost any other life, would never have been ours. The difference between the two of us, though, was that I still had a chance to put things right. I may not have won back the girl of my dreams that weekend, but I didn't see myself lying on any pavements in the near future, either. Before the war, I was scared of dying and I'd been scared of living ever since, but I was determined to change that now.

Bella was back in my life, and I had a feeling that it wouldn't be too long before I saw her again. In fact, a few weeks later – just a short while after he'd called her a hussy and she'd railed at his cruelty – Bella rang to tell me that Ross Sinclair and Poppy Alcott were to be married. It was hard to imagine them as a couple, but at least it solved the problem of who should inherit Cecil's estate.

To put that into context, the estranged daughter of a murdered film star's dead wife married her deceased boyfriend's elderly father. Or, to say it another way, people are strange, and love is even stranger.

It had not unfolded entirely as I would have hoped, but my night away in the countryside did inspire me to write again. As soon as I got home (and I'd made it through the rigmarole of my family behaving as though I'd been gone for several years) I sat down to start chapter three of *A Glimpse of a Blood Moon*.

Though I didn't know it just then, the book would write itself. The words seemed to jump from my pen as though I'd already composed every last one of them in my head. I'm sure you'll be pleased to learn that I included a large number of very short chapters so that Bertie would pay me enough to cover all my debts.

Sitting in my study with the finished manuscript on my desk, I reflected on my time at Everham Hall. It occurred to me that I should have known that Wilson was involved as soon as I discovered that he'd enjoyed my book. If anyone has the ability to devise a fiendish murder, it's fans of detective fiction. They're simply not to be trusted.

A LETTER FROM THE AUTHOR

Many thanks for reading *Murder at Everham Hall*, I hope you were glued to the book as Marius and Bella raced to unmask the killer. If you'd like to join other readers in accessing free novellas and hearing all about my new releases, you can sign up to my readers' club!

benedictbrown.net/benedict-brown-readers-club

If you enjoyed this book and could spare a few moments to leave a review, that would be hugely appreciated. Even a short comment can make all the difference in encouraging a reader to discover my books for the first time.

Becoming a writer was my dream for two decades as I scribbled away without an audience, so to finally be able to do this as my job for the last few years is out of this world. One of my favourite things about my work is hearing from you lovely people who all approach my books in different ways, so feel free to get in touch via my website.

Thanks again for being part of my story– Marius, Bella and I have so many more adventures still to come.

Benedict

benedictbrown.net

 facebook.com/benedictbrownauthor

ABOUT THIS BOOK

This series came about quite unexpectedly. My new baby, Osian, had just been born, and I was looking forward to a relaxed publishing schedule and plenty of sleepy afternoon naps with my son. Happily for Marius Quin, and sadly for my lazy days, an editor at Storm happened to read a book in my other 1920s series and reached out to see whether I would like to write something for a new publisher. I really liked the idea of collaborating with a team of people, and it was too good an opportunity to pass up. It was also rather fortunate that Osian is the world's sleepiest baby, as that gave me the time I needed to write.

I had a few ideas for a spinoff series from the Lord Edgington books, but rather than sticking with my usual type of characters, I wanted to challenge myself by creating something different. Marius is smoother and more confident than my existing narrators, but he's also facing a major predicament in work, love and life in general. I thought a broken-hearted (and broke) writer with writer's block was a good starting point for a series, and I hope you're excited for what comes next. I've always wanted to write a really compelling romance, and I'm eager to find out how the relationship between Marius and Bella will develop.

In terms of the setting, I based the unusual look of Everham Hall on the Elvetham Hotel in Hampshire. I absolutely love this unique building and, after coming across it online, I e-mailed the managers to see whether I would be allowed to use an image of it on the cover. Sadly, I never heard back from them. Oh well!

One of the reasons I love it so much is for the centuries of history that have unfolded there. The medieval residence that formerly stood on its grounds was in the Seymour family for three hundred years, and it was there that Henry VIII met and fell in love with his third wife, Jane Seymour – which might sound romantic if it weren't for the fact he was with his second wife at the time, who he put to death the following year, before asking Jane to marry him the very next day. Such a nice guy!

There is evidence that King John, Queen Elizabeth I, and (perhaps) even William Shakespeare all passed through the estate at different moments. The building was extended, rebuilt and burnt to the ground a number of times over the centuries before the then owners paid the architect Samuel Sanders Teulon to redesign the house in a Gothic style with red and white polychromatic brickwork. The place now looks like something from a fairy tale. It combines countless different international architectural features and is covered all over with towers, turrets and chimneys. If anything, I made Everham Hall slightly simpler than the real Elvetham, which may be one of the most spectacular buildings I've used as inspiration for my books so far.

I wanted to have a glitzy and glamorous murder victim, which is why I chose a film star, and it was really interesting finding out about the growing British film industry of the 1910s and 20s. This is the third of my books in which actors feature as suspects, and I'm not sure why they fascinate me, but they certainly make easy targets for humour. As a child, my brother and I did a lot of drama, and we used to compete in amateur dramatic competitions, often against rather pompous adult companies who took the whole thing too seriously. Perhaps by plotting Cecil Sinclair's death, I was serving an ever so cold dish of revenge. Either way, I've really enjoyed meeting this bunch of calculating characters and getting to know my amateur detectives. I hope that you have too.

HISTORICAL RESEARCH

When I started writing my first 1920s series, "Lord Edgington Investigates...", I realised just how many fascinating facts I came across when researching my stories. From the second book on, I've included a chapter like this one to describe some of the most amazing things I've learnt. Not only has that section grown with each new entry in the series, my existing readers have really come to love it, so here we go again...

One of the very first things I discovered (to my horror) when writing *Murder at Everham Hall*, was that there was no such term as "writer's block" in 1927. In fact, though people such as F. Scott Fitzgerald, Rachmaninoff and the early Romantics suffered from the condition, it was not until 1947 that an Austrian psychiatrist called Edmund Bergler named it. He decided that it was caused by the sufferer having an irregular love life, or perhaps because their mothers bottle-fed them. Today we are a little more enlightened, and it is commonly accepted that a range of factors influences the condition – with the way you were fed milk unlikely to be among them. I'm happy to say I have never had writer's block... yet. I really hope I never do, either, as I have a lot of books to write.

Although I'd seen a few classic silent films over the years, I knew very little about the state of the British film industry in 1927. We were still in the silent era, with the first full-length British talkie, Hitchcock's *Blackmail*, not released for another two years. Hollywood had a head start on us, but Britain was catching up, and one figure who had enabled that success was the producer/director and entrepreneur, Will Barker.

Barker set up his first film company in 1901, using a hand-cranked camera and charging the public to see short documentary films of everyday life. By 1902 he'd taken a house in Ealing, West London, and then bought up land around it in order to build three stages for filming in all weather. In fact, because of London's notorious tendency for grey skies, the stages were built with high glass walls to make the most of the light – California, it was not. Through his desire to make large-scale epics to compete with Hollywood's output, he helped make Britain the second most important film-making nation of the day.

By 1912, Ealing Studios were probably the biggest in Europe, and Barker invested in lavish historical productions about Henry VIII and Queen Victoria and even paid famous theatrical actors to appear in them. But his real legacy is the studio itself which continues to exist over a century later and became synonymous with British cinema, especially for its comedies in the forties and fifties such as *The Ladykillers* and *Kind Hearts and Coronets*. The studio was subsequently owned by the BBC for forty years before, more recently, making major films again such as *The Importance of Being Earnest* and *The Imitation Game*. It even became the setting of the downstairs scenes from *Downton Abbey*.

From film stars to swans – I can't remember why I mentioned them, but just go with it – I perhaps foolishly hadn't realised that the term "swan song" came from the belief that the ever-mute birds would, upon their death, release a beautiful song with which to exit this world. Aristotle, Plato and Socrates all bought into the idea, though this sounds to me like something that could be disproven really quite easily.

What I did know was that there's a widely held belief that all swans in the UK belong to the crown. This turned out to be closer to the truth than I assumed as, ever since the twelfth century, the monarch of the day can claim ownership of any unmarked, non-privately held swans. This goes back to a time when the birds were a great delicacy and only the king or queen could grant hunting or ownership rights. In fact, since medieval times, there has existed the essential role of Keeper of the King's Swans. It is this lucky person's duty to round up and examine any such birds on the Thames once a year, though his duties have recently been shared with a helper. That's probably a good thing, considering how long the river is.

I knew that the Heimlich Manoeuvre was a fairly recent method, first written of in 1974, and so it wouldn't have been used to save Alma from the not-poisoned peanut. Before then (and since, it seems) people would have been more likely to use back slaps to remove an obstruction. What's particularly interesting, however, is that, despite the manoeuvre's ubiquity, there doesn't seem to be much evidence that it is more effective than back slaps and, according to the family of the inventor of the technique, Henry Heimlich's greatest achievement was his talent for self-promotion. He claimed to save two people's lives using his namesake manoeuvre, but according to his son, neither act actually occurred.

Moving swiftly on, nail polish! It turns out that coloured nail polish didn't become popular until the twenties. At the same time that car manufacturers developed a new range of colours for their vehicles, vibrant shades became more popular in make-up too. However, in those early days, it was uncommon to polish the whole nail and so the tips and nailbed were normally left unpainted.

There are two important addresses in the book which have

a story to tell: 15 St James's Square and 22 Cresswell Place. The first is the insanely fashionable and expensive address where Marius lives, and it is a truly beautiful Georgian building if you ever get a chance to stroll around that exquisite garden square. In reality in the 1920s, the building was used as the headquarters of the General Medical Society. To be honest, I doubt that even a successful mystery author would have been able to afford the down payment on a flat in St James's, as highlighted by the other address I used.

Marius's publisher's home address, 22 Cresswell Place, is on a very pretty mews in West London but, in reality, it was where Agatha Christie moved after her divorce. She bought it in 1929 and, unlike many of the properties she owned, never sold it. It is a very small former stable where she lived with her daughter. Of course, if Marius hadn't been trying to show off, he would have opted for something similarly affordable.

I try to check my facts for even the briefest references, and I was interested to discover that Dalmatian dogs were introduced to Britain in the eighteenth century. Before becoming famous in Dodie Smith's book and the subsequent Disney film, Dalmatians were known to be the best kind of carriage dog. It was their job to run alongside horse-drawn carriages in case of an attack by highwaymen. They would fight off the bandits, giving their masters time to take appropriate measures. The richer the occupants of the carriage, the more dogs they would have, and the term "carriage dog" became synonymous with this breed. They were also used to escort fire-engines and helped clear the way through crowds in emergencies. What helpful little fellows!

One thing that really made me choke up as I researched the book was reading about conscription and those who volunteered to fight in the Great War. I needed to check whether Marius would have had any time off between his basic training and being shipped out, and then I fell down a research rabbit hole, and it really affected me to learn of the sacrifices young men and their families made. Soldiers were typically given ten days' holiday before being sent to the continent but, towards the end of the war, when Marius came of age and numbers were low, some soldiers wouldn't have been able to return home to say goodbye to loved ones.

The thing that really had me sobbing, though, was something called "pals' battalions". The British government went on a massive recruitment drive to get men to fight in the war. One initiative was to persuade them to sign up with friends. The result was that battalions of hundreds of men from the same town, or even small villages, would come together to fight shoulder to shoulder with names like the "Grimsby Chums" and "Preston Pals". Sadly, this also meant that they died in a similar fashion. In one case, in a battalion of 700 men, 235 were killed and 350 injured in the space of twenty minutes in a particularly fierce battle. I found that absolutely heartbreaking. We sometimes read historical accounts without thinking about the real people who were affected, but this example brought the reality of the First World War home to me.

Another feature of the war I had to look into was trench raiding. This was where a small team of soldiers would use stealth to cross no-man's-land in order to gain ground, prisoners or information. It was quite common for British troops to sneak into an enemy trench under the cover of darkness and round up the men there for questioning. This was one of the techniques which enabled the Allied forces to have such accurate information before the Hundred Days Offensive that saw them outmanoeuvre the German army.

As Marius explains on his night-time raid to the old part of Everham Hall, the Allies would also send bilingual men over the top to listen for German plans. I can only imagine how frightening such a mission would have been and, reading accounts of similar moments on the website of the Imperial War

Museum in London, I found the bravery that so many men showed in order to achieve their goals quite incredible.

I've become something of a classic car fan since starting my 1920s books and Marius's 1927 Invicta 3 Litre is rather special. The relatively unprolific Invicta marque was dreamt up by racer, engineer (and father of Le Mans 1955 driver Lance) Captain Noel Macklin. With the backing of Oliver Lyle, an heir to the Lyle sugar family, he had grand ambitions for the cars, believing they could rival Rolls Royce for quality and be as powerful as contemporary American vehicles whilst remaining safe enough to drive on European roads. I can't say whether they succeeded in these goals in the ten years they produced cars, but they did have a lot of success in races. Having served alongside him in the First World War, Noel's sister-in-law, Violette Cordery, was a pioneering long-distance and racing driver. She once managed to drive 30,000 miles in 30,000 minutes and even drove 10,266 miles around the world in five months, and she did it all in Invicta cars.

I put a lot of thought into the names I choose for my characters, but Marius Quin came quickly. I had used the name Marius as a victim in a previous book, but I changed it just before publishing in order to keep it for this series. I thought it was a perfectly mysterious and unusual name which most people will have heard of because of the character in *Les Misérables*, but without very strong geographical ties. Quin came because of Christie's short story collection, *The Mysterious Mr Quin*, the allusion to which I found fitting for my brooding hero. Quin is a semi-supernatural figure who keeps popping up through the course of the stories to lead the detective figure, Mr Satterthwaite, to the solutions of various mysteries.

Bella's name came from a family of children I used to spend half the week with when I was a toddler. The daughters of the family were called Isabel, Abigail and Sophie and, I've no idea why, I always picture them in blue velvet Victorian dresses. My Bella got her surname from Romeo and Juliet, of course, but the House of Montagu (without an e) is an ancient family in Britain with the Duke of Manchester at its head. They were a prominent clan in the Middle Ages but, judging by the current duke's criminal record, may not command the same respect they once did.

My books almost always have a song or three in them and, as this one is set at Christmas, I looked for lesser-known Christmas folk songs to include. "The Cock Sat Up in the Yew Tree" is a wassailing song which has its origins in the counties that border Wales in the west of England. With a wassailing bowl in hand, it would have been sung from house to house on Twelfth Night in exchange for gifts.

When you read about old British folk songs, you'll often see a number given as part of the Roud Folk Song Index. Its creator, a man named Steve Roud, was formerly a librarian in Croydon, near where I'm from. He set out to preserve and collate all the traditional songs that have been handed down to us by categorising similar songs into specific numbers. It's interesting that a song like "The Cock Sat Up in the Yew Tree" may have totally different lyrics in another part of the country and different variations branching off from the often lost original. Roud not only compiled existing records, but travelled around the country to make field recordings, and the index now has over 250,000 references for 25,000 entries.

This song has an index number of 230 which it shares with "We Wish You a Merry Christmas". The lyrics, with talk of hens and pies, may seem strange, but wassailing songs often contained good wishes for those listening and, like Amazon wish lists today, items that the singers would like to receive as payment. The famous line about figgy pudding suddenly makes sense.

A more modern song, however, is Jack Pleasants' "I'm

Learning A Song for Christmas" that Uncle Stan is singing as we meet him. Pleasants was a northern English music hall comedian and singer at the turn of the twentieth century. He died at the ripe young age of forty-nine after coming off stage at a pantomime. After his death, people feared that the production was cursed as, with Jack already dead, the lead actress was washing her hair with some nasty substance, and the room caught fire. Luckily, her and her mother's screams were so loud that their landlord heard and put the flames out with a carpet.

I have to confess that I am a frustrated songwriter. When I was a teenager, I was in a band with my friends, but as I was only the drummer, I didn't really have the musical acumen to compose music of my own. Instead, I would write lyrics to melodies that only ever existed in my head. I wrote hundreds of the things and never did anything with them – which is lucky as I'm certain they were all terrible. Sadly for all of you, these books give me the chance to continue my appalling lyrical adventures whenever I can't find a real song that fits my need. And so the song that Bella sings, "Without My Man," is a Benedict Brown original. A woman's reliance on her boyfriend is probably not the kind of message you would include in a modern pop song, and I apologise for everything about it.

The past was a dangerous place! People used flammable spirits in place of shampoo! Isn't it lucky that we live in the nice, safe twenty-first century where nothing bad ever happens? Well, that might not be totally accurate, but at least we have better haircare now.

I'm sure there are twenty other interesting facts that I've already forgotten, but that was some of the good stuff. See you again next time.

ACKNOWLEDGEMENTS

I have to say a massive thank you to my always cheerful and encouraging editor, Emily Gowers, without whom this series would never have existed. You have been a great source of support from the beginning, so thank you very much. I also have to thank my hardworking and patient alpha readers, Bridget Hogg, and Joe and Kathleen Martin. I wouldn't be able to sit in a lonely room for twelve hours at a time to get books written in a few weeks if it weren't for your companionship.

My family deserve truckloads of appreciation as well. Most of all my wife Marion, who works so hard to keep our life propped up as I disappear off to the 1920s, and my kids Amelie and Osian for being so darn cute and cuddly and occasionally getting me to stop work to do something more fun. My mum and much-missed dad are absolute legends, and everything I do is thanks to them. Even my brothers are on hand when needed, and I appreciate their support.

But there wouldn't be any point in writing these books if no one read and fell in love with them, so thank you to every last reader. My ARC readers are so helpful and I'm grateful to all of you. In fact, I appreciate every last person who even takes the time to read the blurb on one of my books, as it means that the dream I've had since I was a child is a reality, and I'm doing the job I love.

WORDS AND REFERENCES

Crab-stick – a grumpy person.

Sillikin – a silly person.

Jellyfish – a cowardly person.

Faugh! – sixteenth century word for "yuck" (which itself didn't exist until the 1960s).

Druggard – a druggy person... I mean, a drug addict.

Dryasdust – a boring person.

Blue bore – ditto.

The American Bar – one of the most famous bars in London that became well known for its cocktails and also features in my Lord Edgington book *A Killer in the Wings* which introduces Marius as a character.

Bufflehead – a mild insult for a stupid person.

Shell-back – an experienced sailor.

Nosey Parker – an overly inquisitive person – this is the spelling from the nineteen twenties.

Get one's dander up – to become angry. Originally American, but already in use in the UK by 1850.

Chicken-heart – a cowardly person.

Nerve-shaken – nervous.

Dote – a less than intelligent person.

Whoopee (noun) – a big party.

Petticoat pensioner – the male equivalent of a sugar baby. A man paid by an older woman to be her companion.

Lackwit – a stupid person.

CHARACTER LIST

Marius Quin – soldier in the Great War with a broken heart, turned mystery novelist with writer's block.

Bertrand Price-Lewis – Marius's publisher and friend.

Lady Isabella Montague – Marius's childhood friend, the daughter of the Duke of Hurtwood.

Gilbert Baines – Bella's boyfriend, a rather charmless banker.

Cecil Sinclair – Bella's friend and Gilbert's client, a debauched film star who is throwing a party on New Year's Eve 1927.

"Just Poppy" – Cecil's girlfriend and a wannabe actress.

Anton Cavendish – a well-known film director who has directed several of Cecil's films.

Alma Cavendish – Anton's wife and the leading lady in many of his films.

Ross Sinclair – Cecil's ageing father, a former sailor.

Edith Havelock – Ross's far-too-young girlfriend, a former receptionist.

Carl Wilson – not the lead guitarist from the Beach Boys, but a junior clerk at Gilbert's bank. He is shy and nervous and a big film and book fan.

Perkins – the butler of Everham Hall.

Philip / Matthew – the footmen of Everham Hall (and also the names of two of my cousins).

Uncle Stan, Auntie Elle (her name was originally Elfride, but I kept forgetting how to spell it) and Marius's mum – I think those names are self-explanatory.